AF350506

QUEST FOR THE SEA'S REVENGE

QUEST FOR THE SEA'S REVENGE

ALEX VEGA

IngramSpark

Contents

Copyright © 2024 by

All rights reserved. No part of this book may be reproduced in any
manner whatsoever without written permission except in the case of brief
quotations embodied in critical articles and reviews.

First Printing, 2024

Acknowledgements

I want to give special thanks to my editor, Clara Carlson-Kirigin from Prometheus Editorial LLC, and my cover artist Viergacht from selfpubbookcovers. I also want to thank Dr. Ellen Foster, my parents, and my friends Edward, Shannon, Brooke and Frog for their help and support through this process. This book wouldn't have been possible without all of you.

Map

YARLFORD
DIELDARA
THAWPEAK
BORRA
EMPIRIS
N
W E
S
THE QUEEN'S QUARTER
THE TEMPLE
KIRAL
THE SILVER ISLES
THE WELL
TALLIX
EVERSYN
VOLDEN
ZARRA
CARRAN
THE INTERIOR SEA
THE MAELSTROM TAVERN
SAKSI
VALDORIA
THYS
ORLOXI
XEPHOV
SELKIS
VENSIA
AREL
TOROKAI
KARSTAN
SYRRA
KOTO
LISSWEN
DAWL
REDHIL
DEAD MAN'S ISLAND

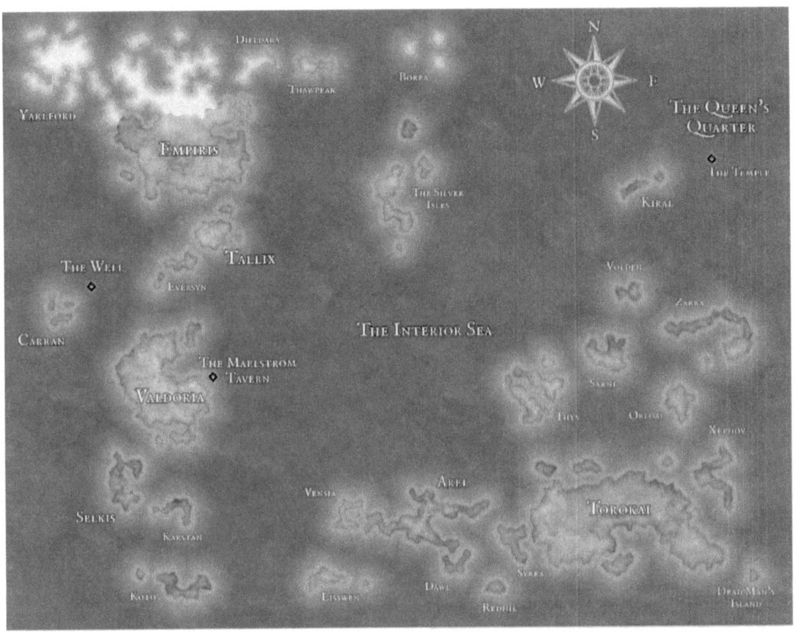

I

Part 1

I

Valdoria

The sun was just beginning to rise, casting a dull gray light through the mist-shrouded docks, but the atmosphere was already bustling. Shouts and barked orders rang through the air, accompanied by a cacophony of rattling chains, creaking wheels, and the sharp thuds of boxes and crates being tossed to and from cargo holds. Waves lapped against the rocky seawalls, and birds screeched and fought over scraps of food. The smells of dead fish, smoke, and unwashed bodies hung thick over the port.

As the mist began to clear under the warm sunlight, a large elegant ship glided up to an unoccupied pier. Planks lowered and the passengers began to disembark. A woman wearing a green and gold satin dress, hair in an extravagant updo, stepped out onto the plank from one of the upper decks. Jeweled necklaces, bracelets, and earrings glittered with a blinding radiance as she walked slowly and carefully toward the dock.

As she meandered through the crowd, she was stopped in her

tracks by a gaunt, pale boy running directly into her. He stumbled back, surprised.

"My goodness!" she exclaimed, her three chins wobbling with indignation.

"S-sorry," muttered the boy as he continued past her, quickly vanishing into the crowd. She wouldn't realize until he was long gone, swallowed up by the fog and the throng of people, that her jeweled bracelet and pocketbook were missing.

The boy made his way toward the edge of the roadway and jumped down from the pier to the narrow strip of mud and sand that ran the length of the seawall. He kept to the shadows as he darted between the barnacle-encrusted piers.

To an outsider, the docks seemed a chaotic jumble of workers, passengers and guards, fishermen and stevedores, townspeople and visitors. But each of the wooden walkways had a purpose, and each had their own usual cast of characters.

The fifth western pier, for instance, was a space for vendors to display their goods and sell their wares to wealthy visitors. The ninth eastern pier was less friendly to tourists, a place for illicit gambling and other shady dealings. The third eastern was a location for fishermen to gather and exchange tall tales, as well as sharing insider information on the best spots to cast their nets. The tenth western was for the ships of the Empire's Army, while the tenth eastern was reserved for unloading and exchange of cargo. The first pier, perfectly centered in the bay, was considered neutral territory where all classes of people intermingled.

The boy ducked under the very last pier, waiting for a group of guards to march past before running to an old wooden ladder that hung from the side of the seawall. He climbed up and dashed across the open walkway before disappearing into a dark alley between two ramshackle buildings.

Surrounding the docks of Valdoria were clustered, run-down

storefronts, bars, factories, and apartments, divided by narrow cobblestone roads and polluted canals. Here lived the fishermen, stevedores, and vendors, along with many of the thieves, gamblers, and other criminals who made their livings in less than legal ways.

Some of the canals were larger and cleaner than others, and these cut through the slums and to the larger, nicer homes of the merchants and military. On the hilltops, located above the houses of splendor, lay the lavish mansions, courts, and dwellings of the wealthiest members of Valdoria society.

The boy hurried across a bridge over the Bay Access Canal and down a dark street paved with broken stones, ultimately reaching a dilapidated bar. An old, barely legible, partly broken sign hung over the door: "The Golden Eel Tavern."

He pushed the door open. Despite the early hour, it was alive with activity. The air was smokey and thick with the smells of alcohol and sweat. Several of the tables were occupied with groups of shifty-looking individuals deep in conversation around heavy mugs of ale and beer. Tavern maids wound through the smoke and maze of tables to serve their shady patrons. From the dusty rafters hung hammocks filled with snoring figures, sleeping off the long night.

Perched at the bar, wiping down the counter was a thickset woman with frizzy hair and several missing teeth. She glanced at the boy as he approached.

"Cas!" she rasped, smiling. "What you got for me?"

Cas slid into a barstool and pushed his messy brown hair out of his eyes as he retrieved the bracelet and pocketbook from his worn leather bag.

"The ship was coming in from Tallix. It was a nice-looking one, too," he said as she took the bracelet from his dirty hand and examined it closely.

"Tallix, huh? That's a good sign, means it's probably genuine.

Worth a lot." She opened the stolen pocketbook to reveal a pile of gold coins. "Excellent! You did well."

"So, what are you gonna give me for it, Nan?" he asked. She reached below the bar and pulled out a burlap sack. Inside was bread, fruit and dried meat.

"Good enough for you, kid?"

He smiled, took the bag, stood and slipped past her.

"Yeah. I'll see you later, then."

"Ey, Cas," she said, making him pause. "Where's your friend been? Scout? I haven't seen him around for a while."

"He's been having some bad luck. He's fine, though, don't worry."

"Good. Tell him I hope his luck improves." Cas nodded and returned to the street, where the air was cool and refreshing. With the sun up and the day truly begun, the narrow streets were teeming with people, carts, and wagons. Cas kept his head down and maneuvered quickly through the crowd, trying not to draw attention to himself.

He blended into the background of the slums. His unkempt hair covered much of his thin face. With his patched-up trousers and dirty, ragged jacket, very few of his neighbors would give him a second glance.

His appearance did tend to catch the eyes of guards. He ducked into an alleyway as he heard their heavy boots and clanking breastplates. A group of six guards marched by, propping their long rifles on their shoulders, metal masks glinting in the sunlight. He waited until their footsteps faded into the distance before emerging from his hiding place.

He finally reached his destination: a dry canal with a large drain pipe opening. He jumped down to the canal bed and ducked into the grimy pipe.

"Scout!" He called, his voice echoing through the enclosed space. After a moment, he heard a rustling in the darkness ahead of him.

A thin figure emerged into the light, walking hunched over to avoid hitting his head on the low ceiling.

"Cas!" Scout said with a beaming smile. "Looks like you brought me something."

"Nah. This is all for me, mate," Cas said.

Scout laughed, and the two sat down facing each other. Cas opened the bag and retrieved the goods. They ate ravenously.

"Nan's worried about you. I told her you're still alive, just bad at pickpocketing."

"Bad at pickpocketing? I taught you everything you know!" Scout said with a laugh.

Cas rolled his eyes.

"I've just been having bad luck. The guards are always watching, and I can't exactly steal in front of them."

"Yeah, I know. They're increasing security. One of the guys down at the tavern said it's because they're starting one of those purges, trying to get rid of all the pirates."

"Like that'll ever happen. They can start as many purges as they want. The pirates always show back up after a while."

"We'll just have to get better in the meantime. And by we, I mean you."

"Ah, shut up. I'm getting too old for this," Scout said.

Cas rolled his eyes again. "You're only 17!"

Scout grew quiet, staring down at his meal.

"Yeah, 'bout that," he said. "I don't expect you to get it, being a kid and all . . ."

"I'm only a year younger than you."

"Exactly, a kid. But, be that as it may, I'm thinking I should . . . I don't know. Do something other than stealing coin purses and rings in exchange for food."

"Like what?"

"I'll be eighteen in a few months. I could join the Empire's Army.

Then I can send you money, and maybe you could actually get a decent place to live . . ." Cas raised his eyebrows.

"You? In the Army? As if they'd take you."

"Hey, I could do it! All they do is march around intimidating people," Scout said, throwing a fruit pit at Cas. "Besides, you don't want to live like this forever, do you?"

Cas was quiet for a moment. As much as he hated to admit it, he didn't remember a life other than this. He and Scout had been on the street since he was five, first as beggars and then taken in by Nan as thieves. Before that, he had only vague memories of living in a small apartment with his mother. The notion that he could have a better life was something that rarely crossed his mind.

"I suppose not," he said finally.

"Well, unless you want to go work in a factory, this is the only option I can see."

Cas cringed. The only thing worse than living on the street was working in the factories. Workers usually lasted only a few years before they succumbed to exhaustion, disease, or injury.

"I still don't know what the Army would want with a scrawny criminal like you," Cas said. "But I guess it is as good a plan as any."

They finished their meal and wrapped up the remaining food, tucking it into an adjoining pipe that held their other few possessions. They had two tattered blanket to keep warm at night and a bag of trinkets they had decided were too interesting to sell: a ring that was also a tiny compass, a miniature painting of an unfamiliar city, an ivory comb with an inscription that neither of them could read, and a pocket watch with an elaborate golden pattern. Cas also had the necklace his mother had given him shortly before she died.

He pulled it on before they left. He never left it there if neither of them was around; he couldn't risk his one precious item getting stolen.

The two boys sat idly on the seawall, scanning the crowd for potential targets and occasionally skipping rocks across the calm bay. Waves rolled in from far out in the open waters, growing taller and taller before finally breaking with a curl of white foam, crashing against the harbor break beyond the port. Far past the rocks that kept the wild ocean at bay, a single ship cruised slowly toward the horizon, sails stark against the pale blue sky. As it faded into that hazy barrier separating their vision from what lay beyond, Cas felt a pang of envy deep in his chest; he often wished he could just sail off into the blue.

If he watched the sea for too long, he would often lose himself and forget why he came here. Luckily, Scout didn't have that problem.

Scout nudged him with his elbow. As Cas glanced over, his friend nodded toward a group of well-dressed men looking at the vendors' stalls. They wore the jeweled headdresses common with the nobility of Torokai, along with numerous gold rings and earrings. The pair stood and slowly approached them, heads down and hands in their pockets.

One of the men stepped away from the rest, and Scout headed for him. The two bumped into each other, and Cas saw Scout's hand slide into the man's pocket and pull out a wallet. Scout quickly began to walk away.

Cas noticed movement out of the corner of his eye. From the tenth western dock, a group of twenty guards were marching toward them. Cas's heart dropped as he saw the man who had just been robbed checking his pocket.

"H-hey!" He yelled, turning to point at Scout. "Thief! He took my wallet!"

The front line of guards turned their attention to the shabbily dressed boys. Scout met Cas's eyes.

"Run, Cas!" he yelled. Several of the guards took aim at Scout, as several others drew their rifles at Cas. As the two boys sprinted in opposite directions, gunshots echoed through the bay. Scout cried out in pain.

Cas paused, spinning around to see his friend clutching his side as he disappeared into an alleyway. Suddenly, the butt of a rifle slammed into Cas's head, sending him to the ground. Three guards surrounded him. Their masks grinned down at him, fangs seemingly poised to strike.

The guards pulled him roughly to his feet, tying his hands behind his back.

"Get off me, I didn't do anything!" Cas cried.

"We know what you are, you filthy little thief," one of the men growled, dragging him back the way they had come. As they passed the alleyway Scout had run down, Cas saw a trail of blood.

The guards marched him down the winding streets to a tall stone building in the center of Valdoria. A chill ran down Cas's spine as he recognized the prison. Plenty of his fellow pickpockets had gone into that building, but few ever came back out.

Inside, his captors forced him down a series of long, dark stone hallways lined with iron-barred cells. The air was heavy with the smell of rot and waste, as well as whispered voices and distant cries of pain. Turning down a final hallway, they shoved him into a small cell. The barred door slid shut behind him.

"Let me out!" he yelled after them. "I didn't do anything, I have to get back to my friend!" They ignored him, disappearing around the corner. Cas shook the bars, half hoping the door would pop open.

He groaned and collapsed onto the thin straw mattress. His head was pounding, and the only thing he could think about was the blood on the cobblestones.

"Ey, don't I know you from somewhere?" He jumped as a raspy voice came from the cell next to him. In the half-light of the prison, he hadn't realized there was an adjacent cell. Nor had he realized that another prisoner was present inside.

The man was middle-aged, incredibly thin, and hunched over, with wild hair and a scraggly beard. He was dressed in rags and had clearly been in prison for some time. He gazed at Cas intensely.

"No, we've never met," Cas stammered. The man's eyes suddenly lit up, and he gasped.

"Caspian Thane! You're Lyra's kid, ain't you? How's she doing?" Cas stared back at the man, mouth falling open in surprise. He was certain he had never seen this person before, but he somehow knew his full name and his mother's.

"She's dead," he said tentatively.

"Oh. Well, that's not good. Sorry to hear that," the man said matter-of-factly.

"How . . . how do you know me?" Cas asked hesitantly.

"Well, technically, I don't know *you*. I knew your father. Caspian Thane Senior. I worked on his ship. You look just like him . . ."

"His ship?" Cas interrupted. "My father had a ship?"

"Yes. He was a pirate captain. Of course he had a ship."

Cas was silent for a long moment. He hadn't known anything about his father, but he'd never imagined that he was a pirate.

"Do you still know him, or where he might be?" Cas asked finally.

The man shook his head. "Nah. I joined another crew years ago. Last I heard though, he was missing. Hasn't been seen for a long time now."

"Missing?"

"I suppose no one should be surprised. He was always talking about finding the *Sea's Revenge* . . ."

"The *Sea's Revenge*?" The name brought to mind long nights in the Golden Eel Tavern, listening to drunk seafarers tell increasingly wild stories. "I thought that was made up."

"Oh, it's real alright. You've heard of it?" Cas shrugged, and the man continued. "It's a great story. The best pirate ship that ever sailed, it raided countless merchant ships and collected more wealth than you could possibly imagine . . . And then one day it just disappeared, and it was never seen again. People have searched for it, but no trace of it has ever been found. Whoever finds that wreck would be rich beyond their wildest dreams." He stared off into the distance for a moment, a far-off look in his eyes. Then he focused on Cas again and extended his hand through the bars. Cas shook it.

"First off, I'm Jesper. Second off, what're you in here for, anyway? I don't see many boys your age here."

Cas glanced around to make sure no guards were around before answering. "Pickpocketing."

"Pickpocketing, well, I—" he stopped mid-sentence, eyes fixed on Cas's chest, then suddenly reached out and grabbed the necklace Cas wore.

"Hey!" Cas cried as he tried to pull away.

"Where'd you get this?" he asked excitedly.

"Wha—my mom gave it to me! What are you doing? Its mine, let go!"

"Do you know what this is? You don't, do ya? It's a map." Cas once again tried to pull away, but Jesper held the crystal tightly.

"You're crazy! Let go of me!"

"Calm down, just let me see it for a minute and I'll show you."

"No way! Let go!"

"What are you worried about, that I'm gonna steal it? I'm in prison, where would I take it?" Jesper asked as he pulled off his own necklace with his other hand and offered it to Cas. It was a leather cord with a gold luck charm, in the shape of a spiral snail shell. "Here. This is my most prized possession. You can hold on to it while I look at yours, okay? Deal?"

Reluctantly, Cas allowed Jesper to take his mother's necklace and shoved the charm into his pocket. Jesper held the crystal up to the torch that hung on the wall nearby.

"What are you doing? You're going to burn—" Cas's words turned into a gasp of amazement as a pattern was suddenly thrown across the far wall.

Jesper laughed. "It's like a prism, or whatever those things are called, where you shine a light on 'em and they make a rainbow? Except there's a map inside this one," he explained. "Pirates used to use these to sneak maps and letters and things past the authorities."

"What's it a map to?" Cas asked.

"It's . . . hard to tell," he said, examining the patterns on the wall. "This would be easier to see with a better light and a smoother wall, but . . . it looks like the Queen's Quarter to me."

Cas knew what that was. He had heard stories about it at the Golden Eel. It was a place all sailors feared, a place of shifting mist, storms, monsters, and ghosts. According to legend, many ships had disappeared there, never to be seen again.

"Do you think that's where my dad is?"

"I'd say there's a good chance of that."

"So I could follow that map? Could I use it to find him?" asked Cas as the echoes of boots approached down the dark hallway. Jesper tossed the necklace back to Cas and lowered his voice to a whisper.

"People don't go to the Queen's Quarter no more, on account of the fact that so many have disappeared. But I know of someone who may be willing to take you if you were so inclined, and stupid enough to go . . ." A grating noise made him pause and spin around. The heavy deadbolt on the hallway door was being pulled open. He turned back to Cas, his voice barely audible. "There was one ship that came back after vanishing into the Quarter. They say it glowed with a ghostly light, completely abandoned aside from one . . ."

The guards threw the hallway door open and walked toward the two of them. Jesper ignored them.

"Go to the Maelstrom Tavern and ask for the captain of the *Riptide*."

One of the guards clicked the key in the cell's lock. Jesper cowered back, but they grabbed him by the arms and hauled him into the corridor.

"C'mon, pirate, your friends are waiting for you," one of them snarled, and they all laughed. As they pulled him away, Jesper called back to Cas.

"If you find your dad, tell him I said hi!"

The heavy door slammed shut, and Cas found himself all alone, his head spinning with thoughts. As he put the necklace in his pocket, he realized he still had Jesper's luck charm.

2

Voyage

Without windows in the cell, it was impossible to tell how much time had passed since Cas had been captured. Bored and fearful, he paced around the cell for what seemed like hours and eventually fell asleep on the scratchy straw bed. When he woke up, he found himself still alone in the cold prison. He was beginning to worry that the guards had forgotten about him.

Finally, he heard footsteps approach and the deadbolt slid open. A lone guard approached him and unlocked the cell.

"Get up, kid. You're free to go," he said.

"I am?" Cas asked, shocked.

"Yeah, get going before we change our mind," the guard said gruffly.

Cas didn't need telling twice. He hurried down the hallway and out the prison door, not meeting the eyes of the other guards for fear they would throw him back in the cell.

He took a deep breath of the fresh air, thankful to finally be outside again. The sky was dark and overcast, but based on the low tide and sparse people on the docks, Cas determined that it was early morning.

Cas ran as fast as he could down the alleyways and across bridges, thinking of nothing other than getting back to Scout. As he neared the dry canal they lived in, he saw drops of dried blood leading into the entrance pipe. He leapt down into the canal and ran into the pipe, panting, sweat dripping down his face.

"Scout?" he called. There was no response. He stepped inside, following the blood trail deeper into the sewer.

As kids, they had explored the network of underground tunnels that connected the many canals that drained excess city runoff into the sea. The labyrinth acted as overflow valves and a system to drain waste from the canals. The pipe they usually sheltered in ended in a large, circular room with more tunnels branching off, and they often went there to hide. It seemed as though this particular pipe and canal had been permanently sealed off from the flow of water, although neither boy knew why.

As Cas grew close to the chamber, he could hear ragged, pained breathing over his own. His heart was pounding as he emerged into the room, calling for Scout once again. This time, he heard a weak response.

As his eyes adjusted to the darkness, he saw his friend lying against the far wall. He ran to Scout's side and kneeled next to him.

His friend was deathly pale, trembling, struggling to breathe. His clothes were stained with dark dried blood, and as he coughed Cas could hear gurgling in his throat. He took Scout's hand, finding it was cold.

"Nice of you to come back," Scout said with a short, forced laugh. "It doesn't look good for me, does it?"

"You . . . you're going to be okay," Cas forced himself to say. "We'll get you to Nan. She'll know what to do . . ." He put his arm around Scout and tried to sit him up. Scout cried out in pain and Cas dropped him. "I'll go get her and bring her here, okay?"

Scout grabbed Cas's arm before he could turn away.

"Don't leave. Please!" Cas swallowed the lump in his throat, sitting back down next to his friend and holding him close.

"Okay."

"Cas . . . I need to know you'll be alright." Scout said weakly.

"Of course I'll be alright. And so will you," Cas insisted.

Scout let out a weak laugh again. "Do you remember when we used to sit in here during storms?"

Cas nodded. He had been terrified of storms. He would hide in the room, where the thunder and rain were muffled, and Scout would hold him and tell him everything would be alright, that the storm would pass. "You're not scared of storms anymore, are you?"

"Of course not!" Cas said with a laugh. He had outgrown that years ago.

"Good. Because I . . . I can't . . ." his voice trailed off. Cas felt tears stinging his eyes as he pulled Scout closer.

"I know," he whispered. "It's okay."

Cas wasn't sure how long he sat there. He held Scout long after his breathing stopped. He didn't want to let go. Sobs racked him as he held Scout's lifeless body.

*

"You sure you want to leave? Life as a pirate ain't much easier than life on the streets," Nan said. Cas stared down into his drink, still untouched on the bar in front of him.

"I'm not becoming a pirate. I'm going to find my dad."

"With a pirate."

"That's my only option," Cas sighed and looked up at Nan. Although she rarely showed emotion, he could see in her eyes that she was concerned about him. "I can't stay. I have nothing left here."

"I know, Cas. I know. I'll miss Scout too, but .. .." she paused, deep in thought. "How can you even be sure this Jesper fella was telling the truth?"

"He knew my name. How could he know that if he didn't know my father?" She shrugged.

"Just promise me you'll be careful."

"I will."

"If you've made up your mind about this, let me give you something to help." She pulled a cloth pouch from her apron and put it on the counter. "This should cover your fare to the Maelstrom, and a bit extra in case you need to bribe anyone. You'll want to take the *Sea Sprite*. It usually sets sail from the second west pier." Cas smiled and tucked the pouch into his pocket.

"Thanks, Nan."

"Now you'd better get going. And remember, if this doesn't work out, you can always come back here. I'll put you to work mopping the place," she said with a laugh. Cas grabbed his bag and departed.

The *Sea Sprite* was easy to find; it was a big, bulky vessel, tied up at the very end of the second western pier. A group of sweaty, husky men were busy loading crates and barrels into the cargo hold, while the captain stood on the dock barking orders.

Cas approached him. "Excuse me?" he asked. The captain turned, looking the boy up and down with suspicion.

"Yes?"

"Are you going to the Maelstrom Tavern?" he asked tentatively.

The captain stared at him for a moment, then burst out in laughter. "No, I ain't got a death wish!" he said.

"Oh. I . . . I was told you could take me there," Cas muttered, feeling his heart sink.

"Ah, well, we can *take* you there, but we're not *going* there. You got any money?" Cas nodded and pulled several coins from his pocket.

The captain took them and motioned for Cas to get onboard, then without another word went back to shouting at his crew.

Confused but encouraged, Cas jumped on the ship. By the time the sun was directly overhead, they were slowly making their way through the bay, toward the open ocean beyond. Cas stood at the front of the ship, heart pounding with excitement.

"Ey." He jumped as a voice came from behind him. He turned to see two of the crew members, one tall and broad, the other short and thin, regarding him suspiciously. The tall one spoke. "You the kid going to the tavern?"

"Yes."

"You a pirate? You look a bit young to be a pirate."

"No, I'm . . ." Cas paused. What was he, exactly? "I'm just meeting someone there," he said finally.

"Well, then, you'd better be real careful," said the shorter man. "The Maelstrom's a den of thieves and murderers. They'll cut your throat as soon as look at you."

"I'll be careful, but I can handle it." Even as he said it, he felt doubt creeping into his voice.

"You sure you ain't a pirate?" the bigger one asked. Cas nodded. "Good. Cause we don't like pirates around here." The two men looked past him to something up ahead, both grinning. Cas turned.

They were approaching the jetties that bordered the entrance to the bay. Hanging from beams along the jetties were metal cages, just large enough for a person to fit inside.

Cas shuddered. He knew what those were, although he had never seen them up close, nor did he want to. This was the Empire's method of executing pirates.

The cages, although exposed at low tide, would be completely submerged by high tide. Cas knew it wasn't just about executing criminals, but also striking fear into others with the threat of a horrific death. He knew, from the time he'd spent at the Golden

Eel listening to sailors, that the one thing every seafarer feared was drowning.

According to superstition, those who drowned would eternally be bound to the water, never resting, cursed to wander the waves forever. Upon finding themselves on a sinking ship, many sailors ended their own lives with a bullet or sword rather than drown and lose their soul to the sea for all eternity.

As they passed the jetty, Cas couldn't help but look down at the cages. Inside were bodies in varying stages of decay, left to be eaten by birds and fish. One of the bodies was fresh, most likely only dead for a few hours. Cas gasped.

Although the face was discolored, the pale eyes staring blankly across the waters that had taken his life, Cas recognized Jesper.

He quickly turned away, clutching the golden shell charm tightly in his hand. The ship picked up speed as they exited the bay, the sails billowing out and the bow cutting through the waves.

He took a deep breath to calm himself. He was on his way toward a new life. At least, he hoped it was a life and not an early death.

3

The Maelstrom Tavern

"Get up, kid!" Cas was shaken awake by the thin man from earlier. He rubbed his eyes and looked around, confused. It was the middle of the night, and he had fallen asleep on a pile of ropes and extra sailcloth at the bow of the ship.

"What's going on?" he asked.

"Your stop's coming up."

"Huh?" He looked around, growing even more confused. There was no land in sight, just an endless expanse of dark water shimmering under the dim light of the moon and stars. He realized the bigger crewman was untying one of the small wooden lifeboats from the side of the ship. The captain emerged from his cabin and gestured. He pointed out to the horizon, at a small spot of light barely visible above the waves.

"You're gonna want to follow that light. Make sure you keep your eyes on it."

"Wait, what? The ship's not stopping?"

"No way. We've got valuable cargo on here. We ain't just gonna hand it over to those criminals. Oh, and speaking of value, that life-boat will cost you five." Cas handed over the coins, and the captain pushed him toward the lifeboat. Reluctantly, he climbed in and was lowered into the sea. He held on tightly as the little boat was buffeted by the wake of the bulky ship.

"Good luck to ya!" The captain called down. The *Sea Sprite* continued on its path, leaving Cas alone in the vast ocean.

After taking a moment to collect himself, he angled his boat toward the pinpoint of light and began to row.

Although the sea was calm that night, the waves slowly but steadily turned the lifeboat away from his destination. Every time he readjusted, the current would pull at him again, threatening to throw him off course. The water felt thick as tar as he dipped his paddles in again and again. The strong current didn't seem to want him to reach his destination.

He paused, panting, sweat dripping down his face, and turned again to see that the light he thought he was headed toward was once again off at an angle, and he was rowing toward the darkness of the open sea. It didn't seem any closer, either.

A chill ran through him as a thought occurred to him; what if he couldn't make it to the tavern? What if he became so exhausted that the relentless current swept him out, far from land or any ship path, to float in this lifeboat until he died? He had already almost finished the little food and water he'd brought with him.

He shook his head and angled the prow back toward the light. He had to stay calm. He would reach the tavern, find the captain, and find his dad.

Ignoring the burning pain in his back and arms, he pushed the tiredness from his mind and he focused on the rhythmic rowing, stopping only to adjust his course now and then. Finally, just when he worried his strength would give out, he felt the lifeboat bump against something. He turned to see a tall dock rising above him.

He sat in the boat for a minute, catching his breath. His shirt was damp with sweat and his whole body ached. He wanted to just lie down in the small vessel and go to sleep, but his journey wasn't over yet. He grabbed his bag and pulled himself to his feet, tied the boat to the nearby post, and climbed up onto the dock.

The Maelstrom Tavern was unlike any other place Cas had seen. It was a huge, wooden platform floating on the surface of the ocean, with docks extending outward like the points of a compass and dozens of ships tied to them. In the center of the platform was an angular three-story wooden building, the windows glowing with warm light and music pouring out.

He stared at the bizarre structure, noting how the entire place rolled and flexed with the waves just like a ship. Now and then, a jolting shudder would run through the floating platform, and he realized there must be a chain anchoring the false island to the sea floor.

Fascination overcoming his exhaustion, he looked up at the building. It seemed inviting, despite its strangeness, but the words still echoed in his head: "a den of thieves and murderers, who will cut your throat as soon as look at you."

But he couldn't turn back now, even if he wanted to. He walked forward and pushed open the heavy door.

Inside was a familiar tavern scene, one that wouldn't have been out of place in the Golden Eel. There was drinking, dancing, singing and discussion, and no one even looked at Cas as he walked in.

He pushed his way through the crowd and toward the counter. A young tavern maid was serving drinks to those seated around the bar. She looked to be around Cas's age, curvy and wide-eyed, with deep brown skin and a cloud of black hair pulled back with a bandanna. She looked up at him as he approached.

"What can I get you?" she asked.

"Actually, I'm looking for someone," he said. "The captain of the *Riptide*."

She looked surprised.

"Y-you're looking for Nyx?"

"Yeah, I guess,"

She blinked, shook her head, and composed herself. "In the back," she pointed. Cas thanked her as she moved to another customer, then made his way to the back.

The tavern was bigger than it seemed from the outside. The far corner was quiet and dark, at odds with the raucous atmosphere near the bar. A few shady-looking people lurked at tables, watching Cas out of the corners of their eyes.

In the very back, cast almost entirely in shadow, a lone person sat at a table, wearing a long oversized black coat, their face obscured by a black tricorn hat. A bottle sat in front of them on the roughhewn table. Cas approached the table.

"Captain Nyx?" he asked softly. The captain slowly looked up, the shadow from the hat falling away from her face. Cas took a step back.

She was bony, sharp-featured and pallid, almost ghostly, with black hair that was pulled into two nearly waist-length braids. But what caught Cas off guard were her eyes—or, rather, eye.

Her left eye was covered by a black fabric patch, with a long scar extending above and below it. Her remaining eye was a bright, unnatural blue, which almost seemed to glow in the darkness of the tavern.

"Who're you?" Her voice was rough, as if she hadn't spoken in a long time.

"My name is Cas," he said, pulling out the chair across from her. "Um, may I?" She nodded. He sat. "I . . . um . . ." A few moments ago, he had been certain of what he was going to say, but under her intense gaze he suddenly forgot. He tried to pull himself together.

"I, well, uh—I have a map. My father, he, um, disappeared, and . . . This is my only clue to where he might be. I was told you might be able to take me. It's in the Queen's Quarter . . ."

"Well, that's where you're wrong, because I'm not going back there."

"Are you sure? Will you at least look at the map?" He offered the necklace to her. She stared at it for a long moment, her face impossible to read. Suddenly she snatched it out of his hand and stood.

"Come on," she snapped. He jumped up and followed her as she quickly wound her way through the maze of tables and tavern occupants. She led him out into the chilly night and down the west-facing pier. At the end was a medium-sized ship, battered and old yet surprisingly elegant, its twin masts adorned with jet black sails.

He followed her across the gangplank. As she walked into the dark captain's quarters, Cas hesitated in the doorway. He realized that if she wanted, she could simply kill him and steal the map.

Inside, Nyx lit a candle and held the necklace up to the light. The map appeared on the wall, this time much clearer. Cas realized it wasn't just a pattern, it was a series of islands, coordinates and arrows. She read it with increasing interest, her mouth moving along with the words.

He glanced around the cabin nervously as she examined the map. Although it was a rather large space, it was sparsely furnished, with only a hammock hanging in an alcove near the large window, a big wooden desk, and a bookshelf along one wall crammed full of strange items. Taking a step toward it, he noticed a variety of music boxes; some were simple and others ornately trimmed with gold and ivory. There was even one that appeared to be made of oyster shells. Multiple canvas paintings leaned against them, each depicting a stormy seascape.

He paused in front of a small box, glancing over at the captain to make sure she wasn't looking before peeking inside. It contained a collection of eyepatches, from plain black cloth ones to leather to lace, some jeweled and others in the shape of skulls and flowers.

"Where did you get this?" she asked abruptly, making him jump back from the shelves. He turned and realized she was referring to the map.

"My mother left it to me, just before she died."

"This is promising," she said, thin lips curling into a smile. "I've seen maps like these before, but this one . . . this one has the flag of the *Sea's Revenge*." She gestured to a symbol in the bottom corner.

"Yeah! Jesper told me .. ." She wasn't listening anymore. She had begun muttering to herself as she rifled through the drawers of her desk, pulling out scrolls and old papers with other illustrations of maps.

"So, will you take me?" he asked meekly.

She didn't respond. He stepped closer. "Captain?" She jumped and looked up at him as if she had forgotten he was there.

"Huh?"

"Will you take me?"

She smiled, revealing several gold teeth.

"Oh. Yes, I suppose I will. Yes, I believe that I will take you. Welcome aboard, Cuff."

"Cas."

"Whatever. But, we have just one problem. We don't have a crew."

"You don't?" he asked, surprised.

"No. I had one, but they, uh . . ." her eye glazed over, and for a long moment she stared off into nothingness. "They disappeared." She shook her head, focusing on him again. "So, if we want to go anywhere, we'll need to hire a new crew. You got any money?"

"Yes, actually." He pulled the coin pouch from his pocket, and she snatched it away from him, quickly examining the contents.

"Good. Hopefully this will be enough."

"Where are we going to find a crew?" Cas asked.

"Where do you think? Here, of course. The Maelstrom is full of sailors looking to sign on with a ship." She tossed the pouch and the necklace into a desk drawer and closed it, her chipper mood disappearing. "Now get out of my room, I have plans to make."

Cas retreated back to the deck of the ship, and she slammed the door behind him. He stared at the door to the captain's quarters, wondering exactly what kind of person he had just signed up with.

*

Cas was surprised by the number of people that showed up that next morning when Nyx announced they were recruiting. There were at least twenty in front of their table, and it was still the middle of the day, long before peak tavern hours.

"How many crew members do we need?" Cas asked.

"Including us? At least ten, although more would be better," Nyx said.

When some of them heard the pay, only three coins each—one up front and two once they were on the ship, with the promise of more later—they laughed and quickly left the line. But some of them stayed.

One sat down across from Cas and Nyx. He was tall and lean, good-looking with long thick blond hair half braided and half down. He flashed a smile at the two of them and extended his hand. Cas shook it.

"Name and qualifications?" Nyx asked.

"I'm Gryph. Pleased to meet ya," he said. "I don't know how 'qualified' I am, per se. My parents were fishermen, but I hated fishing, so I took a sailboat and started doing a bit of piracy: raiding lobster traps, taking stuff that fell off ships, that sort of thing. I'm a quick learner, though, and I want to be a real pirate."

Nyx nodded. "Welcome to the crew, Gryph." He was given his payment and sent to pack his bags.

Someone else took his place across from them. He was short and scrawny, with dark brown skin and long locs intertwined with beads and gold cuffs, and he spoke in a surprisingly high voice.

"I'm Splinter. I worked on a pirate ship since I was twelve when I was hired as a cabin boy, and after a while I worked my way up to first mate." He frowned. "Until the Navy sank my ship and killed my crew."

"Sounds like you're qualified. You're hired," Nyx said.

As he left, another man plopped down into the chair, and the whole tavern seemed to shake. He was tall and bigger around than the table was wide. He was tan and bald, with a lumpy scar across his square jaw.

"I'm Tig," he said.

"Tig? Really?" Cas said. Nyx glared at him.

"Yeah. I was in the Empire's Army for a while, specifically in the Navy, but they kicked me out for . . . less than upright behavior. Mostly drinking and gambling. And some fights. So, figured I may as well embrace it and join a pirate crew."

He was accepted. As the day went on, Cas couldn't help but notice a man lurking just outside the crowd that was gathered around the table. Although his face was hidden by a hat pulled low, it was obvious he was watching them. Before he could bring it up to Nyx, another man joined them.

He was short and stout with unruly blond hair and a short beard. When he spoke, Cas noticed an accent that he normally only heard in wealthy academics.

"Gyles is my name. Pleased to meet you. I studied navigation for several years at the college of Tallix, but then I got thrown out of school after a bar fight. I'm still a damn good navigator, though, if I do say so myself."

"Good! We need one," Nyx said quickly. "You're hired. I'm sure your skills will come in handy on this voyage."

The next person was a woman. She was a head taller than Cas and muscular, with olive skin and a partly-shaved head with a braided mohawk. Covered in tattoos and battle scars, she had a frighteningly intense gaze, one that made Cas shrink back and cower.

"I'm Cimik," she said. "I served in the Selkis Armada before it was disbanded." Cas had heard of the Armada, a tribe of vicious female warriors from the island of Selkis, who opposed the Army for decades before the Empire finally got the upper hand. "I'm an expert sailor, fighter, and I can keep people in line."

"I think we can use someone like you. You're hired."

A wiry man with tawny skin, long braided black hair, and a gold ring in his nose came next. He had an odd twitchy, restless way about him.

"They call me Knives. I was a gambler for a while at different taverns, but I wasn't too great at it, so I stowed away on a ship to avoid debt-collectors. When they found me, they put me to work. Then we got attacked by pirates, so I joined them for a while. But, um, I sorta got left behind here." Nyx seemed unsure about this one but hired him anyway as they didn't have much choice overall.

Replacing him was a pale, thin, stooped man with long curly dark hair, missing two fingers on his left hand and one on his right. He didn't look either of them in the eyes and spoke in a low voice.

"I'm Fenix. I've worked on lots of ships doing a lot of different things, and I'm avoiding the law anyway," he said simply, glancing around to make sure no one else had heard.

"Don't worry, all of us are. You'll fit right in," Nyx said. She hired him as well.

Several hours ticked by, and although they interviewed several more people, Nyx deemed them too inexperienced, or decided that they seemed too untrustworthy. The tavern quieted down as people went to the rooms upstairs or back to their ships. Finally, two men approached.

One of them sat down in the chair while the other stood behind him. The first man was thin and sharp-featured, with sleek black hair and shifty eyes. The second was big and burly, with dark hair pulled back in a ponytail and a braided beard.

"I'm Zadicus, but you can call me Zad, and that's Kaymin," the thin man said in a posh accent. "We've worked on a few other ships, but none of them were a great fit for us. We're hoping yours will be. We can do just about anything that needs to be done, so we will serve you well in whatever capacity you decide."

"I hope so too," Nyx said, giving them each their payment. As they left, someone quickly slid into the chair. It was the tavern maid Cas had spoken to the night before.

"Prisma," she introduced herself. "I don't know anything about sailing but I can cook, clean, and I know lots about medicine." Nyx was silent for a moment, contemplating the young girl.

"Normally I wouldn't hire someone who has no experience sailing, but I'll make an exception for you, Prisma." She gave the maid her coin, and Prisma smiled widely and ran off to pack.

As Nyx and Cas stood up and gathered their things, Cas realized the man who had been standing nearby and watching them the whole night was approaching.

Although the hat was still pulled low over his face, Cas could now see something strange about him. The faint candlelight revealed a face lined with wrinkles, but also raised marks that Cas had to assume were scars. He had a thick silver beard and a metal hook in place of his left hand. He spoke quietly, in a deep voice.

"I was wondering if I could speak to the captain privately," he asked, glancing at Cas.

Nyx shrugged. "Sure. Just so you know, we don't have any money left, if you were thinking of joining . . ."

"Don't worry, I won't be needing payment," he said as he and Nyx stepped away.

Cas gathered his few possessions and returned to the *Riptide*.

As he strolled along the dock, he could hear loud singing and laughing coming from the ship. The new crew was roaming around the deck and taking their bags down into the cabin. Gryph was yelling the lyrics to an old shanty while he stood at the helm.

"Hey, pretty boy!" Splinter yelled from the hatch. "Get your bags down here or they're going overboard!"

"There's nothing in them that can't get wet!" Gryph replied.

"Watch this," Knives said to Gyles as they walked toward the prow. He took a running leap and grabbed onto a rope hanging from the mast, which promptly slid from its loose knot and sent him tumbling to the deck. He looked up, confused. "This ain't a very good rope."

Cas felt himself smiling as he watched them. He glanced back at the tavern and saw Nyx and the old man walking toward the ship. The crew paused their antics and looked to the captain as she approached.

"This is Vyn. He'll be joining us," Nyx announced. "And we'll be taking a slight detour from our original destination. Everyone get to work. We leave at dawn!"

The crew ran to different posts, seeming to know instinctively where to go and what to do. Cas looked to Nyx, unsure of what he should be doing.

"Cimik!" Nyx called. She stepped forward. "You're in charge of the cabin boy."

"Cabin boy?" Cas cried, his good mood evaporating.

"Yes, is that a problem?"

"I'm the one who found the map and paid for the crew. Don't I get a more important role than that?"

Nyx laughed.

"No," she stated before quickly disappearing into her quarters with Vyn.

Cas stared open-mouthed in shock after them. Cimik grabbed a mop and bucket from where they leaned against the quarterdeck and thrust them into Cas's hands.

"I want this ship looking like new by the time we leave," she growled, her intense eyes making him bow his head and stare at his feet. Reluctantly, Cas began mopping the deck.

"It could be worse," a voice came from behind him. He turned to see Prisma smiling at him. "They could've just stolen your map and money and shot you."

"Thanks, that makes me feel so much better," Cas said sarcastically.

"Just sayin'. There's much worse fates on a pirate ship." She winked at him. "I'll see you around, cabin boy."

He watched her as she walked down to the lower levels. Across the ship, he heard Cimik yell. "I don't see you cleaning, kid!"

He quickly returned to work.

4

A Pirate's Life

At first, being at sea was thrilling. The salty wind, the intoxicating motion of the waves, seeing nothing but the ocean in all directions; Cas felt at home on the sea. The longing he'd felt deep in his soul every time he sat on the seawall was finally satisfied. Not to mention, it was a welcome surprise to be given three meals a day and a comfortable place to sleep.

Unfortunately, it all came with a price, and that price was that he was kept constantly busy by Cimik. From dawn to dusk she had him cleaning, cooking, and performing ship maintenance.

Constant exposure to seawater and sweat meant that he was covered in salt, and it burned his skin as the wind dried it. At the end of each day, he was exhausted and sore, with increasingly more cuts and abrasions on his overworked hands.

"I really think Cimik hates me," he muttered as Prisma applied yet another layer of bandages over his hands.

"She doesn't hate you," Prisma said. "She's just doing her job."

"How long have we been sailing now, anyway?"

"Two and a half weeks."

"And we're going in the opposite direction of the map, aren't we? I know the Queen's Quarter is east of here, and we're going west."

"That's because we're going to The Well." Prisma lowered her voice. "I overheard Nyx talking to herself about it. Vyn convinced her to go after some ship, and he heard that's where they would be."

"What ship?" he inquired.

She shrugged.

"And what's The Well?"

"You've never heard of it?"

Perhaps he had, late at night in the Golden Eel, but so many stories had blurred together in his memory that he couldn't pick apart which were which. "It sounds familiar," he said finally.

"The Well is a bottomless pit out in the middle of the ocean, surrounded by violent storms that take out even the strongest ships. But along the outside is a ring of islands, and that's where a lot of pirates used to meet in the old days, before taverns like the Maelstrom popped up."

"And we're going there?" Cas couldn't keep his voice from shaking.

"Apparently."

"Can I ask you something?"

"Sure."

"Is the captain a little . . ."

"Crazy? Yes."

"In the tavern, she said she normally wouldn't hire someone without sailing experience, but she'd make an exception for you. Do you two know each other?"

"Kind of. She and her crew were regulars at the tavern, and I used to serve them sometimes. But then they just disappeared . . ."

"In the Quarter?" Cas finished.

She nodded. "Yeah. They were gone for almost three years. We all assumed they were dead, until the *Riptide* came back one night." She paused, laughing. "Maybe I shouldn't tell you. I don't want you to think I'm crazy too."

"No, you can tell me. I won't think you're crazy. I promise," Cas insisted. After a moment of silence, Prisma continued.

"It was really late one night, just before dawn actually. Just about everyone was asleep, or had already left. It was me, a couple other maids, and the tavern keeper, Jois. I was cleaning tables when suddenly the whole tavern shook. We looked outside and saw that a ship had run straight into one of the docks, but that wasn't the strange part.

"The ship was . . . glowing, with this eerie blue light, and it was covered in barnacles and seaweed like it had been sitting at the bottom of the ocean for years. When we walked out onto the pier, it all started to fall away. The barnacles and slime and weeds sloughed off in big chunks like it was shedding its skin, and the glow started to fade. When that happened, we recognized that it was the *Riptide*. Jois and I went aboard to look around and realized the whole ship was abandoned. The crew was gone.

"Jois told me to wait where I was and she went up to the helm, and that's when I noticed that the ship wasn't *completely* empty. Nyx was slumped over the wheel. At first, we both thought she was dead. Just like the ship, she was soaking wet and glowing, and she was pale and skeletal. But then she woke up, like our presence had startled her awake.

"She seemed . . . *wild*. She screamed and clawed and fought Jois, and then collapsed to the ground crying and muttering nonsense to herself. Jois pulled her to her feet, and she just went limp. She must have fainted.

"We brought her inside and tied the ship up. I took care of her while she recovered. That's how she knows me.

"Like I said, I didn't know Nyx well before. She was just one of the many pirate captains that hung around the tavern. But she always seemed serious, level-headed, and tough. The Nyx that came back wasn't the same. The glow faded and she started to recover, but she always acts strangely now. And, of course, with no crew she couldn't go anywhere, so we just took her in at the tavern. She still slept on her ship but we gave her free food and drinks and all."

"What happened? Did she ever tell you?"

"Not really. She just kept saying that her crew disappeared, and talked about ghosts and monsters . . . but it never made much sense. Whatever happened, though, she's the only person I've ever heard of that disappeared into the Quarter and came back out. So, I guess she's the perfect person to be leading us there, huh?"

"Cas!" Cimik's voice came from the door, making them both jump. The boatswain glared at him from the ladder. "Get back to work." He stood as she climbed back up, but paused as Prisma jumped to her feet.

"Oh, I almost forgot!" she said excitedly. She reached under the medic cot and pulled a sheathed sword from beneath it. "I found it down in the cargo hold, tucked behind some boxes. I guess it must've belonged to someone in Nyx's old crew." She offered it to him. He took it, sliding the shiny silver blade from its cracked leather casing. The razor-sharp edge glinted in the lantern light.

"You don't want it?" he asked.

"I have a sword. Besides, you need a weapon if you want to be a pirate. That is kind of a requirement for the job."

He smiled and fastened it to his belt. "Thanks."

"Now get up there, you don't want to keep Cimik waiting."

Up on the deck, the crew was busy. Nyx was at the helm. Tig, Knives, and Gryph were adjusting sails, Gyles kept watch from the nest, while Fenix and Splinter were up in the rigging. All of them were shouting at each other.

"I said port! Port, you idiot! That's starboard!" Splinter yelled down.

"I'm trying!" Gryph snapped. "Why don't you come down here and do it yourself?"

"He can't, he's too small," Knives said with a laugh. Splinter's shoe flew down from the mast and hit him directly in the head, making him stumble back and fall. Gryph doubled over in laughter. Tig rolled his eyes.

"I'm not getting paid enough to put up with you people," he muttered.

Out of the corner of his eye, Cas noticed Zad stumble up onto the deck and vomit over the side of the ship. Zad and Kaymin normally kept to themselves down in the lower levels, but anytime the sea grew even a bit rough it would make Zad sick. Cas walked over to him.

"I'll tell you what, kid," Zad groaned, pushing his slick hair back under his hat. "I can't wait to get wherever we're headed."

"What did you do on the other ships?"

Zad looked at him, confused. "Huh?"

"You said you worked on several other ships before this one. Didn't you get sick on them, too?"

"Oh! Well, uh, they were much bigger ships. They were steadier in the water than this one." He wiped the sweat from his forehead. "I hope we're getting close to our destination."

"I don't think you're going to like it."

"What? Why not?"

"I heard, or, I guess, Prisma heard, that we're going to The Well." His eyes grew wide and he leaned closer to Cas.

"The Well? Why are we going there?"

Cas shrugged. "Apparently there's a ship out there. I don't know, it's Vyn's plan."

"A ship? One that we're meeting or attacking?"

"I don't know. It must be important, if we're going weeks out of our way for it."

"Yes," Zad muttered. "Very important. It's Vyn's plan, you said?" He glanced toward the quartermaster's cabin. Vyn spent most of the days inside, emerging at night to act as a lookout. Cas had hardly seen the man since they'd met in the tavern. "Does he seem a bit odd to you?"

"I . . . I guess so. A little."

"I hope Nyx knows what she's doing. A strange man approaches you at a tavern and demands you go to a remote and dangerous location . . . And I worry that Nyx isn't in her right mind most of the time."

"What do you mean? Do you think it's a trap or something?" Cas asked.

Zad shrugged. "Don't know. But I'd be ready for anything if I were you, kid." He turned and retreated down to the lower decks. As Cas worked, he found himself staring at the door to Vyn's cabin.

By the next night, word had spread through the crew about where they were supposedly going. The galley at dinner time was always rowdy and loud, with everyone laughing and drinking and Gyles playing the violin. The only two absent were Nyx and Vyn, who typically ate in their cabins. Cas sat down next to Prisma at the long wooden table in the center of the room.

"This ship we're attacking better have some good food," Gryph was saying. He picked up the biscuit from his plate and hit it against the table, producing a thud. "These things could be weapons." Splinter hit him on the back of the head with one, and he cried out.

"You're right, they can be used as weapons!" He said. He threw one at Gyles, but Cimik caught it in midair and glared at Splinter.

"Don't waste food," she snapped. The table went quiet for a minute.

"Anyway, we don't know we're attacking the ship at all," Knives said finally. "It could be another pirate ship. Maybe we're joining forces."

"If we're meeting another pirate ship, why couldn't they meet us halfway? Nah, we're going after prey," Gryph insisted.

"Or, we're being set up," Zad suggested, his eyes darting between the crew. His gaze landed on Cas, who nervously looked down. "After all, what do we really know about Vyn *or* Nyx?"

"You're questioning the captain?" Tig asked, his voice low and menacing.

"No, no, of course not!" Zad quickly laughed. "We're all just listing hypotheticals here."

"He's got a point," Gyles said, pausing his music. "What do we know about them, really?"

"I trust Nyx," Prisma spoke up.

"Sure, you two are friends, aren't you?" Zad asked.

"I wouldn't say we're friends, but I trust her," Prisma said quietly.

"She's the captain. We should all trust her," Cimik said.

"Yes, you're right. We all *should* be able to trust a captain," Zad muttered. Kaymin nodded.

"Yeah," he grunted. Kaymin rarely spoke, aside from agreeing with Zad. Cimik glared at the two of them, and they both returned to eating.

Gyles continued playing music, and Knives, Gryph, and Splinter descended into an argument about whether the bread should be called "biscuits" or "rolls." When Fenix entered, Cas realized he hadn't even noticed him leave.

A few moments later, he heard boots heading toward them. Nyx and Vyn walked into the galley. The room went silent. Nyx sat down in an empty chair with her feet up on the table. Vyn, hat pulled low over his face, stood behind her in the doorway.

"I heard there's some talk about where we're going," she said, looking between each member of the crew. "And some of you aren't too happy." Zad avoided looking at her.

"We were just curious, is all. We don't know anything about it," Gryph said.

"Alright, then I'll tell you. Vyn informed me that a ship carrying valuables is waiting at The Well for reinforcements. They've recently lost several crew members, and given that they're in a bad position, he thinks we can easily take them and be set for the trip to the Quarter," she explained.

"I know the ship. I worked on it," Vyn continued. "We can get in and out with everything we need before they even realize we were there."

"And what's in it for you?" Zad asked.

"Excuse me?" he asked.

"You didn't get paid to be here, and you asked the captain to take you straight to this ship. Surely you're not just doing this out of the goodness of your heart?"

"They stole something from me, and I want it back," Vyn said sharply.

"And we're risking our lives going after them for your sake?"

"This isn't a Navy ship. We're a democracy here," Nyx continued. "So, let's put it to vote. If you want to go after the undermanned ship carrying valuables, raise your hand."

Splinter, Gryph, Knives, and Fenix immediately put their hands up. Cimik and Tig paused, glancing at each other and at the others, before raising theirs as well. Prisma and Cas exchanged a look.

This was going to be their first ever act of piracy. After this, there was no going back. As Cas looked into her dark eyes, he knew what she was thinking: they were aboard a pirate ship, and sooner or later this was going to happen. It may as well be sooner.

Both of them raised their hands.

"Well, that's a majority vote." Nyx looked at Zad, Kaymin and

Gyles. "Tell you what, boys, you can stay on the ship and look after things while we get the treasure." She left without waiting for a response.

"I have nothing against taking on this ship," Gyles muttered. "I just don't like going into things without more information, y'know?"

"You're a pirate now, mate. Get used to jumping into fights without much planning," Vyn said. Then he turned and followed the captain out.

On a normal ship, there would be multiple night lookouts posted when they were at sea, but with most of the crew needed during the day for sailing, Vyn was the only one awake once the sun set. Although Nyx and Prisma stayed in private cabins, Cas and the others slept in hammocks strung up below deck. He was quickly growing used to the nighttime antics of the crew, even beginning to find them comforting.

"Everything I own is wet," Zad muttered as he climbed into his hammock. "Isn't the point of the ship to keep things dry?"

"Only in theory," Tig said.

"You're in my hammock," Splinter said.

"How is this *your* hammock? I don't see your name on it," Gryph asked.

"Get out, you prick!" Cas opened his eyes a crack to see Splinter attempting to wrestle Gryph out of the hammock.

"Would you two idiots cut that out?" Cimik yelled.

Cas soon drifted off to sleep, lulled by the gentle rocking of the ship and the quiet bickering of the crew.

He woke up with an unsettled feeling deep in his chest. The lanterns that kept the room lit had gone out, plunging the lower deck into almost total darkness aside from the faint moonlight coming in through the cracks in the hull. He could hear the sounds of snoring and people shifting in their hammocks, and he seemed to be the only one awake.

At first, he couldn't figure out what had awoken him. Then he heard it: a low, ominous rumble, the kind that he not only heard but felt. He jumped out of bed and hurried up to the deck.

Everything seemed normal. The sea was calm and reflected the clear sky like a mirror, millions of stars glittering above and below.

A flash of light caught his eye. Directly ahead of the ship, although still distant, was . . . something. Cas squinted, trying to make it out. It was a black spot, far darker than the background of the night sky. Another flash came, and he realized that he was looking at black clouds hovering on the horizon, discharging jagged bolts of lightning.

The low growl of thunder echoed over the sea again, sending chills down his spine. Perhaps he wasn't over his fear of storms after all.

"What are you doing up, kid?" Surprised, he spun around. Vyn was standing by the wheel looking down at him, gray hair glowing white in the moonlight.

"Oh. Um. I heard the storm," he said.

"That's not just any storm. That's The Well."

Cas looked back at the imposing dark mass on the horizon, swallowing hard.

"That's where we're going?"

"This is nothing. Next destination is the Quarter, and that's going to be far more challenging. The Well isn't too bad, as long as you stay out of the worst of it."

"Have you been there before?"

"Yes, as a matter of fact, I have. Back in the day, pirates from all over the map used to meet here."

"That's what Prisma said. It just seems . . . dangerous," Cas said.

"We're pirates, kid. Danger is what we do."

Cas stepped up to the helm. For the first time since they had met, Vyn's hat was off, and Cas found himself examining the old pirate. Now that he could see his face more clearly, Cas couldn't figure out what could have caused such a disfigurement.

His scars looked similar to knife slashes, but of varying size and depth. They covered the entire left side of his face from chin to forehead and continued down his neck and under his coat, and Cas could see bare patches in his hair and beard that revealed even more.

Vyn glanced over, and Cas quickly looked away.

"You said you used to work on the ship we're chasing?" Cas asked in an attempt to deflect the situation.

"Yes," he said simply.

"And you said they stole something from you?"

Vyn was silent for a moment, his pale eyes fixed on the storm that hovered far ahead of them. "They stole a lot from me," he said finally. "But there's one thing in particular that I need back."

"What is it?"

"The less you know about it, the better."

Cas decided not to press the issue further. "Is The Well really bottomless?" he asked after another long pause.

Vyn chuckled. "You ask a lot of questions, huh?"

Cas shrugged.

"I have no idea. I suppose it can't truly be bottomless. Everything has to end somewhere. But it's deep, real deep. I heard a man tried to measure it once and lowered down miles and miles of rope with a cannonball attached. As far as I know, he never hit the bottom. Of course, maybe the rope just got sucked up by the current."

"You said there was a cannonball at the end, though."

"There was. But I wouldn't doubt that the currents in The Well are strong enough to pick up a cannonball. I've seen what they can do to a ship . . ."

"What did it do to the ship?" Cas asked, partly horrified and partly intrigued. Vyn leaned in, smiling.

"Ripped it in half, and as soon as the crew hit the water it sucked them down never to be seen again."

Cas recoiled. Vyn seemed amused.

"Don't worry though, kid. That's in the center of The Well. We're only going around the edges."

"That doesn't make me feel much better." Cas said nervously.

"You should try to get some sleep. Tomorrow we'll be arriving."

5

The Well

The storm reared up before the ship as the crew rushed about, making preparations to survive the treacherous conditions of The Well. Cas tied a rope around his waist and the other end around the mast. The wind that whipped his hair back was surprisingly cold and brought the smell of rain and a hint of sulfur.

His heart pounded in his ears as thunder crashed and blue-tinged lightning lit the sky. This wasn't like any storm he had seen before. Even the hurricanes that occasionally rolled in from the south seemed tame in comparison to the greenish-black clouds that filled the sky ahead.

"Everyone tied in?" Nyx shouted above the howling wind. She was met with confirmations from her crew. "Prepare for impact!"

The ship pitched downward into a deep trough. Cas's heart skipped a beat as he saw the next wave towering over them in impenetrable wall of water.

As they crested the top of the wave, the clouds finally engulfed what was left of the sunlight. Rain poured down in sheets, pounding against the deck like drumbeats interspersed with cacophonous crashes of thunder.

Cas wiped the water from his eyes and almost wished he hadn't. Another wave was bearing down on them, even bigger than the last, edged with menacing white foam. It crashed over the deck, knocking him off his feet.

He pulled himself up, coughing and sputtering. He grabbed the mast and clung on, squeezing his eyes shut.

Around him, he could hear the ominous creaking of the ship and the frenzied cries and shouts of the crew. He tried to block it all out, trying to imagine himself back with Scout in the sewers. He felt tears stinging his eyes as it hit him that, even if he survived this, he would never be with Scout again.

Someone grabbed him and pulled him away from the mast.

"Get up, kid!" Vyn yelled. "We're taking on water, we need you below—"

Before he could finish, the ship listed sharply to the side. They both stumbled and fell against the railing.

For a terrible moment, Cas was certain this was going to be the end. The ship was going to capsize, and they would all drown.

But then the rain subsided into a dense, clinging fog, and the waves calmed. Cas pushed the wet hair from his eyes and looked around.

The fog made it difficult to see much, but the ship seemed to be in good shape, all things considered. The crew were pulling themselves to their feet, untying themselves, and ensuring that no one was injured. Knives slung his long, dripping braids away from his face, splashing Gryph where he sat nearby.

"That was fun. We should do it again," he said.

"Is that it? Are we through?" Cas asked shakily.

"Not exactly," Nyx called down from the helm. "The Well is divided into three sections: the outer ring of storms, the inner ring, and the central pool. We're through the outer ring. Everyone to your posts, and keep an eye out for an island."

Cas was sent below deck to help bail out the water that had poured into the ship from an improperly sealed hatch. As he reached the lowest level, he splashed down into cold seawater past his knees. Prisma stepped down behind him.

"This doesn't look good," she sighed.

They began scooping out buckets and passing them up to Tig, who dumped them out the porthole. They worked for what seemed like hours before a cry went up that an island had been sighted.

Prisma and Cas raced up to the deck. A dark shape was slowly emerging through the mist: an island, devoid of plant life, with sheer cliff faces on every side that plunged down into the cold waves. Up on the helm, Nyx and Vyn were quietly discussing something while looking through their spyglasses.

Cas leaned out over the side of the ship and squinted into the fog. As he did, he could make out a huge cave tunneling into the near side of the island. Faint firelight came from within.

"Is that where we're headed?" Gyles called down from the crow's nest.

"Yes," Vyn replied. "But slowly, and quietly. The less warning they have, the better."

The *Riptide* crept forward into the dark cave. The main cavern was enormous, easily allowing the ship to pass through. Huge dripping stalactites hung down from the ceiling, and strange rock formations like melted wax rose up around them. The wind produced an eerie whine as it whistled through the caves.

In the flickering light, Cas saw that smaller passages branched off the main tunnel. Some were tiny, others big enough for several people to walk side by side into them. As they passed by one of the larger passages, he saw something retreat back into the darkness. Something big. He swallowed hard and focused on the cavern ahead.

They approached a bend in the cavern and slowed to a halt near a jagged outcrop of rock that concealed whatever lay beyond. Zad, Kaymin, Gyles, and Prisma stayed behind to ready the ship for a quick getaway, while the others jumped into the two lifeboats and began rowing toward the dim light.

As they circled the bend, Cas's mouth dropped open. The cave expanded into a massive chamber, large enough to contain a whole fleet of ships. Curved walls gave the cavern an almost cathedral-like quality. From the center rose a gigantic outcrop that looked disturbingly like a half-melted human skeleton.

Anchored to the skeletal rock was a ship, the deck dimly illuminated with lanterns. It was an impressive ship, larger than the *Riptide*, with three tall masts and an elegantly curved prow. The hull was sleek and shiny black. As they drew closer, the name appeared in gold lettering: *The Queen's Curse.*

"She was an Empire Navy ship," Vyn muttered to no one in particular. "Beautiful vessel, and surprisingly easy to handle. And now it's in the hands of that bastard Lucien . . ."

"Who?" Splinter whispered. Vyn shook his head.

"Never mind."

"Where is everyone?" Tig called softly from the other boat. Cas realized with a start why the ship seemed so strange to him: there was no one on the deck, in the rigging, or even keeping watch from the crow's nest. It seemed to be abandoned.

"I told you, they recently lost most of their crew. I assume the survivors are below deck," Vyn said.

"What happened to the crew?" Gryph asked.

"Captain killed them," Vyn answered.

"Huh?" Knives asked. Vyn didn't elaborate. Instead, he grabbed the grappling hook and rope that sat next to him and threw it up to the deck. Nyx did the same, and the two climbed up.

The rest of the crew soon joined them, making as little noise as possible.

"Everyone fan out, grab as much as you can, and get back to the boats. Be back in exactly twenty minutes." Nyx whispered. Vyn gestured to the two hatches on the deck.

"The closer one leads down to the cargo hold. That one over there is the kitchen and cannon room." Gryph, Cimik, Tig, Fenix and Knives jumped down the nearest hatch, while Splinter and Nyx headed to the far one.

Cas took the far hatch as well and crept down the ladder to the lower deck. He saw bright candlelight pouring out of a room nearby, and he could hear laughing and talking. He caught a glimpse of a table with several people sitting around it inside. Behind him, he heard a door creak and spun around, expecting that he had been caught. Instead, he saw Splinter, who quickly slipped inside the dark room.

Cas quickly continued to the next level. He found himself inside a long room full of cannons and barrels of gunpowder. Nyx was dragging the barrels to one corner and arranging them in a pile.

"What are you doing?" Cas whispered. Nyx smiled and gestured down to the floor. There, starting at one end of the room and leading up to the barrels, was a trail of powder.

"We can't have them coming after us, now can we?"

"You're going to blow the ship up?" Cas gasped.

"Vyn's suggestion."

Cas quickly went back up the ladder. If Nyx was planning to set the whole place on fire, he sure wasn't going to stay onboard. He would wait in the boat.

As he reached the main deck, he saw that the boats were already filled considerably with boxes, barrels, and bags.

Cas jumped as a shout and a crash came from the captain's cabin. He heard raised voices below him, and then the sound of people rapidly ascending the ladder just as Vyn came running out of the cabin.

"To the boats!" he yelled.

Cas didn't need to be told twice. He ran and jumped off the ship, landing awkwardly in one of the lifeboats. Above him, he heard confused cries turning into anger, and then the sound of gunshots and swords clashing together.

One by one, the rest of his crew joined him in the lifeboats. As they began to paddle away, bullets flew past them, missing them by inches. The crew of *The Queen's Curse* began to ready their ship to give chase.

A bullet hit the lifeboat, punching a hole clean through the bottom. Water began pouring in. Cas pulled off his jacket and shoved it against the breach, temporarily stopping the flow of the water.

The enemy ship's sails unfurled, and the anchor was pulled up. It began to move toward them, slowly at first but gaining speed. For a moment, Cas was sure they were going to be caught.

Then they rounded the bend and reached the *Riptide*. As quickly as possible, they hauled in the lifeboats and ran to their posts. The *Riptide* lurched away as soon as the anchor was pulled up, and the sails filled with wind as they headed for the cave entrance.

The Queen's Curse appeared around the corner. It raced toward them, surprisingly fast for such a large ship. As they approached the entrance, Cas realized the other ship was attempting to come up alongside them and drive them into the rocky walls.

Then they were out, back on the fog-shrouded sea. The strong wind caught and the sails billowed out, and for a moment, the *Riptide* shot forward. Cas thought they would get away.

But as soon as the *Curse* exited the cave, the wind filled its sails and it came rushing toward them. Cas felt like a prey animal, pursued by a much bigger, much faster predator. As the *Curse* pulled up along their flank, he expected the crew to start swinging over to the *Riptide*.

Instead, it turned into them. The prow crashed into the side of the *Riptide* with a horrible crack, and Cas was thrown to the ground. Above the shouting and creaking of wood as the two ships separated, he heard Nyx yell.

"They're trying to push us into the center!" Before Cas could find his footing, the *Curse* rammed them again and the ship listed to the side.

The sails above his head suddenly turned inside out and the *Riptide* was dragged away from the *Curse*. He could hear laughter and taunting cries from the enemy ship.

As Cas pulled himself up, several things happened at once.

Nyx shouted orders at the crew, to stow the sails and seal the hatches, and for everyone to tie themselves in.

Then a huge explosion tore the *Curse* apart. Everyone dropped to the deck as bits of flaming wood and sailcloth shot in every direction. It left Cas's ears ringing and briefly blinded him. As his vision cleared, he saw the remains of the once mighty ship burning, scattered across the ocean.

Cas let out a shrill laugh of surprise and relief. Out of the corner of his eye, he saw Vyn staring across the water, hat off in a sign of mourning.

"Cas, tie yourself in!" he heard Prisma yell. As he turned, the fog cleared, and he caught sight of what lay on the other side of the island and where the wind was taking them. His relief instantly turned to horror.

The storm swirling around the outside of The Well was nothing compared to what lay in the very center. A huge, disk-shaped mass of dark clouds rose up into the sky like a solid wall. The water below almost seemed to be boiling, bubbling and frothing as it tossed up huge waves, spinning around and around beneath the low-hanging clouds.

As they were picked up by a wave, Cas caught a glimpse of what lay in the middle, what they were being pulled toward: a massive whirlpool.

Although his legs felt weak with terror, he forced himself to move. He grabbed a rope and tied himself tightly to the mast once again, hands shaking, mind blank.

"What do we do?" Zad's voice, just as frightened as Cas felt, came from nearby.

"Pray to the deity of your choice," Vyn replied, voice cracking.

The current swept the ship along like a paper boat in a river. Waves came from every direction, chaotic and ceaseless, preventing Cas from standing up. He held tightly onto the mast. Above everything else, he could hear the ominous creaking of the ship as it threatened to shake apart.

Captain Nyx had tied herself to the helm and was somehow still standing. Her jaw was set in fierce determination, and her eye held a frightening intensity. She looked down at the crew and shouted over the storm.

"Drop the anchor over the port side!" The crew paused, their captain's voice seeming to snap them out of their panic.

"Captain, I don't . . ." Tig protested.

"*Drop the anchor, now!*" she screamed, eye flashing a brilliant blue.

Cimik pulled the lever and Cas watched as the anchor disappeared into the dark water. The chain rattled as more and more fell away into the sea. Then, with a terrible crack, it pulled taut.

The ship nearly turned on its side, sending Cas sliding across the deck until his safety rope stretched tight. The anchor chain strained, and wooden beams snapped cleanly off the side of the ship and fell away into the sea. As they crested a wave, Cas stared down into the gaping black maw of the whirlpool.

Then the weight of the anchor shifted. It began to drag them away from the center of the pool. The next thing Cas knew, they were at the outer edge. Nyx ordered the crew to pull in the anchor, and as it was hauled in the ship righted itself. Nyx angled the *Riptide* straight with the flow of the current and, like a slingshot, it sent them flying away from the swirling interior of the whirlpool.

They found themselves back in the calm, fog-shrouded waters of the inner ring. Cas slowly released his white-knuckled grip on the side of the ship and drew in a shaking breath. Miraculously, they had survived.

Nyx sliced through her ropes with her sword and came running down from the helm, heading for Vyn. He slowly pulled himself to his feet, staring at her with a combination of shock and respect.

"Nyx, that was—" He didn't get to finish. She drew back her fist and punched him square in the jaw, dropping him to the floor.

"You told me this would be easy, that they didn't have enough people to sail!" she yelled. "Well, I hope you got what you wanted. You nearly killed us all and we lost half what we took, not to mention the damages to my ship!"

"I . . . I'm . . ." he stammered.

"I want you off my ship at the next port. And count yourself lucky I don't just throw you overboard," she growled, turning and marching back to the helm. "The rest of you, get to your posts! We head for Carran."

6

The Hunt

They limped into the port of Carran several days later. There were times that they worried the ship wasn't going to make the journey. Both sides of the ship were heavily damaged, as were the sails and masts. Even with their preliminary repairs, keeping water out of the hold was a full-time job. When Gyles first sighted land, everyone breathed a sigh of relief.

Carran was a group of three sparsely populated, rocky islands, constantly battered by storms blown in from The Well. The port was small compared to Valdoria's, not much more than a few docks and a cluster of weathered buildings tucked into the mountainous terrain.

Stepping out onto the dock after weeks at sea was strange. Cas felt awkward and wobbly, like he was still moving up and down on the waves despite having solid ground beneath his feet.

Most of what they took from the *Curse* had to be traded for repairs. The rest was distributed evenly among the crew, although it was only enough for a few nights in the local Inn and a few good meals.

The night before they set sail, Cas and Prisma walked down to the tavern with the last of their share. The tavern was quiet, with only a few locals hanging around, none of which seemed particularly interested in the newcomers. The bartender paused as the pair passed him their money.

"Interesting coins. Where'd you get them?"

"On our travels." Prisma said.

"I ask because a few weeks back, I got some of these from pirates that stopped here. You ain't pirates, are you?"

Prisma and Cas quickly shook their heads.

"Yeah, I figured you'd be too young to be part of the crew of *The Queen's Curse*."

"*The Queen's Curse*?" Cas gasped.

The bartender paused and regarded him suspiciously. "You know it?"

"We were attacked by that ship." Prisma said. "When we were passing by The Well. But it sank in the storm."

"Good riddance. That ship and its crew have been a menace for decades, it's about time something destroyed it."

"What do you mean?" Prisma asked.

"You don't know about Captain Alistair?" the bartender asked. When the pair shook their heads, he set down the glasses he was cleaning. "Alistair was one of the best damn pirates that ever lived, with a crew of vicious criminals and thirty cannons to back him up. People called him the Demon of the North Sea. He raided hundreds of ships over the years and had a sadistic side. He would have his fun killing the crew in very . . . *inventive* ways. For the higher-ranking officers, he would tie them to the masts and sink the ship.

"Rumor has it, Alistair had some kind of supernatural sense about where other ships would be. He never plotted a course ahead of time, just set sail and happened upon every merchant in the area. Some said he could predict the future. He fought off an entire Navy fleet once, and he couldn't have done that if he hadn't seen it coming. I met a man that was part of that fleet. He said Alistair was terrible, more creature than man, with a shout like a cannon's roar and eyes like fire. He was invincible, they all believed."

"So what happened to him?" Prisma asked.

"For a while, no one knew. He just disappeared for a few years. But when the ship came here, a few of the pirates told me the story. Apparently, Alistair's first mate mutinied and killed him, as well as a sizeable portion of the old crew, and they were headed to The Well to wait for reinforcements." The bartender chuckled. "I guess the reinforcements didn't get there in time. Serves them right."

Cas and Prisma finished their meal and walked back to the Inn, slowly. Both were quiet, the true gravity of their battle finally setting in, as well as the knowledge that things could have been much worse than a damaged ship.

The next morning, they were up bright and early and heading down to the dock. In the tavern, Cas saw the hunched figure of Vyn at the bar.

"I'll be there in a minute," he told Prisma, and he walked inside. Before he could approach Vyn to tell him goodbye, Nyx pushed past him and stepped up to the bar.

"Don't worry, I'm not planning to rejoin you," Vyn started.

"Actually, that's what I want to talk about," Nyx interrupted. "Thanks to you, I don't have enough money left over to hire a new crew member. And we still need someone to work the night shift, so as far as I'm concerned, you're stuck with us." Vyn looked up at her, confused. "We'll be waiting." She quickly turned and left the tavern. Vyn noticed Cas, who shrugged.

"I guess you better come with me," Cas said. A smile crept over Vyn's face.

"I guess I better."

They set off into a beautiful morning, hardly a cloud in the sky and a warm breeze coming from the south. Cas and Prisma gazed out over the sea as the prow angled west and the sails caught the wind and billowed open.

"I think this is a good sign," Cas said. "Maybe the worst is behind us."

"Let's hope," she responded.

"Cabin boy!" Cimik shouted from across the deck. "Deck needs cleaning!"

Cas sighed. "Maybe not."

*

Cas was awoken from his sleep by shouts and someone shaking him. He sat up and looked around. Everyone was out of their hammocks, frantically getting ready.

"What's going on?" Cas asked.

"We're going hunting!" Splinter said with a fierce excitement. Cas jumped out of his hammock and joined them as they ran up to the deck. Nyx was at the wheel with Vyn by her side, pointing toward a light in the distance.

"Merchant ship ahead! Lower the sails and raise the flag," she called. The crew jumped into action. The *Riptide* lurched forward as the sails billowed out, and the black flag adorned with a white skull unfurled at the top of the mast.

The *Riptide* began to close the distance to the ship. Across the water, Cas heard a yell as the merchant's lookout woke the rest of the crew. White sails, bright against the midnight blue sky, sprang open as the ship began to flee.

The *Riptide* raced toward it, prow slicing through the waves, and it quickly became clear that the smaller pirate ship was much faster and more agile than its lumbering prey. Soon, Cas could hear the panicked cries of the crew as they struggled to outrun their pursuers.

He jumped as gunshots from the merchant vessel echoed through the night. The pirates raised their own guns and fired back, and Cas could tell their intention wasn't to hit the ship, but to intimidate the merchants into compliance. The *Riptide* drew alongside the merchant ship, and Cimik tossed a hook toward it, snagging on the rigging and connecting the two vessels.

Nyx let out a crazed laugh, which tapered into a low, menacing snicker as she picked up the metal megaphone from where it sat by the wheel. Her voice boomed across the sea.

"Surrender now, or die!"

Moments after she spoke, a white flag came up from the merchant ship.

"Ah, they gave up easy! I like a little more of a fight," Splinter said as he climbed down from the rigging.

"Yeah, I haven't even gotten a chance to try out the cannons yet," Tig said.

"Everyone out on the deck, and put all your weapons in a pile!" Nyx ordered the merchant crew. Cas watched as they reluctantly obeyed. Nyx jumped to the merchant ship and climbed up to the deck as the rest of the crew followed. Cas came aboard last, heart pounding as he traversed the treacherous space between the two ships.

Most of the pirates were heading down to the cargo hold, while Nyx, Cimik and Vyn stood on the deck, monitoring the merchant crew. Nyx in particular seemed to be enjoying herself as she kept her pistol aimed at the captain while giggling and humming.

Cas joined the others below deck to help take the cargo aboard the *Riptide*. He began to feel a bit of guilt gnawing at his stomach. He certainly had no objection to stealing, but this felt decidedly different from taking a wallet or some jewelry. This was someone's entire livelihood.

After the majority of the hold was empty, Nyx gave the order to stop.

"That'll do," she said. "Now let's get going."

Out of the corner of his eye, Cas saw movement. One member of the merchant crew had lunged for the pile of weapons and drawn a gun. Before he could fire, Nyx whipped around and shot him.

Eye blazing with fury, she turned back to the rest of her prisoners.

"Anyone else want to try something?" she snarled. They stared down at the ground, clearly terrified, not speaking. Nyx motioned for her crew to return to the ship. As Cas jumped back to the *Riptide*, he heard Nyx speak again.

"You're going to wait here until we're out of sight. If you try to chase us or signal for help, we'll come back, and we won't be so nice."

She slid down the ropes and landed on the quarterdeck, and they quickly made their getaway. Soon the lights of the merchant ship disappeared into the night.

As soon as they were a safe distance away, a jubilant change came over the ship. They spent the rest of the night eating, drinking, dancing, and singing under the stars.

While Cas celebrated with the rest of the crew, the guilt and fear he felt aboard the merchant ship began to fade away.

When the first haze of dawn appeared on the horizon, the dancing and singing had tapered out. Cas relaxed on a pile of rope, watching the sunrise break across the clear sky as they swapped tales of their past adventures.

"My very first trip with the Navy, we ran into some pirates," Tig said. "One of 'em gave me this," he pointed to the scar on his jaw, "before we captured them. Always thought pirates were horrible.

Never thought in a million years I'd end up joining them. But I'm glad I did!"

"I remember my first time fighting the Navy," Cimik said, a nostalgic look in her eyes. "It was a big Man o' War sent to break up the Armada. Two shots from our cannons and the whole thing burst into flames. We had hit their gunpowder supply with the second shot. I got this afterward." She unbuttoned her shirt to show a tattoo of a flaming ship on her chest. "I miss the Armada."

"I don't," Vyn said. "I ran into you once, when I was younger. You almost sank my ship and you killed half my crew. I'd rather take on a whole Navy fleet than mess with the Armada again." He glanced around at the others. "You're all too young to remember the Armada, ain't you? It's been gone, what, twenty years now?"

"Twenty-one, actually," Cimik said bitterly.

"I may be too young to remember it, but I gambled once with a former Selkis captain," Knives said. "I got a lucky hand at the last minute and took all her money, so she caught up to me after I left the tavern, beat me senseless and took it all back. Tough ole gal!"

"That's how I got kicked out of school!" Gyles said. "I tried gambling with a pirate and he was furious when I won. We ended up in a huge fight in the middle of the tavern. I even got a nice scar from it." He lifted his shirt to show a long slash mark across his stomach. "He got me with a broken bottle. The guards got involved to pull us apart, and I hit a few of them. After that the college didn't want me around anymore. It was 'bad for their image' or something, they said."

"When I got into a fight with a pirate, he offered me a job on his ship," Splinter laughed. "That's how I became a pirate in the first place. I guess he thought I was brave, being a little 12-year-old trying to fight a big tough criminal."

"I was about that age when I first tried to become a pirate," Gryph said. "I didn't think to join a crew, though. I just took my little sailboat and climbed onto a merchant ship and started taking things! Of course, I got caught, but since I was young and obviously stupid, they let me go."

"I worked on a lot of merchant ships, and I'd have let you go too," Fenix said. "Most of the workers are slaves, they don't care if the cargo gets to its destination or not. Once when a little group of pirates came aboard, I helped them carry things off! The merchant captain didn't like that, of course. I much prefer working for pirates than merchants."

"Merchants can be surprisingly vicious," Nyx said, and glanced over at Cas and Prisma. "Don't think every raid is as easy as the one we just had. I lost my eye during a fight with a cargo ship, right after I became captain. A little cabin boy with a sword jumped out and got me." She flipped her eyepatch up, revealing an empty socket underneath. "Of course, Prisma, you've probably heard plenty of stories of failed raids at the tavern."

"Yeah, I have. Too many, probably," Prisma said with a laugh. As the group began to tell stories they heard of other pirates' experiences, Cas realized two members of the crew were missing.

"I'll be right back," he whispered to Prisma, and he descended to the lower deck. He found the galley and the crew's quarters were both empty. As he walked back to the ladder, he heard voices from below.

Cautiously, he descended into the hold and glanced around, one hand still on the ladder. At the opposite end of the room, hiding by a stack of boxes, he could see Zad and Kaymin, backs turned to him. They were talking quietly and urgently.

"We have the cargo, we have the map, let's just do it now!" Kaymin said. Cas was surprised, as this was the most he had ever heard Kaymin speak.

"No! We need to wait until we're closer to the Quarter. Neither of us knows how to run this ship. I barely even know half the orders the captain gives us." Zad stated.

"You shouldn't have told her you worked on other ships."

"She wouldn't have hired me if I didn't have experience! Besides, I won't have to run the ship very long. We just get the treasure and head back home to Tallix."

"And then we'll both be rich again," Kaymin added.

"Yes, that's the goal. But we can't get to that goal if we take over too early. We have to wait for the right time. And according to the map, the right time should be just as we enter the Quarter." Zad pulled a familiar necklace from his pocket, and Cas involuntarily let out a gasp. Both of the men spun around, and the three stared at each other for a long moment.

Then Cas bolted up the ladder, Zad yelling at Kaymin to stop him. A moment later, Cas felt someone grab his ankle and pull, making him lose his grip on the rungs and fall hard to the ground. As he lay on his back, trying to catch his breath, Zad and Kaymin stood over him.

"You should've minded your own business, kid," Zad snapped. "Kaymin, tie him up."

As Kaymin grabbed the struggling Cas and began to wrap a length of rope around him, Zad continued talking.

"This is going to change our plans. They're going to notice if he doesn't come back up. So, we'll just have to attack today, and figure out how to captain the ship as we go."

"Sounds good to me, boss," Kaymin said.

"Stick to the plan. We kill Cimik, we kill Vyn, we take the captain hostage to ensure the rest of the crew is on our side. Then we kill her too."

"Isn't the standard to maroon the old captain?"

"Even better," Zad agreed.

Tied and gagged, Cas could do nothing as the two men climbed up the ladder and shut the hatch behind them.

7

Mutiny

Cas squirmed against the ropes for what felt like hours, but it was no use. They were too tight, and he only succeeded in scraping his wrists on the rough bindings.

Eventually, he gave up, lying against the side of the hull, panting. Zad and Kaymin were going to stage a mutiny, and there was nothing he could do about it. If they succeeded, he and the rest of the crew would either have to join them or die.

Then he heard the hatch creak open. He expected Zad or Kaymin, but instead Prisma appeared. She stared at him in shock.

"Cas?" she asked, astonished.

He tried to tell her to untie him, but, of course, it didn't come out coherently. Even so, she jumped down from the ladder and began slicing through the ropes with her knife.

"Zad and Kaymin are going to try and take over the ship," he said as soon as he was free of the gag.

"What? How?"

"They're going to kill Vyn and Cimik and then hold Nyx hostage until the rest of the crew agree to join them."

"They can't do that!"

"No, they can't. We need to stop them," he agreed.

They quickly ascended the ladder, to find the upper deck abandoned. Cas ran toward the captain's quarters, but before he could knock, the door flew open.

Nyx and Zad stood in the doorway. Zad was holding one of the captain's arms twisted behind her back and had a gun to her head. Nyx looked very angry.

"Too late, cabin boy," Zad sneered. "Why don't you make yourself useful and wake the rest of the crew? We have something to discuss with them." Cas paused, looking at Nyx.

"Go ahead," she said.

Entering the crew's cabin, Cas was relieved to see that Cimik was still alive. He quickly woke her and the others.

"What's going on?" Tig asked groggily.

"Zad and Kaymin are staging a mutiny," Cas said.

"*What?*" Tig cried, now very much awake.

"I overheard them in the hold. They were planning to wait until we got to the Quarter, then kill Vyn and Cimik, and hold Nyx hostage until you agreed to join them . . . But I messed up their plan. Now they have Nyx and they want all of you up there," he explained, guilt evident in his voice. If he hadn't been seen, he could have snuck back up and warned Nyx before this happened.

"So, what's our plan?" Fenix asked.

"Huh?" Cas asked.

"I'm certainly not going to let them take over or kill anyone. Are the rest of you?" Fenix asked. His question was met with a resounding no. "Then we have to stop them. So, what's our plan?"

*

Zad paced back and forth on the deck nervously. In front of the quarterdeck sat Nyx, Vyn and Prisma. Kaymin stood behind them with his pistols out and aimed at the captives.

"You seem anxious, Zad," Nyx said.

"Shut up," he snapped.

"You worried things aren't going to go your way?" she asked mockingly.

"I said, shut up," he said, drawing his gun and pointing it at her. She smiled up at him.

"Go ahead, shoot me. I dare you."

"I'm not going to shoot you. I need you alive, for now." He went back to pacing.

"Do you really think the crew is just going to accept you as their new captain, and not get rid of you as soon as they can?"

"I'll make a great captain. Much better than you," he snapped. He turned to face the hatch, his finger moving to the trigger of his pistol. "What's taking that idiot cabin boy so long?"

A few moments later, Cas re-emerged from the hatch, with the rest of the crew following. Zad smiled unpleasantly.

"Nice of you to join us. Now, let's discuss the terms of this new arrangement. I will be taking over from now on. We will complete this quest, and, if you all behave, I'll make sure you're rich when we find the treasure," he announced.

"And if we don't join you?" Cimik asked.

"Then we kill you, hire a new crew, and we still get the treasure. It's going to be much better for everyone if you just agree. At least you'll be alive, and like I said, you'll get your share of the treasure if you don't make any trouble for us."

"Aside from remaining alive, what's the benefit of having you as a captain?" Tig asked.

"The benefit?" Zad asked with a laugh. "The benefit is that I, unlike your previous captain, am of sound mind! Nyx is a raving lunatic, and you all know it!" Nyx shrugged. "See? She's not even denying it! I was waiting at the tavern for a week before the cabin boy showed up. I heard her telling stories! Did you know she *shot* her old quartermaster?" he asked.

"Not on purpose!" Nyx interjected. "I thought he was the ghost of my father."

"Precisely! Out of her mind, she is! I may never have captained a ship before; I'll give you that. But I can learn. And more importantly, I'm not her."

"Alright." Gyles said, stepping forward. "I'll join you."

"Excellent! I had expected you would. You're an intelligent man." Zad said.

One by one, the rest of the crew stepped forward. As Cas did, he saw a flash of movement on the quarterdeck, as a figure pulled themselves over the railing and ducked behind the wheel.

"I think we'll all get along quite nicely now that everything is peaceful," Zad was saying. "Who knows, you might even come to be friends with me. It's like my parents said before they cut me off, I'm a very likable person." He paused, looking between the pirates that stood before him. "Say, weren't there thirteen people on this ship? There's Kaymin and me, the captain, the quartermaster, the medic, shouldn't there be . . . more of you?"

Before he could finish his thought, Fenix leapt down from where he was hiding on the quarterdeck and smacked Kaymin over the head with the hilt of his sword. Kaymin collapsed to the ground.

Zad spun around and immediately began to fire shots in their direction. Fenix rolled out of the way and Vyn, Nyx and Prisma scattered. Cimik, sword drawn, lunged at the mutineer.

Kaymin groggily glanced up, saw Cimik, and jumped to his boss's aid. Their blades crashed together, throwing sparks up into the air.

The rest of the crew sprang into action, pulling their weapons from their holsters and firing at Zad. He dove behind a pile of crates, shooting blindly from around the side, forcing the rest of the crew to take cover as well. Cas quickly ducked behind a barrel.

Prisma cried out in pain, and Cas turned to see her grab her arm.

"Prisma!" he yelled, jumping up from his hiding place. He had only taken three steps when it felt like someone kicked his leg out from under him. He fell to the ground, confused for a moment. Then pain overwhelmed him. It radiated up and down his leg like fire, so intense it made his head spin.

Cimik knocked the sword from Kaymin's hands. The sun caught her blade as she swung it, a brilliant flash of light followed by a spray of blood. Kaymin fell to the ground. His head landed several feet away.

Zad, realizing his bodyguard was dead, fired the rest of his bullets and made a dash for the lifeboat. He didn't make it far before half a dozen bloody holes appeared through him, and he collapsed to the ground, a lake of crimson spreading around his lifeless body.

The last thing Cas remembered was Prisma gazing down at him, her lips moving but no sound reaching him. Then everything faded away.

2

Part 2

8

A Leg to Stand On

"Try putting more weight on it," Prisma said. Cas shifted and immediately fell. Prisma caught him. "Alright, maybe not." She helped him sit back on the medic cot.

"This isn't going well," he muttered.

"You're getting better. It's going to take a lot of practice." Prisma stood and walked to the door. "I have to start dinner. We bought some nice things at our last stop at port—we'll bring you some."

As she left, Cas stared down at the wood-and-metal frame that now replaced the lower half of his right leg. It felt strange to try and walk on the device. Feeling the pressure of each step in his knee and thigh was dramatically different from walking on his foot. It certainly didn't feel like a leg.

He had hardly left the medic cabin since the attempted mutiny, and he was growing restless. He had hoped the new leg would allow him to go back to his normal activities, but it was much harder to adapt to than he expected.

The first week or two after he was shot had been a blur. He was unconscious most of the time, and it wasn't until the second week that he was coherent enough to understand that his lower leg was gone. The bullet had shattered his bone and an infection had taken hold. The only way to save his life had been to remove the leg below the knee.

After that, his world had been restricted to the medic cabin for what felt like an eternity. He could walk with the help of crutches and someone to support him, but it was difficult on the constantly moving ship, and it was almost impossible to climb up and down between the decks.

Cimik had designed the new leg. Part of her job in the Armada had been making prosthetics for those who lost limbs in battle. In form, the leg was surprisingly elegant. Although similar in design, it was much nicer and supposedly more comfortable than the simple wooden peg-legs Cas had seen other sailors using.

He couldn't help but feel it was his own fault that his leg was gone. He had been impulsive and stupid. If he had just stopped and looked closer, he would've seen that Prisma's injury had just been a graze from the bullet, enough to draw blood but not seriously hurt her.

Sitting on the cot, he again shifted his weight to the new leg, feeling the smooth frame pressing against his thigh. Perhaps he could get used to it. He would just have to figure out how to balance with it, and then life wouldn't be so different from before.

"Cas." He looked up as Vyn entered the cabin, holding two plates of fish and biscuits. He handed one to Cas and sat down in the chair across from him. "How are things going?"

"Difficult." He felt his eyes straying to the quartermaster's hook. "How long did it take for you to get used to it?"

"I don't think I can say I am used to it. Sometimes I still expect a hand to be there. But it'll get easier."

"Can I ask you something?"

"Sure."

Cas paused. He had wanted to ask how he lost his hand, and, additionally, how he got all his scars, but at the last moment he changed his mind.

"Why are there so many things named after a queen?"

"What?"

"The Queen's Quarter, *The Queen's Curse* ... We don't have a queen."

Vyn chuckled, and that familiar mischievous smile crossed his face. "That's referencing the Drowned Queen, kid. You've never heard of her?"

"Oh, um, actually, I may have. From sailors at the tavern," Cas said. "She's an evil spirit, right?"

"No, she's not evil," Vyn snapped. Then his voice grew softer again. "There's many versions of the legend, of course."

"What's your version?" he asked.

"Well, this is the one I heard as a kid, and it's always been my favorite.

"There was once a kingdom, now lost to time, that was a lot like our Empire. They had a king with absolute power, nobility and barons who lived lavishly in palaces, a strong military to enforce the laws, and a population of peasants, thieves and beggars. When the king died, his teenage daughter, his only child, was next in line for the throne.

"His daughter quickly gained a reputation for having unusual ideas about how the kingdom should be run. She believed in fairness and equality and wanted to help the poor by redistributing money from the rich, and she even intended to use the royal treasury for this purpose as soon as she was allowed. This did not go over well with many of the so-called elite. In fact, the nobles and barons were so outraged by these ideas that they began to conspire against her.

They bribed the commander of the military, and his men to get rid of her.

"On the eve of her eighteenth birthday, the day she would formally become the Queen, the commander kidnapped her. He and a small crew took her to their frigate and sailed off into the night.

"When they were away from the island, far out in the deep sea, they chained a cannonball around her ankles and threw her overboard. Satisfied that they had met their goal, they set sail for home.

"As the ship came within sight of the harbor the next morning, the inhabitants of the kingdom noticed something strange. Despite clear skies and a calm sea, the ship seemed to be having trouble. They began to signal for help. The rest of the military fleet, knowing their commander was onboard, immediately responded.

"Upon reaching the distressed vessel, several of the more cowardly men jumped ship and returned to the shore, for what they saw terrified them far more than the threat of punishment for desertion.

"Back on shore, they watched as dark clouds appeared from nowhere. Lightning flashed and rain obscured their view. They could hear the snaps and crashes of ships being torn apart, and the screams of their less fortunate comrades. When the clouds dispersed, the whole fleet was gone—swallowed up by the sea.

"When they were asked what they had seen, the deserters recounted a strange tale.

"The frigate was caught in a tide of sorts, pushing it away from shore. The commander shouted something, but his words were swept away with the wind.

"Then, from out of the sea, the dead Queen appeared. She hovered just above the surface of the ocean, her eyes glowing with an unearthly light. She raised her arms, and a whirlpool formed before them. It dragged down the commander's ship and began to pull the rest of the fleet toward it. That's when they ran.

"One of the men claimed that the Queen watched them as they

fled, and he knew in his heart that she was *letting* them escape. She *wanted* them to tell the kingdom what had happened.

"It seems as though, after disposing of the fleet, the Queen returned to the sea, as she wasn't seen again by anyone from her kingdom. But she wasn't done with her vengeance just yet.

"A strange mist descended over the island. Ships began to disappear as they traveled to or from it. Terrifying apparitions were seen. Fleets were attacked by sea monsters. Soon, everyone believed that the kingdom was too dangerous, and all trade with the island ceased. Many of the poorer people became pirates, heading off to take their chances on the high seas.

"The last person to ever leave the island was a pirate named Alrac, and he said the kingdom had fallen into disrepair. With no connection to the outside world, people were losing hope and losing their sanity. He said the nobles and barons had barricaded themselves in their palaces, convinced that the mists would soon lift and trade would resume as normal.

"He tried to return to the kingdom a few years after he left. Despite his best efforts, he could no longer find the island. It was as if it had vanished, consumed by the mist. And it hasn't been seen since. Eventually, that strange, confusing patch of fog in the middle of the sea was named . . ."

"The Queen's Quarter," Cas finished.

"Exactly. But, although the kingdom seems to have disappeared, its Queen is still seen from time to time. Some people say she conjures storms and rogue waves to destroy ships and drag sailors to their deaths beneath the sea. Others say she's more . . . benevolent. They say she offers protection and guidance, if she believes you're a worthy soul. In fact, I once knew a man who swore up and down that he'd encountered her."

"What did he say?"

"He said that he fell overboard in a storm one night. The crew either didn't notice or didn't care, and the ship sailed away, leaving him to die. As he was struggling to keep his head above water, he saw a light out of the corner of his eye. He turned, but instead of a ship, he saw a woman, hovering just above the waves. She reached out her hand and he took it, and then he found himself on a beach. Somehow, he had been transported from the middle of the ocean to the nearest island in a split second." Cas listened with fascination.

"Do you believe him?"

"I take all claims made by drunk pirates with a healthy degree of skepticism," Vyn said with a laugh. "But I believe that the legend of the Queen is true, and that she is a force of both good and evil, depending on your perspective." The door opened, and Prisma entered, a smile on her face.

"You talking about the Drowned Queen?" she asked.

"Am I the only one that didn't know about this story?" Cas asked.

"Yeah, probably. I heard about her from pirates at the tavern. You know, there was a whole religion devoted to her once. It's mostly gone now, though."

"Ah, yes, I've heard of that," Vyn said. "Although I heard they were more of a cult than a religion."

"From what I've heard, it started out as a religion," Prisma explained as she hurried around the cabin, making Cas's daily medicine. "But they got greedy and corrupt. They lost sight of what the Queen stood for and began acting just like the people who killed her."

"And they all disappeared, didn't they?" Vyn asked.

"Yes. I heard some of their records survived, and they were writing about having to abandon their temple due to a horrible storm. But the nearest island was reporting clear skies the whole time, so it was a storm that only affected them."

"Do you think the Queen sent the storm?" Cas asked. Prisma laughed.

"Do *I* think she did? No, because I don't think she's real. I don't believe in ghosts or spirits or dead people who control the weather."

"Even after seeing Nyx show up, glowing and all?" Cas asked.

"I think that was very weird, and scary, yes. But Nyx isn't a ghost, and neither is this ship. They're both real, tangible things. I don't know what happened to her out in the Quarter, but I don't believe it was ghosts."

"And that's how I can tell an experienced seafarer from a brand-new one," Vyn said. "All experienced seafarers believe at least a little in the supernatural." Prisma shot him a skeptical look.

"That's because most of them are drunk most of the time."

"I can't argue with that," he said matter-of-factly.

"Here, Cas. Drink this," Prisma said as she handed him a cup full of a syrupy red liquid. She gave him some new combinations of herbs and tinctures every day, and while he wasn't quite sure what it was, it certainly seemed to help with the pain, and he was healing faster than anticipated. The drink left a strange tingling sensation in his mouth and throat.

"Huh. That's . . . interesting," he said.

"Get used to it. With this, we'll have you walking around in no time," Prisma said with a smile.

Although visits from the crew and Prisma's care kept him occupied during the day, there were no such interruptions at night. For the first weeks, it was pain and anxiety that kept him awake, but now his mind was finding other things to dwell on as he lay in the medic cot.

He often imagined Scout sleeping nearby. In a half-asleep state, lulled into a sense of security by the dark, damp night that reminded him so much of his old resting place in the canal, he would turn over to search for the warmth of his companion, only to awake with a jolt when he touched the cold wall instead. Worse were the times when he didn't immediately wake up, and instead his dreaming mind would conjure the image of his friend's cold, bloody body lying next to him.

Cas was now very aware of Scout's absence. During the first weeks onboard the *Riptide*, everything was so new and different and distracting that he'd barely had time to think about it. But lying awake and alone, his missing friend was more noticeable than his missing leg. His ears rang with the silence that Scout's laughter and snarky comments once filled. When he wiped the tears from his eyes, there was no one there to pull him close and tell him it would be alright.

He wondered if Scout would have accompanied him on this voyage, had he survived. Cas remembered once, many years before, as the pair sat on the seawall, Scout had remarked that life on a ship seemed like it would be awfully boring, stuck on the same vessel for months at a time with nowhere to go. Scout rarely stayed in one place for long, growing bored and restless if Cas wanted to hang around the tavern listening to stories.

When Cas did sleep, his dreams often involved Scout. As the pair sat on the seawall overlooking the rolling waves of his subconscious, his friend smiled and nodded toward the shiny metal frame of his new leg.

"Too bad about that infection, huh? We could've had matching scars." He looked down at his side, where the hole torn in his shirt revealed a healed circular mark. His smile faded. "Too bad about a lot of things, really."

*

Cas gazed down the narrow corridor that linked the medic cabin to the ladder, where Prisma stood illuminated by the flickering candlelight.

"You've walked this far before; you can do it," she said encouragingly.

"Yeah, with crutches," he said nervously.

"You can still use them if you need them."

He didn't want to use them. They made it easier to walk, yes, but he was going to need his hands free if he was going to climb up to the deck.

The ship rocked heavily as it crested a wave, and Cas stumbled against the wall. He regained his balance and took a tentative step forward, keeping his hand on the wall to steady himself. Shifting his weight fully to the prosthetic, he took another limping step and then fell.

"Maybe we should try this tomorrow .. ." Prisma said as she ran to him.

"No!" Cas snapped. "I can do this."

"Cas, I know you want to be able to walk, but you're going to hurt yourself."

Cas sat in the corridor, not meeting her eyes, frustration burning in his chest. He had spent days in the medic cabin practicing, pacing back and forth for hours with the help of crutches, getting used to the feeling of the prosthetic. But it still wasn't good enough. He felt tears stinging his eyes and quickly blinked them away. Prisma held out her hand.

"Come on," she said firmly.

He took her hand and pulled himself up, leaning against her as he tried to walk once again. He stared down at the floor and took a step, this time noting how his prosthetic moved slightly out of sync with where he expected his foot to be. With the next step, he adjusted accordingly and didn't stumble.

He let go of Prisma as they neared the ladder. Looking up the hatch, he could see a bright blue sky. He began to climb, using his upper body strength and one leg, not wanting to try balancing on the rungs with his prosthetic. Prisma followed behind him.

Emerging onto the deck, he found his footing and stood, with

Prisma nearby to steady him if he needed. Feeling the wind and salty spray in his face was like coming home after a long day. He paused, looking out across the sparkling blue sea, finally free after so long in the dark cabin below deck.

"I told you; we won't be getting to the Quarter for another three days! Your prediction was way off," Gryph was yelling.

"We'll be gettin' there tomorrow. You can tell by all the mist forming at night!" Splinter yelled back from his perch high up in the rigging.

"Aye, cause mist can't form anywhere but the Quarter, of course!"

"You're both wrong, we're still weeks away from the Quarter," Gyles called from the crow's nest. "We only *just* stopped in Kiral, and the stars aren't aligned for the Quarter yet."

"Stars don't mean nothing, they change all the time," Splinter snapped. Gyles leaned down to stare at him in disbelief.

"What world are you living in where the stars are changing?"

"If you put half as much energy into sailing as you do bickering, we would've been there weeks ago!" Nyx shouted at them.

Behind him, Cas heard Cimik clear her throat and turned to see her holding a mop and bucket.

"Don't think you're going to get out of your work just because of your little leg scratch, cabin boy," she said as she pushed them into his hands and turned to go.

"Cimik?" Cas said. She stopped and glanced back at him. "Thanks." He saw a half-smile cross her face, and she looked down at his new leg.

"It looks good," she muttered before she walked off.

That night, Cas slept out on the deck, admiring the endless starry sky and the dark sea all around them.

9

Vindicator

Cas watched the sea sprites leaping through the ship's wake, their gelatinous bodies glittering in the rising sun as they flapped their translucent wings. The sky was dotted with fluffy white clouds and strong winds filled the sails, the calm sea ruffled like blue velvet.

It had been almost a week now of perfect weather, and they were far ahead of schedule. Gyles estimated that they would be at the Quarter within a few days. The crew was relaxed and happy, hardly arguing as they worked.

"Distressed ship, 10 o'clock on the horizon!" Gyles called down. "Flying an Empire merchant flag!"

Cas leaned over and peered ahead. Distantly, he could see a flash of light as the ship signaled for help.

"Well, perhaps we can help by getting rid of all that heavy cargo," Nyx said with a laugh. Cas felt guilt gnawing at his stomach again.

The prow sliced through the waves toward the merchant ship while the crew laughed and shouted in excitement. The black flag was raised as the pirates fired their guns into the air, the echoes rolling across the open sea like little crashes of thunder.

This ship was much bigger than the last one they had attacked. It was massive, comparable to the largest merchant galleons Cas had seen in Valdoria, the hull a resplendent mahogany trimmed with gold. Although the sails were tied, the three masts towered over the *Riptide*. Written across its side in black letters was its name: *Vindicator*. Strangely, there only seemed to be a few people up on the deck.

There was no attempt to put up a fight as the *Riptide* drew close and Nyx climbed aboard. The men didn't even seem to have weapons. Cas and the rest of the crew joined Nyx, swords and guns out.

All at once, as though on an unspoken command, the doors to the cabins and the hatches burst open and dozens of men in Navy uniforms charged out. It happened so quickly that Cas didn't even comprehend what was going on for a moment, he just stood in stunned silence as rifles were aimed at him.

"Drop your weapons and raise your hands," a soldier barked at them. Cas threw his sword aside. The other pirates complied as well. As they put their hands up, Gryph leaned over to Splinter.

"Do you think it's too late to take the flag down and pretend we're not pirates?" he asked with a nervous grin.

"Yeah, I think it's just a bit too late," Splinter snapped.

Several of the men stepped forward, forcing the crew to sit in a line and tying their hands behind their backs. Cas sat next to Prisma, and the fear on her face made him realize the gravity of the situation. They had been captured by the Empire's Army, and they were likely about to be put to death for piracy. His heart began to pound wildly, and he felt light-headed as he looked at the soldiers around him.

As their captors tried to push Nyx to the ground, she resisted and shoved them back. A brief struggle broke out, with the captain quickly being overpowered and held back by two burly guards. Before they could tie her up, a shout rang out from the helm.

"Wait." The soldiers turned their attention to a man descending from the quarterdeck. He was tall, attractive, in his mid-20s, with neatly combed blond hair, wearing a long, dark blue coat that signaled a rank of commander. He approached Nyx, looking at her intensely. He smiled unpleasantly.

"I thought you looked familiar. Captain Nyx, isn't it?" he asked confidently.

"Have we met?" she asked.

"You don't recognize me. I can't say I'm surprised. Do you happen to recognize this?" He drew a rapier sword from his belt and held the point close to her face. For a moment, she seemed confused, then her eye lit up.

"Oh! Are you that kid that stabbed my eye out? You've certainly grown up," she said with a grin.

"Yes, I am, and it's thanks to you that I joined the Navy. After witnessing you disgusting criminals up close, I knew I had to do something about you."

"You've been searching for me this whole time? How romantic."

He recoiled, prompting a laugh from her. He quickly recomposed himself. "You look worse than you did last time I saw you. Piracy not treating you well?"

She shrugged.

"In that case, perhaps you and your crew will prefer prison." He turned to face the pirates lined up on the deck, regarding them one by one.

"I recognize you," he said as he stopped in front of Splinter.

"Yeah, you sank my ship," Splinter said through gritted teeth.

"Ah, that's right! I thought we had killed everyone aboard, but I guess we missed one. Won't happen this time, though," he said with a smile.

"I'm guessing you got this shiny new ship and a promotion as a reward for that, huh?"

"I earned my ship and my position as commander with my hard work, something *you* wouldn't understand." He moved on down the line, pausing to look at Cimik next. He used the tip of his sword to trace the tattoos on her neck. "Selkis Armada? And a high-ranking member, if I'm reading these correctly."

"I was a boatswain on the warship *Tempest*," she said.

"And I suppose you're angry and bitter about being defeated, so you've turned to piracy as an alternative. I've captured plenty like you before. They were all put to death, and I assume you will be as well." He walked past Knives, Tig, Gryph, and Gyles, and stopped at Fenix. "You look familiar."

"I believe you're mistaken; I've never met you before," Fenix muttered. The commander motioned to his men, and two of them grabbed Fenix, pulled him to his feet, and pushed him up against the mast face-first. The commander used his sword to slit open the back of his shirt.

Fenix's pale back was crisscrossed with long, raised scars, and on his left shoulder was a brand mark in the shape of an S.

"You're a runaway slave, aren't you? I saw your wanted poster back in Empiris. Your owner claims you stole valuables from him before you ran . . ."

"That's not true, I didn't take anything from him," Fenix interrupted.

"All criminals profess their innocence. Regardless, you'll be returned to him now that you've been caught."

They pushed Fenix back to the ground. The commander cast his steely gaze on Prisma and Cas. "You two seem rather young to be pirates."

"They're not pirates," Nyx said quickly. "They're the cabin boy and the ship's medic. We forced them to join us." Cas opened his mouth to speak, but the captain's glare silenced him.

"Well then. You two will probably be allowed to go free, *if* you can convince the judge of your story. As for the rest of you, you'll either be sentenced to death or, if you're lucky, imprisoned for the rest of your miserable lives. If you survive the next few weeks aboard this ship, that is. And you, Captain . . ." He turned back to Nyx with a grin. "I'll ensure you receive the maximum punishment for your crimes."

"Draigh!" The commander immediately snapped to attention as a man stepped out of the cabin. He was older, in his 60's, with short gray hair mostly hidden beneath an admiral's hat. "If you're done playing with your latest captives, we do have a schedule to keep."

"Sorry, sir," he said quietly.

"Get these pirates down to the brig and . . ." The admiral paused as his eyes panned over the crew. He suddenly went pale, and a look of terror filled his eyes. "*You?*"

Everyone turned to see what had frightened the admiral so much. To Cas's surprise, he was staring at Vyn. Vyn smirked at him.

"Admiral Caine, it's been a long time . . . although, can you still be called an 'admiral' if all but one of your ships sank?"

"You're supposed to be dead. The official reports say you were mutinied and thrown overboard—" he gasped. Vyn laughed again, a dark cackle that Cas had never heard from him before.

"You should know killing me is harder than that."

"I'm sorry, sir, but how do you know this pirate?" Draigh asked. The admiral tried to compose himself, but fear was evident in his eyes.

"You know him too, or at least, you know of him," he said. "That is the pirate who destroyed most of my fleet some fifteen years ago, the so-called Demon of the North Sea, Captain Alistair." The crew stared at Vyn in disbelief.

"And *I* caught him!" Daigh exclaimed, smiling proudly.

"You said your name was Vyn!" Splinter said.

"It is. My last name, that is. Well, Vyncin," Vyn replied.

"Oh, this is even better than I could've hoped," Draigh said to himself. "Not only did I catch Nyx, I found one of the most famous, or notorious I should say, pirates of our time. Just wait till we get back to Empiris . . ." He trailed off and looked to his men. "Get them down to the brig. And send a small crew to their ship—we'll bring her in too. Perhaps she can become a Navy ship."

"What?" Nyx shouted, her almost casual demeanor replaced by rage. He turned to face her, seeming to enjoy her anger.

"Or maybe she could become a merchant vessel," hissed Draigh.

"How *dare* you . . ."

"Or sell it at auction. I'm sure some baron or noble would love to own an authentic pirate ship."

Nyx was silent for a moment, teeth bared, eye blazing with fury.

"Would you rather we scrap her?" he asked mockingly.

Nyx spit directly into his face. He cried out in surprise and disgust.

"Take the rest of them down to the brig," he growled. "I'm not done with this one yet."

Cas was pulled roughly to his feet and dragged down below deck with the others. The brig was in the lowest section of the huge ship: a dark, damp room with several cells lining the walls. He was shoved into one along with Prisma.

As soon as the soldiers retreated back upstairs, Knives spoke up.

"This ain't looking good for us."

"No, it's not," Cimik said, leaning up against the bars. "Good thing we have legendary pirate Captain Alistair Vyncin here."

All eyes turned to him. He was standing in the corner of the far cell, looking down at the floor. He glanced up.

"I assume you all want an explanation?" he asked.

"Yes, I think that's in order," Cimik replied.

"Alright. I am, in fact, Alistair, and I'm sure the rumors of my life have been somewhat exaggerated, but many of them are, sadly, true."

"Why did you have us attack your own ship?" Gyles asked.

"Because it's no longer mine. My first mate staged a mutiny and left me in a lifeboat to die, but I was picked up by a merchant ship and, luckily, none of them recognized me. I decided I would rather see *The Queen's Curse* destroyed than allow it to remain in the hands of my mutineers."

"Why didn't you tell us who you really were?" Prisma asked.

"The less you knew, the safer you would be. And that still applies, so I think we're done here." Cas stared at the man. He still couldn't believe Vyn, someone he considered a friend, was really the monster he had heard about.

10

Empiris

Gyles kept watch through a small hole in the wall, reporting on where they were going by the stars and wind patterns.

"We're heading northwest," he had announced that morning. "With the polar winds, we'll be in Empiris in no time."

"Do you think they killed Nyx?" he asked.

Cas snapped out of his own personal misery. Over the past days, everything had begun to blend together. In fact, Cas wasn't even sure exactly how much time had passed since they were captured.

The sun rose and set, but the amount of light in the brig didn't change much. The waves lapping against the walls outside, and the crew's voices created a background noise that never fluctuated much, except when Gyles made his announcements. A couple times a day, one of the soldiers came to deliver meals of stale bread and water.

But what really made Cas grow numb to everything was the pain. Without Prisma's medicine, he quickly grew uncomfortable. Discomfort soon turned into near-constant shooting pain down his leg. Or rather, where his leg used to be. Since it was no longer there, there wasn't much he could do about it.

Cas had spent most of his time in the brig sitting in the corner of the cell, only moving when he had to. Everything had been going so well, and now he was back in a cramped, dark cabin, unable to walk yet again, and knowing that the only thing that awaited him at their destination was a trial and possible death sentence.

But Gyles asking about Nyx made Cas remember that the captain had never been brought down to the brig. What *had* they done with her?

"I wouldn't be surprised if they did kill her," Cimik said. "The only reason they're taking the rest of us to Empiris is because that commander of theirs wants to show off his catch. Normally, we would've just been killed as soon as we were captured."

"Nah, he wouldn't have killed her. You heard the way he talked about her, he wants everyone to know that he caught her. He wants to show her off," Tig replied.

"Then where is she?" Cimik asked.

"Don't know. But I'd be willing to bet she's alive and still on the ship somewhere," Tig said.

"What's the difference? We're all going to die at the end of this anyway," Knives piped up, voice edged with fear.

"Cheer up, you might just get life in prison!" Gryph said. Knives glared at him.

"Yeah, that sounds worse."

Prisma turned from where she had been standing by the door of the cell and sat down next to Cas.

"Do you think they're going to let the two of us go?" she asked quietly.

"I don't know," he replied.

"And if they do, what then?"

Cas hadn't considered that. They would be alone and stranded in

Empiris. He supposed they could hop a ship back to Valdoria, but what then? Returning to a life of pickpocketing?

Cas felt a lump rise in his throat as he imagined going back to his home, walking into the canal pipe and seeing what remained of Scout's body . . . No, he couldn't do that. He would never go back to Valdoria. He would have to start a new life, somewhere else.

"I don't know," he repeated after a long moment.

Prisma leaned against him, head on his shoulder. "Just promise you won't leave me."

"Of course I won't."

As Cas fell asleep that night, the brig faded away. The sleeping forms of the crew turned to patients lying in rows of cots as the room became a vast hospital. The floorboards were stained with blood and the air was thick with the smell of rot and vomit. Distant screams came from rooms deeper in the building.

Exactly what was wrong with the patients, he didn't know and he didn't want to know. Anyone who was sick and potentially contagious was sent there, not to try and help them so much as to keep them from infecting others. Cas stayed close to the masked doctor as he led the young boy between the rows of beds.

They finally reached the cot where Cas's mother lay. The doctor stepped away and Cas approached her bedside.

He didn't really understand what was happening to her. He knew that she had become weak and tired, and then she was brought to this frightening, disgusting place and he wasn't allowed to see her anymore.

Lyra Thane was a shadow of her former self. She was painfully thin and pale, her once thick golden-blonde hair thinning to sporadic clumps still clinging to her head. Specks of dried blood covered her lips.

She smiled as he approached.

"I'm glad you're here, Cas." Her voice was a rasping whisper. "I need to give you something."

She pulled off the necklace she wore and pressed it into his hand, her voice becoming more urgent.

"Take care of it," she said. "And don't lose it."

"I won't," he promised. He looked down at the teardrop-shaped jewel in his palm, confused. "What is it?"

She didn't seem to hear him. "I love you, Cas," she whispered.

Before he could reply, she began to cough violently. The spasms quickly turned to convulsions. As she writhed on the cot, dark blood running down her chin, Cas was swept away by one of the doctors while his colleagues rushed to attend to his mother.

Cas squinted against the bright sunlight as the doctor led him outside. The door slammed shut, and Cas realized he was now by himself.

Scared and alone, Cas sat on the steps until the sun dipped low in the sky and long shadows covered the cobblestone street, hoping that someone would emerge from the building and tell him what to do or where to go. No one ever did.

"Ey," a voice said. Cas looked up to see a boy around his age standing at the base of the staircase. "You waiting for someone in there?" He gestured up to the hospital.

"Yeah," Cas replied.

"Me too. You can come wait with me if you want." Cas stood, shoving the necklace into his pocket.

"I'm Cas," he said as the pair began to walk down the darkened street.

"Nice to meet you, Cas. I'm Scout."

Cas awoke disoriented, unable to make sense of his surroundings at first. Then everything came back to him. He hadn't had that dream in many years, and he had almost forgotten those events.

Prisma was still lying by his side, her eyelids fluttering slightly. He wondered what she was dreaming about.

The sound of footsteps descending the ladder snapped him back to reality. He sat up as a man arrived with their breakfast. The man delivered hunks of stale bread and old alcohol bottles filled with water, yelling at the pirates to wake up. It was the same routine as every morning.

The same routine, that is, until a second man came running in, dragging Nyx along. Cas was taken aback when he saw her. There was fresh blood on her face, down her neck and staining her shirt, stark red against her pale skin.

The sailor opened one of the cells and roughly shoved her to the ground. The man quickly locked the cell door and hurried away, acting like one might when caging a dangerous animal. She pulled herself into a sitting position and grabbed the bottle of water that sat nearby, messily downing half of it.

"What happened to you?" Gryph asked. She glanced up at him as she began to wipe away the blood. As it came away, Cas realized she was bruised and scratched across her face, and her wrists were raw from rope burns.

"They had me tied up on the main deck," she said, her voice hoarse. "At first Draigh and his friends were having fun, y'know, hitting and whipping me, but after a while they got bored with that and just left me to see how long I'd live without food or water. Until this morning, when one of them got drunk and started getting handsy with me. So I bit him."

"You *bit* him?" Tig asked. Nyx laughed as she began eating her ration of bread.

"Yeah, I bit him. I ripped a big chunk out of his face. Obviously, he started screaming and crying, so the admiral told them to put me down here since I'm clearly too dangerous to have on the deck."

"So that's not your blood, then?" Vyn asked.

"Nah, it's his."

"You should've just ignored that commander when he started talking about the ship. You could've avoided all this."

"Hey, when you threaten someone's ship, you make it personal." She glanced at him. "So, are we calling you Vyn or Alistair now?"

He paused. "I suppose you can call me Alistair now, if you'd like."

"Good to know," she answered.

"How far are we from Empiris, Captain?" Splinter piped up.

"Not far. You know how fast the north winds are."

"Great," Knives muttered. "Glad we're making good time to our funerals."

"Speaking of." Nyx pulled something out of her shirt pocket and tossed it through the bars of the cell to Cas. He caught it and was surprised to see it was the necklace. "I hope you find your dad someday, kid."

"I thought that map was to the *Sea's Revenge*," Splinter said.

"It is, that's where his dad is," Nyx said.

"What's your dad doing on that ship?" Splinter asked.

"He can't be *on* the ship, otherwise he would've come back with the treasure," Tig said.

"Unless he was captured!"

"Captured by who? That ship disappeared 150 years ago; the crew's not still alive!"

"Yeah, but maybe someone else found it and started sailing . . ." Tig said.

"Or maybe it's being sailed by their ghosts!" Gryph suggested.

"What are you idiots going on about?" Cimik snapped. "The ship was never found because it probably sank, and any treasure it had is at the bottom of the ocean."

"If you don't believe the ship is still out there, why'd you even come to look for it?" Splinter asked.

She rolled her eyes. "Because it's not the *ship* we're after. It's the island that they hid their treasure on! That's what the map is for!"

"What? I've never heard that before. I always thought they just kept everything down in the cargo hold," Gryph said.

"How would that work? You can't have a map to a ship! It can move!" she pointed out.

"I agree with Cimik, it's got to be the location of the island," Fenix said.

"There are many versions of the legend. Some say it's a ship, some say it's an island, some say it's a shipwreck on an island. I've heard them all," Nyx said.

"Which version do you prefer?" Prisma asked.

"I prefer the one my dad always told me," Nyx said. "The *Sea's Revenge* was the ship of Captain Eris Black, the greatest pirate who ever lived. This was back in the early days of the Empire, and he held them in a reign of terror for ten years, single-handedly taking down countless merchant ships and sinking Navy vessels. In fact, he was so feared that ships would go out of their way to avoid his territory.

"Although his territory spanned much of the North, he had a lair somewhere near the Quarter, where he knew he wouldn't be found. That's where he stored his treasure. See, he had a plan. He didn't just want to steal enough to survive—he desired true wealth and power. Once he had accumulated enough, he would return to Empiris and live like a king. But no amount was ever enough for him. No matter how much he took, he needed more.

"Many people knew that he had a treasure trove somewhere out in the Quarter, and countless pirates went after it. Captain Black couldn't always be there to guard it, so he came up with another plan to protect the island.

"He sent out hundreds of fake maps to his treasure. Each of them appeared to be real, but each would lead deep into the confusing fog and treacherous tides of the Quarter, ultimately sending the would-be thieves to their deaths."

"Tell 'em how the captain distributed the maps. That's my favorite part," Splinter said with an evil grin.

"Unlike many pirates, Captain Black would take prisoners. He would slit their throats, tie them to barrels, stuff a map down inside them, and toss them overboard. Then it was just a matter of time before the bodies would wash ashore on an island or be picked up by another ship," Nyx said.

"Gross!" Cas cried.

"It was intended as a warning; if you follow the map you found inside a dead guy, you're probably going to end up dead as well. But still, many people read them as real maps, or believed they could stitch together a true map from all the fakes." She paused, her voice losing its luster for a moment. "That's what I tried to do. I collected all the maps I could find; I averaged them all up and calculated where the treasure *should* be. But that doesn't work either." She shook her head, and went on with the story.

"There's really no way to know how many maps he made and sent out on the ocean, because I'm sure many of them were lost. But regardless, none of the maps were real. He kept the only real one with him, inside his necklace.

"Over the years, not only did Captain Black's hoard grow—his greed did as well. He began to take unnecessary risks. One night, he attacked a Navy fleet that was allegedly carrying the contents of the royal treasury. It didn't end well for him.

"He barely escaped, his ship heavily damaged and many of his crew fatally wounded. They sailed off into the fog of the Quarter and were never seen again. It was assumed the ship sank and everyone aboard died."

"Until . . ." Alistair said when Nyx paused.

"Until many years later," she continued. "One morning, off the

Eastern Shore of Kiral, a fishing boat spotted something strange. It was a barrel with a decaying body tied on. They dragged it back to the beach and one of them cut the ropes, only to realize something was very, very wrong. The corpse *spoke*.

"Although the man should have been dead, he wasn't. His skin was rotting off, bones exposed, his crumbling body covered in barnacles and parasites, but he was somehow still alive. One of the fishermen ran to alert the authorities, but the others stayed. The man told them that he was part of the crew of the *Sea's Revenge*, and they had become shipwrecked on their island hideaway.

"The crew waited to succumb to their injuries, but they just . . . never died. Even all these years later, they were all still alive even as their bodies rotted away, stranded out in the Quarter, awaiting help. But he wasn't going to wait any longer, so he escaped. And he brought the *real* map with him.

"By the time the authorities arrived, the man had died. They took the real map and intended to bring it to Empiris, but it never arrived. Some people say the authorities kept it for themselves. Others say the carrier ship was attacked by pirates and it was stolen."

"And now it's here, on its way to Empiris again," Cimik said.

Cas stared down at the jewel in his palm, recalling his dream. What a journey the necklace must have taken to get to him.

*

"Captain Alistair," the judge's voice echoed through the room, reverberating off the high marble ceilings and wooden viewing boxes that stood empty above the pirates. Although the Navy had sent word of Alistair's capture to Tallix, none of the noblemen or merchants they were expecting had shown up to the trial.

Cas glanced down the line. The crew was standing before the judge's stand, hands and ankles shackled, with guards posted at every entrance. Several of the Navy men, including Admiral Caine,

Draigh, and the bandage-clad soldier that Nyx had bitten, stood off to one side. Draigh listened with intense interest to the judge's every word.

"Captain Alistair, you have been accused of many crimes, including piracy, murder, destruction of property, torture, and assault. How do you plead to these accusations?" There was a long pause.

"Guilty," Alistair said finally. The judge nodded, and the scribe wrote down the plea.

"Captain Nyx," the judge continued. "You have been accused of piracy, murder, destruction of property, and at least one case of assaulting a Navy man. How do you plead?"

"I will admit to being guilty of all but the assault. That was self-defense," she said stoically.

"We'll keep that in mind." His voice was laced with disdain.

As he continued down the line, each of the pirates confessed to being guilty. Finally, he reached Cas and Prisma.

"According to the testimonies of your captain, the two of you were forced to join the crew. Is this true?"

"Yes," Cas said quietly. Prisma echoed the statement. Cas didn't want to abandon his crew. It felt cowardly. But Nyx had made the decision, and he wasn't going to go against her.

"In that case, you will be pardoned and are free to go." The guards stepped forward and unlocked their chains. "The runaway slave will be returned to his owner, at his owner's request. The rest of you are hereby sentenced to death for your crimes and will be executed at the next high tide."

The guards escorted Cas and Prisma out of the courtroom and down the elegant hallway to the large double doors. As soon as the two stepped outside, the guards shut and locked the doors behind them.

Prisma sat down on one of the polished steps that lead up to the building, staring out at the sprawling city around them.

Empiris was one of the largest cities in the world. Although Cas had arrived as a prisoner, he couldn't help but be amazed. The outskirts of the city seemed familiar; a slum of taverns, inns, apartments, and ramshackle houses, much like the scene around the docks of Valdoria. The city center was dominated by towers made from marble and stone, rising up taller than any building he had ever seen before.

In the very center of the town was the palace. Cas hadn't been able to glimpse much of it during his journey from the shipyard to the prison, but what he could see looked spectacular. He could see the very top of it between the towers now. Glistening white spires contained crystal windows that cast rainbows onto the city around it, while walled-off courtyards held exotic plants and manicured gardens. That was where the emperor lived, he knew.

"What now?" Prisma asked, drawing his attention away from the palace. He sighed.

"We can't let them die," Cas said.

"How can we stop it? They're not going to just let us walk back in."

"I don't know. We'll just have to think of something .. ." He trailed off, scanning the darkening city streets. His eyes locked on several guardsman uniforms hanging out to dry by the nearby bath-house. "And I may have just thought of it."

11

Escape

Cas adjusted the heavy mask that covered his face, attempting to stay in line with the other guards as they marched up the steps while trying to hide his limp as much as possible. He glanced over at Prisma, almost unrecognizable in the uniform with her hair and face concealed.

The guards were ushered inside the building. As soon as no one was looking, Cas and Prisma broke off from the group and started down the long, dark hallway to the prison cells. As they walked, they heard a commotion ahead.

They stepped aside as Fenix was led down the hall, flanked by a couple guards and a muscular, tattooed woman brandishing a whip. Fenix was bleeding from a gash across his eyebrow.

"Have to make up for what you stole from the captain, won't you?" The woman sneered as she shoved Fenix along.

"I didn't steal anything!" he insisted. "I . . ." He paused as they approached Cas and Prisma, blinking in surprise and recognition. Before they could say anything, Fenix was pulled away by the guards.

"Just wait till we get back to *North's Bounty*. We'll have some fun with you," the woman's cruel voice drifted back along the hall.

Cas and Prisma stepped into the prison room. Several other guards were lined up inside, as if waiting for something. The two impostors stepped into line, unnoticed. In the cells were the rest of the crew, sitting or pacing in silence.

After a long minute, Draigh and the admiral marched in, looking condescendingly at the guards.

"Tide's coming in. Let's go," Draigh snapped.

The docks of Empiris were crowded and noisy but seemed to grow quiet as the convoy of soldiers and pirates approached. Cas felt hundreds of eyes on him as they walked to the last pier and heard countless whispered rumors as to who the pirates were and what they had done.

The final pier was empty, guarded by only two soldiers. At the end, the *Riptide* was anchored, the hull polished and tattered sails repaired.

"I finally decided what to do with your ship," Draigh said as they approached. "What better way to serve the Empire than by carrying criminals to the execution docks?" He smiled at Nyx, who silently glared back.

With the pirates and soldiers onboard, the sails were unfurled, and they began their short voyage to the far side of the bay. Several strips of rock walls bordered the outer edge, each with dozens of hanging cages bolted into the sides. Some were empty, while others contained bodies in various stages of decay. Cas felt his stomach turn as they passed the first row.

Prisma squeezed his hand. He took a deep breath to focus himself. They had a job to do.

"Guard," the admiral barked, regarding Cas. "Make sure their chains are tight. We don't want any surprises."

Cas stepped up to Nyx. He slid the key into the lock that kept her hands chained, clicking it open as quietly as he could. Their eyes met. A slight smile twitched across her face, disappearing just as quickly.

As Cas carefully unlocked the shackles of the rest of the crew, Prisma slowly moved toward the hatch, and when she was sure no one was watching, disappeared down to the lower decks. The *Riptide* slowed as it approached the final rock wall before the open ocean. The guards occupied themselves with pulling the ship smoothly in line with the cages.

"Expect to bring me back out here in a few hours," Draigh announced to the other guards. He then turned to face Nyx. "I want to watch this one die."

"You take too much pleasure in this, Draigh," Caine said, casting a disapproving gaze toward him.

"This is why I joined the Navy, Admiral. Catching criminals and ensuring they pay accordingly for what they've done. Are you telling me you take no joy in knowing that Alistair will be gone soon?"

"Joy is not the right word. I certainly won't be coming out to watch," the admiral said flatly.

"Well, I will enjoy watching them drown enough for the both of us," Draigh said quietly to Nyx, smiling with an evil glint in his eyes.

Cas finished unlocking his friends and stepped back. Out of the corner of his eye, he saw Prisma peek out of the hatch, her arms full of their discarded weapons. She quickly ducked back down. The ship came to a stop, several of the guards jumping over to the strip of rocks to prepare the last cages for their temporary occupants.

"Guard . . ." Draigh said, glancing over at Cas, then paused and did a double take. Cas realized he was staring at his leg.

In one swift movement, Cas pulled the baton from his belt and hit the commander across the head. Prisma jumped out of the hatch, throwing Nyx her sword.

The deck erupted into chaos. The pirates dropped their chains, grabbed their weapons and attacked the guards that remained on-board, filling the air with the sound of metal on metal. Nyx raced to the helm and sliced open the sailor steering the ship. As the rest of the crew fought, she turned the ship away from the rocky jetty.

Alistair locked eyes with Admiral Caine. The two lunged forward, their swords clashing together. They matched each other step for step, seeming to predict the other's next movement with incredible accuracy.

"You took everything from me," Caine hissed through gritted teeth. "My fleet, my men, my dignity . . ." He brought his sword down in an arc, Alistair deflecting it to the side. "You're not getting away this time."

"You can chase after me all you want, Caine," Alistair laughed as he dodged another strike. "But your fleet couldn't take me down, and neither can you."

With a flick of his wrist, Alistair flipped Caine's sword out of the way, and leapt forward, his blade burying itself deep into the admiral's stomach. Caine stared down in disbelief at the sword protruding from his abdomen.

His enemy skewered on the end of his sword, Alistair leaned in and whispered a final insult.

"You couldn't beat me before, and you can't beat me now."

He gave the admiral a shove as he yanked the bloody blade from his torso, sending the soldier stumbling off the side of the ship and into the waves below. Alistair watched as the wake of the *Riptide* turned red, a satisfied smirk creeping across his face.

As the ship pulled away from the rocky wall, Cas bolted to the side and began slicing the ropes of the soldiers as they attempted to pull themselves back onto the ship, leaving them behind in the waters of the bay. The *Riptide* lurched as it hit the choppy waves of the open sea, making Cas lose his balance.

As Cas stumbled to the side, a sword blade buried itself in the railing where he had just been standing. He jumped back as the sword's owner steadied himself and pulled his blade free. It was Draigh, a thin trickle of blood running down his face from the gash on his head where Cas hit him.

"I should've known you weren't innocent in all this," he spat. "You or that medic girl . . ." He swung his sword, narrowly missing Cas as he ducked away. Draigh lunged forward, sweeping Cas's legs out from under him. He fell to the deck, hard, and Draigh raised his sword.

Before either of them could move, someone barreled into Draigh, shoving him with their whole body weight. Draigh let out a cry of surprise as he toppled from the deck.

Tig smiled down at Cas. "You alright, kid?" Cas nodded and pulled himself to his feet.

"You're not going to get away!" Draigh shouted after them from the water. "I'm going to find you!"

"And when you do, we won't go so easy on you!" Nyx called back.

The *Riptide* quickly put distance between them and the soldiers left behind in the bay. Cas knew the commotion would have attracted the attention of the guards back on land, but they would be able to outrun the Navy ships with this much of a head start. They were free.

"Where'd that guard say Fenix's ship was heading?" Nyx shouted.

"Headin' north, along the coast," Gyles called as he climbed up to his usual place in the crow's nest.

"Anyone know the name of the ship?" she asked.

"The *North's Bounty*!" Cas said. "Are we going after him?"

"Of course we're going after him! He's one of us," Nyx said—then added under her breath, "Besides, we hardly have enough people to sail the ship."

Catching the northern winds, the *Riptide* picked up speed, prow slicing through the choppy waves. It wasn't long before they spotted a merchant ship in the distance. Gyles confirmed it was the one they were after.

The flag was raised and the *Riptide* began to pursue the merchant ship. Surprisingly, once again, this ship didn't attempt to escape, and the pirates pulled up alongside the slower vessel. They were met by a short, balding man wearing expensive-looking clothes and a crew of rather despondent sailors.

"Sorry to disappoint you, but we don't have any cargo yet. We're on the way to get it. Feel free to try again later," he said, amused, seeming very unconcerned by the swords and pistols pointing at him.

"We're not here for your cargo, we're here for Fenix," Nyx said.

His eyebrows shot up. "Fenix? The slave? What do you want him for?"

"He's part of our crew. We want him back."

The man stifled a laugh. "He's *mine*. I bought him at auction three years ago."

"In that case, we're stealing him. See how accommodating I am?" Nyx sneered while motioning for the pirates to look below deck.

"You can't just . . ." he took a step toward Nyx, who aimed her pistol at his head.

"You were saying?" she asked.

"N-nothing," he stammered.

He watched helplessly with silent anger as Cas, Prisma, Gryph and Splinter climbed down the hatch.

Below, the four passed through several empty cargo holds until they reached the lowest deck. The smell made Cas gag. It was a combination of rot, waste, and something sharper beneath that; the metallic smell of blood.

"First time in the brig of a merchant ship?" Splinter whispered. Cas nodded. "Merchant ships are kept going primarily by slaves. This is where they bring them when they don't behave."

He peered around the dark space. Chains hung from the walls, clinking softly with the motion of the waves. On one side of the room were several cells. On the other side was a collection of whips and ropes.

Laying in the corner was Fenix, hands tied and back slashed with countless whip marks, his clothes soaked in blood. He was lying so still that at first, Cas thought he was dead.

Prisma ran to his side. At her touch, he twitched, and began to whimper.

"I didn't take anything, I swear . . ."

"Fenix!" she said. He looked up at her.

"Prisma? What are you doing here?"

"We're here for you!" she said as she cut the ropes that tied his hands. "Come on, we have to get you out." She pulled him to his feet, and guided him to the ladder. Splinter and Gryph climbed up after them, helping to steady Fenix. As Cas turned to go, he heard a whispered voice from the opposite side of the brig. He paused.

"Hey!" He took a step forward, and realized with a start that the shape he had assumed was a pile of rags and old clothes was, in fact, a person in the cell. "How about you go get the key over there and let me out?" The man said, a scrawny arm gesturing to a ring of keys hanging on the wall. Cas hesitated. What if he was dangerous? After all, they had locked him in his own cage instead of being tied up like Fenix.

"Come on, I'm gonna end up like your friend if you don't!" he pleaded. The fear in his voice won Cas over. He grabbed the key ring and began looking for the correct one.

The man stepped forward expectantly. He was skinny and dressed in tattered, baggy clothes, with shoulder-length ginger hair and a scruffy beard. But there was something *off* about him. Cas paused, key in the lock, trying to figure out what.

Suddenly, he realized it was the man's eyes. They were the exact unsettling, almost glowing, shade of blue as Nyx's.

The man smiled as the lock clicked open.

"Thanks, kid," he said, and ran for the ladder.

As he quickly climbed up, Cas called after him. "Where are you going?"

The man paused, his eyes glazing over as he stared off into the distance, pondering the question. "I don't know, actually," he said finally.

"Do you want to join our crew?" Cas asked hesitantly. He wasn't actually sure if he was allowed to hire people. The man thought about it.

"Yeah, sure. I suppose."

As Cas and his new companion emerged from the hatch, he could see that there was a commotion on the deck. The owner of the ship was angry. He had been joined by the muscular woman Cas had seen in the prison, and the two were in a heated discussion.

"So you're telling me that the slave didn't steal anything from you?" she asked.

"No, not technically . . ." he admitted.

"Why did you say he did?"

"Because escaped slaves are hardly ever found, unless you report that they stole something valuable from you. I paid good money for him, and I wasn't about to lose my investment," he explained.

"If he didn't take anything, then why have I been interrogating him about it since we left port? Why didn't you tell me not to?"

"Well, I can't have him thinking about escaping again."

"So not only are you a slave keeper and trader, you're also a disgusting specimen of one at that?" Nyx asked. He glared at her.

"I'm disgusting? You're a criminal. A thief and a murderer . . ." He noticed Cas and the man, and immediately shifted his attention to them. "Hey! You got the one you came here for, you can't take that one too!"

"We can take whatever we want. Are you going to stop us?" Nyx snapped, then leaned toward Cas and whispered. "Who is that, and why is he here?"

"Look at his eyes," Cas whispered back. He saw a look of shock cross the captain's face. The man stared back at her, seeming confused. After a moment, Nyx managed to shift her attention back to the owner of the ship.

"Where'd he come from?" she asked the merchant.

"We found him on a tiny little spit of land, a few weeks after your friend escaped," he said. "I was gonna keep him, but he freaks everyone out, so we put him down in the cage instead. I was planning to sell him once we got to the trading post."

"That's a shame. We'll be taking him now," Nyx said.

"What? You can't just—" Nyx cocked her gun before he could finish his sentence, silencing him.

"Get them both onboard," she snapped. "And as for you, good sir . . ." She leaned closer to the ship's owner. "Consider yourself lucky that we're in a hurry, otherwise we'd teach you a thing or two about manners."

"Yeah, but I'm not in a hurry," the muscular woman growled, stepping closer to her boss. "And I don't like being lied to." Cas saw fear flash across his face.

The pirates didn't stick around to see what happened between them. Soon, they were racing north across the open sea, putting as much distance as possible between them and the Navy ships. Fenix was taken down to the medic cabin, while the blue-eyed man remained on deck, seeming to enjoy the fresh air.

"So, what's your name?" Nyx called down from the helm.

He was silent at first, brow creased in confusion, before he seemed to remember. "Niko! Yeah. I'm Niko."

"How'd you get on that island?" she asked.

He shrugged.

Nyx stared at him in confusion. "What do you mean? You don't know?"

"Nope. Can't remember a thing before a couple days prior to them finding me."

"Huh." she was quiet for a second. "Do you know anything about sailing?"

"Yes! I know lots about that."

"Good. You're part of the crew, then. Get to work!"

12

Interception

Fifty miles off the coast of Empiris, dawn was breaking over a scene of destruction. Firelight glinted across the glass-flat sea as an Empire messenger ship burned, the heavily damaged vessel slowly sinking beneath the water.

A large, dark ship glided away from the fiery wreckage, bloodred sails seeming to glow in the morning light. Barked orders, whip cracks, and the occasional cry of pain echoed across the sea as the crew worked relentlessly on the upper deck.

On the lower decks, men hurried to and fro restocking gunpowder and adding their new cargo to the hold. Others drank, toasting to their newly acquired supplies, while some rested in the hammocks. Below it all, down in the dark, dripping depths of the ship, was the tall, imposing figure of the captain.

He stared down at their prisoner, eyes glinting with fascination behind his tinted spectacles. The prisoner, cut and burned nearly beyond recognition, whimpered in pain and fear as the captain regarded him silently.

"Now," he said, voice honeyed and persuasive, "Why don't you tell me the *whole* story this time?"

"I . . . I will," the prisoner stammered. "They sent a messenger to Tallix a few weeks ago."

"Yes, I know that. I intercepted that message," the captain snapped.

"It detailed the capture of Alistair Vyncin—"

"I *know* that." The harshness of the captain's tone made the prisoner flinch back. "What is the *new* message?"

"S-sorry. The message I was sent to relay is that Alistair and his crew escaped during their execution."

"Escaped? How?"

"I don't know," he said weakly.

The captain took a step forward, and the prisoner shrunk back.

"There was some kind of incident while taking them out to the cages! I don't know the specifics!" he frantically stated.

"Is that all?" The prisoner was quiet for a second.

"No. Admiral Draigh said the ship was last seen sailing north. He plans to go after them."

"He won't catch them," the captain mused to himself. "Alistair has a lifetime of experience avoiding the Navy. But if he's heading north, I know where he's going."

"Will you let me go, then?"

The captain looked down at the man, a smile crossing his face. "You've told me everything?"

"Yes, I swear!"

"Then of course we'll let you go." The captain whistled, and a tall, burly man climbed down the ladder. The prisoner was pulled up to the deck and the ropes that bound his hands cut away. The captain motioned to his companion.

Without a word, the burly man picked up the prisoner and tossed him overboard. The prisoner let out a scream of terror, and bobbed up to the surface a moment later, coughing. The captain's smile widened as he addressed the crew.

"Some of you were a bit off the mark during the attack," he announced. "Consider this target practice."

The captain turned away as dozens of gunshots rang out, drowning out the screams of the prisoner. He strode up to the helm and spoke a single word to the woman at the wheel.

"Yarlford."

13

A New Way

Despite the blazing fires that sat in the hearths at each corner of the tavern, Cas still felt the chill of the wind howling through the cracks in the walls. He wrapped his jacket tighter around him, wishing he had the thick fur and wool coats of the locals. At least the tavern was warmer than the deck of the *Riptide*.

Cas had thought he knew what being cold meant. He had been cold many times, especially living outdoors during the winter. But being up here was a different experience entirely.

The air was so cold that taking in a breath made the inside of his nose sting and his lungs ache. The sails were brittle and the ropes had to be constantly cleared of ice. Touching the metal of the chains burned his skin. The cold was all-consuming, numbing, and he couldn't escape it, even huddled in his hammock under every blanket he could find. But this was the pirate's best option.

Yarlford was the last northern landmass not occupied by the Empire, a final stronghold for those who opposed them. The rugged coastlines were dotted with ports and villages run by the descendants of pirates who had settled there, and the icy waters were patrolled by all types of raiders, thieves, and runaways, most notably the last remnants of the Selkis Armada.

Alistair had suggested coming to the frozen island. He had an "old friend" who he said could help them.

"Where are they?" Cimik growled. "He said they'd be here an hour ago."

"Be patient. It's not like we have a schedule to keep," Nyx said. She leaned back and put her feet up on the table, pulling her hat low as if planning to sleep.

"At least it's warm in here," Splinter muttered.

"By 'old friend' . . ." Gyles spoke up, "do you think he meant a *friend*, or . . ."

"In my experience, 'old friend' can mean anything from a spouse to someone who wants you dead. Sometimes both," Nyx said.

"Maybe we should send someone to check on him, then," Gyles suggested.

"Do you want to go out there and look around?" Tig asked. Gyles quickly shook his head.

The tavern door opened, allowing a gust of frigid wind inside. Prisma shivered and leaned up against Cas, her thick, coily hair tickling his nose. He felt his heart skip a beat.

"Glad you're all still here!" a familiar voice said. Alistair strode up to the table, accompanied by a tall, slim man with long salt-and-pepper hair and light brown skin, dressed in thick wool clothes and a fur cloak. "This is Kal."

"Good to meet you," Nyx said. "I assume you're the one who's going to help us?"

"Yes, that's me," Kal said as he and Alistair sat down.

"What exactly are your qualifications?"

"He's qualified, don't worry," Alistair said.

"I'd like to hear that from him," she replied.

"Why? You can't just trust me?"

"No, I can't trust you. You lie to us all the time."

Alistair looked offended. "I do not!"

"You had us calling you by a fake name for the first six months we knew you," Knives pointed out.

"That wasn't a *fake* name . . ."

"To be fair, he doesn't outright lie so much as withhold important information," Gyles said.

"Regardless, no, I don't trust you," Nyx continued. "So, Kal, how exactly can you help us?"

"In this case, Alistair isn't lying. I believe I can be of assistance to you," Kal said. "I used to make maps professionally. Mostly for people that didn't want to be found, if you know what I mean. That's how Alistair and I met. And I believe I've drafted up one that can get you to your destination while also avoiding the Navy." He pulled a folded piece of parchment out of his coat and spread it across the table. The group leaned in.

Cas had seen many maps of the known world. They were all pretty similar: a ring of islands surrounding the Interior Sea, with illustrations of monsters and serpents lurking along the outside of the ring. This map traced a path that took them directly into those unknown outer waters.

"Excuse me?" Splinter asked.

"The Navy doesn't patrol out there. Those are lawless waters," Kal said.

"Yeah, with good reason," Cimik pointed out.

"It's either this or we risk running into the Navy and ending up back in a prison cell. Do we want to go to the Quarter or not?" Alistair asked.

"About that," Gyles said. "I'm starting to wonder if this is all worth the trouble. There's a solid chance we won't even find the treasure and will end up lost in the fog forever."

"That's not going to happen," Nyx snapped.

"Can you be certain?" Gyles asked.

Nyx leaned back in her chair, glancing between the crew. "No, of course I can't be certain. But I wouldn't be going back if I didn't think it was worth the risk, even if we do have to go around the entire Interior Sea to get there." Her voice grew quiet, and Cas thought he detected a hint of fear. "You have no idea what I went through in the Quarter, and it's the last place I want to be. But I'm willing to do it because I believe we can find the treasure this time. I'm not going to force any of you to go if you don't want to."

"This is what we signed up for," Prisma said. "I plan to see it through." The rest of the crew agreed. Even Gyles nodded along.

"In that case, the only way you're going to get there is by traversing around the Empire's territory," Kal continued.

"So we're taking the long way around, basically?" Tig asked.

"Essentially. It'll take me a few days to get a final version of the map and navigation route. The final result be much more precise than this one."

"What do we do about all the monsters?" Splinter asked. Gyles stared at him.

"There aren't really monsters out there, Splinter," he said.

"Wha—then why are they on all the maps?"

"It's for decoration," Gyles said.

"No, actually, there really are monsters out there," Nyx insisted. "Not the same ones you see on the maps, but they're out there."

"We have cannons. I still haven't gotten to try them." Tig said.

"They won't help," Nyx muttered.

"You're all out of your mind," Gyles groaned.

"Once I saw a fish bigger than the ship," Fenix said. "I don't know if it was a 'monster,' per se, but it was *big*."

The table went silent for a moment.

"Anyway," Kal said, "it may be best to trade in your ship for a smaller one, with your crew size."

"No," Nyx snapped. "We're keeping the *Riptide*. That isn't negotiable. You navigate and leave the ship to me!"

"Alright, easy. I'm just saying it would be faster."

"I know it would be. But this is my ship."

Sensing that there was no use arguing, Kal continued. "I'll see what I can do. Plan to stay here for a few more days while I complete my calculations and drafting. The tavern has rooms you can stay in."

"Gladly. I'm not getting back on the ship in this weather," Knives said.

"If you need me, I'll be in my cabin," Nyx said as she stood up.

"Aren't you gonna be cold?" Cas asked.

"Probably gonna be cold either way. I may as well be in my own room," she said as she left the tavern.

*

As Nyx drifted off to sleep, shivering and huddled beneath blankets, the cabin faded away. It was replaced by a comforting darkness, pressing in around her like a thick quilt. It felt strangely familiar, although she couldn't pinpoint when she had felt it before.

"That was a close call." The words, though spoken in a melodic voice, were sharp and made goosebumps rise on the captain's skin. The figure of a woman, outlined in a soft blue glow, appeared in front of her. "For a while, I was worried you were going to die," The woman continued.

Nyx smiled, feeling her heart flutter. "Awe, you were worried about me?"

"You shouldn't have been so stupid."

Nyx's smile faded. "Excuse me?"

"You could have died, not to mention the setback your crew suffered. You're further from the Quarter now than when you started!"

"Hey, you could've stepped in, you know. Like when I was being starved and beaten within an inch of my life? That would've been a great time for a visit, Zephyrine." Nyx snapped.

"These are problems of your own making, and it is not my job to save you." The voice rose in intensity, seeming to come from all directions at once. "I have helped plenty already, in ways you don't even understand yet. Not to mention my goal will help both of us, in case you forgot. You acquire the treasure, and I rid myself of all these treasure-hunters continually entering the Quarter, dying and never leaving!"

"Calm down. I'll get there, it'll just take a little longer." Nyx assured her.

"Don't let it take too long, or I'll find someone else to assist me."

Nyx jolted awake, drenched in sweat despite the frigid air. Her breathing was heavy, creating tendrils of ice fog before her face. She swallowed hard and lay back in her hammock, watching the lantern as the flame flickered low, then went out.

*

In the early hours just before dawn, Cas was finding it difficult to sleep. The tavern's tiny sleeping cabins were cold and drafty, and the small wooden cot was uncomfortable compared to his hammock. After a long night of tossing and turning, drifting off into half-sleep only to be woken by bad dreams, Cas finally climbed out of bed and walked down to the main tavern space. The heat of the fireplaces was welcome after his chilly room.

At this time of night, the tavern was mostly empty. However, Cas immediately recognized someone familiar. He sat down next to Niko at the bar.

"What are you doing up?" Cas asked. Niko shrugged.

"Can't sleep." During the journey to Yarlford, Niko had spoken very little. He was a good sailor and always seemed fairly cheerful, but couldn't hold a conversation.

"Yeah, me neither," Cas muttered.

"Bad dreams?"

"Yeah."

"Me too. Except my dreams sort of feel like memories. But then I can't really remember them when I wake up."

That explained why Niko would occasionally shout and writhe in his sleep, then awake confused and unable to tell them what was wrong.

"So, you really don't remember anything before the island?" Cas asked.

"Nope. Nothing."

"The reason I ask is because of the captain . . ." Cas began.

"Yeah, I know. She's got the same eyes as me. Or, well, eye, in her case."

"Apparently it changed to that color when she was in the Quarter."

"I've heard," Niko affirmed.

Cas must have looked surprised, because Niko chuckled. "I may not talk a lot, but I listen," he said.

"What *do* you remember?" Cas asked. Niko was silent for a moment, staring down at his drink with a look of concentration and confusion.

"I remember water. I assume I swam to that island from somewhere. Probably a ship. But I don't remember that. I just remember water all around me, and it was dark and cold, and I was afraid. And then things get very hazy. The next thing I knew, I was lying on the beach of an island. It wasn't much of an island, just a few trees clinging to a strip of sand in the middle of the ocean. Luckily there was a bunch of fruit on the trees, because I was stuck there for a few days. Then I woke up one morning and there was a big ship passing by. I started yelling and waving, and they moved closer, so I jumped in the water and swam out to them.

"They pulled me onboard and suddenly there were a bunch of guns and swords pointed at me. The captain assumed I must've been a pirate captain who had been mutinied and abandoned there, and maybe I was, I don't know. They didn't kill me, 'cause I guess they needed an extra worker. But, y'know, on account of my eyes and things, the others thought I was some kind of evil spirit disguised as a human, so they locked me up after a while."

"And that's it? You can't remember what you did for work, or your friends or family?" Cas asked. Niko shook his head, and for a moment looked like he might cry.

Then the door flew open, making Cas cringe back at the gust of frigid air that swept into the room. Alistair and Kal stepped inside.

"Oh, good. You're up. Go wake the rest of the crew, would you?" Alistair said.

"Why? The sun's not even up," Cas said.

"Yeah, and we want to be leaving when it comes up. We need time to go over the plan and get the ship in sailing condition."

With the crew gathered, Kal spread the finished map over the table.

"Looks nice," Gyles said, impressed.

"This map includes the constellations you'll need to follow, as well as compass directions," Kal said. "It's a long trip. And it'll take quite a few months, but it'll be well worth your time."

"I hope so," Nyx said. "Thank you, Kal. You do good work."

"Of course. Anything for an 'old friend.'" He shot Alistair an amused look.

"I think we better be going," Alistair said quickly, rolling up the map and handing it to Nyx.

Outside, the crew made their way along the slick walkways. Cas had to grip the railing tightly and lean heavily on his good leg to keep from slipping. Prisma stayed by his side, ready to catch him if necessary.

The *Riptide* sat in the harbor, bobbing alongside icebergs. The black sails were encrusted with a layer of white frost, and icicles hung from the rigging, with ice coating the hull like glittering plates of armor.

"You ready for a long morning, Cas?" Cimik asked as they approached.

"Huh?" Cas asked.

"Cleaning off all the snow and ice off the deck is the cabin boy's job." Cas stared up at the snow-covered ship, watching with dismay as more snowflakes began to fall from the gray clouds overhead.

"Well, then you better be prepared to wait a while," he muttered, grabbing his broom.

14

Uncharted Waters

Alistair stood at the helm, looking out across the ocean with his spyglass. He had a strange feeling in the pit of his stomach. Something was wrong.

The day, however, seemed to disagree. The sea was calm, waves lapping gently against the hull, and the sky was adorned with fluffy white clouds that drifted in front of the sun now and then, casting gold and gray dappling across the ship.

Perhaps he was just nervous because these waters were unfamiliar to him. He had sailed to every corner of the map in his long career as a pirate, but never into uncharted territory. He knew the tales and legends about what lurked outside the predictable Interior Sea and the islands that dotted it, and he didn't like them. Although he was relieved to be back in better sailing weather, he was nervous.

"You can go to sleep, you know," Nyx said from the wheel. "It's daytime. Your shift is over."

"I can't sleep," Alistair replied.

"Why? Sea's calm," she stated.

"I'm worried."

"About what? Leaving the map? The Quarter? The Navy fleet after us?"

"Yes, all of the above." He glanced down at the deck, where Cas was repairing ropes with Prisma. "Do you think the lad's father is really going to be there?"

"Oh, no. He's definitely dead."

Alistair turned to face her; brow furrowed. "Why do you think that?"

"No one gets out of the Quarter alive."

"You did," he pointed out.

"That's because . . ." She paused, staring out across the sea. "Because I was very lucky."

"What about Niko?"

"We don't know what happened to Niko. He doesn't remember, and we can't just assume where he came from."

"So, tell me, what is out there, really? Beyond the map, in the places we draw sea serpents and monsters?"

Nyx was quiet for a moment. "Things we're not supposed to see," she said finally. "Things better left a mystery."

"And you've got no problem going back there?"

She laughed. "I'm terrified to go back. But I set out on my quest for the *Sea's Revenge* years ago, and that quest needs a conclusion. Either we'll find the treasure and come home rich, or we'll die. One way or another, it will end this time."

Alistair raised his spyglass once again, scanning the horizon. There was nothing in sight but the expanse of water all around them. He tucked his spyglass back into his pocket and retired to his room.

The quartermaster's cabin was only about half the size of the captain's, sparsely decorated with a hammock and a desk, with a porthole offering a view of the sea. He pulled open the desk drawer to reveal a single item inside: a small blue velvet box.

Sitting back in his hammock, he glanced at the door to double check that it was closed and locked and then opened the box.

A single, palm-sized piece of polished blue sea glass sat amongst the velvet. He picked it up carefully, feeling comforted as he ran his fingers across the familiar smooth edges. As he angled the flat, reflective surface toward his face, the image shifted.

Instead of the cabin, the glass now showed a rough seascape, the waves glinting blood red and fiery orange. Above the water fluttered brilliant red sails. They were growing closer.

3

Part 3

15

The Calm

Over a month into their journey, Cas had yet to see any horrible sea creatures or unnatural weather phenomena. So far it was clear skies, smooth sailing, and some welcome warmer weather now that they had left the harsh climate of the high north behind. There was no sign of Empire vessels, or any vessels for that matter.

As he cleaned the deck one sunny morning, he could tell that the others were feeling positive too, for the first time since their encounter with the Navy.

"Ey, Splinter! What are you gonna do with your share of the treasure?" Gryph yelled up the mast. "I'm gonna get a big yacht and travel the world!"

"Probably spend it all on stupid stuff and go back to being a pirate," Splinter called down from the rigging.

"Really? You know how much it's supposed to be, right? You'd be set for life!" Gryph said.

"Well, in that case, maybe I'll get my own yacht and join you."

"I'm gonna open a tavern," Knives said. "And a casino. Somewhere warm and sunny."

"Personally, I'm going back to school," Gyles said from the top of the mast. "I could become a certified navigator and cartographer, making maps and charts."

"Really living on the wild side, huh?" Splinter yelled sarcastically.

"I'm going home to Selkis," Cimik said from the bow. "I can buy one of the old warships and live in the bay, shooting down the Empire ships that pass by. Until I get taken out in a blaze of cannon fire."

"Sounds fun," Knives said.

"I intend to get a big mansion and retire in Tallix," Tig said.

"I'm with you, Tig," Alistair replied, lowering his spyglass. "Except I'll be settling down in Yarlford."

"It's so cold there, though," Fenix said.

"I don't mind it," Alistair said, then returned to scanning the sea.

"I'll probably do the same as you two," Niko said. "Get a house. Be rich and happy. Maybe I could go back to that island and try to figure out . . ." He trailed off, staring into the distance.

"I'm headed somewhere tropical," Fenix continued after a moment of silence. "I can get some land by the sea and offer a safe haven for other runaway slaves."

"You're really not selfish enough to be a pirate, Fen," Gryph said. Fenix shrugged.

"I'll be fixing up the *Riptide* and going back to what I do best: sailing the high seas," Nyx said. "And if you're all leaving, I can hire a proper crew."

"As if you could do better than us!" Splinter said.

Gryph rolled his eyes and glanced over at Cas and Prisma. "How 'bout you kids? What are you doing with your share?"

"I guess I could go to school and become a real doctor," Prisma said. "Probably at a really nice school, in Empiris or Tallix."

"I . . ." Cas paused. "I never thought about it."

"What? What have you been thinking about this whole trip, then?" Gryph asked.

Cas shrugged. "This was never really a treasure hunt for me. I want to find my dad."

The crew scoffed and laughed.

"Yeah, but what if you find the treasure *and* your dad?" Fenix asked.

"Then . . . I guess he and I would get a house. I'd never have to steal again. Maybe I could live in the rich part of Valdoria . . ." He paused again, thinking about walking the same streets he once patrolled with Scout, navigating the canals and seeing the taverns he and his friend visited pass by on the way to his mansion in the hills. He decided that it would be too painful. "Maybe not Valdoria. But I'd give some of my money to Nan, the tavern keeper who helped me."

"Yeah, same here. I would share my treasure with Jois," Prisma agreed.

"If you all keep talking instead of working, we'll never get there to find the treasure." Nyx said. The crew went back to their duties.

"If the conditions stay this fair, we'll be there ahead of schedule," Cas heard Alistair mutter. Despite the positive words, there was an air of uncertainty to his voice.

A moment later, Cas noticed a dark shadow pass across the water. He glanced up, confused, as there were no clouds in the sky. With a shudder of horror, he realized the shadow was *below* the water.

He leaned over the deck. The dark creature was twice the size of the ship, jet black against the clear blue water. It swam silently below them, not even creating a ripple as its gigantic tail swayed back and forth. He looked up at Nyx, open-mouthed in shock. She was peering into the water as well, seemingly unfazed.

"Oh, yeah. That's a big one," she said, and returned her attention to the wheel. Swallowing hard, Cas tore his gaze away from the beast and returned to cleaning.

16

The Storm

"Does Alistair seem . . . a bit strange to you lately?" Cas asked the next morning, as Prisma was preparing his medicine. She turned to look at the cot where he sat, fastening his prosthetic in place.

"Stranger than usual you mean? A little, maybe," she said.

"He seems worried."

"He's a superstitious guy, and we're in a part of the ocean supposedly full of horrible sea creatures. Monsters and demons. He probably is worried."

"Yeah." Cas wasn't sure that was it. Alistair was hardly sleeping, spending all day and night pacing the deck and constantly scanning the horizon with his spyglass. Something that the tavern keeper in Carran had said was echoing through Cas's head—that Alistair was rumored to have a supernatural sense. "You don't think he can really see the future, do you?"

"No, I don't," Prisma said firmly. "The man is just lucky."

"You're probably right."

Prisma handed him a bottle of purple liquid. "Drink up. Cimik wants you to scrape barnacles off the hull today."

"Another exciting day as a pirate," Cas muttered.

As he climbed back onto the main deck, an unexpected cold wind ruffled his hair. He looked into it and saw dark clouds hovering in the distance. He swallowed hard, remembering The Well.

Of course, they were far from The Well now. This was just an ordinary storm. He began his daily tasks, trying to put it out of his mind. But each time he glanced up, the clouds were looming closer.

Sunset turned the water brilliant orange and red, the waves like dancing flames as the sea became increasingly choppy. From the helm, Nyx barked orders to prepare the ship for a stormy night.

Suddenly, Alistair gasped.

"Ship! Out in the fog and closing fast!" he yelled. Nyx turned and pulled out her spyglass. Cas squinted into the hazy patch of ocean beneath the storm clouds. He could see the outline of sails, partially hidden by the dense mist.

"Wha—what's another ship doing all the way out here?" she muttered. Alistair ran to the helm and grabbed the wheel while Nyx was distracted.

"Tig! Ready the cannons! Lower the sails! Prepare for battle!" he shouted. Nyx spun around and glared at him.

"What do you think you're doing?" she snapped. "*I'm* the captain, not you, and we are not going into battle!" She shoved him away from the wheel. He stared back, eyes glinting with anger.

"That ship is here to kill us. If we don't do something . . ."

"How do you know it's here to kill us?" she asked.

He blinked and took a step back, seemingly caught off guard.

"Because I know!" he insisted.

"And I'm supposed to risk our lives launching an attack on an unknown ship because you *just know*?"

Cas looked away from the scene on the helm and noticed the

ship was getting closer, red sails fully opened despite the encroaching storm.

"You've got to listen to me . . ." Alistair implored.

"Tell me why I should, and I might," she replied.

"I *can't* tell you. You'll just have to trust me!"

"Then in that case . . ." She was cut off when an explosion echoed across the waves. A second later, a cannonball shattered the bowsprit.

Cas threw himself to the deck, hands over his head. He could hear Nyx and Alistair shouting orders and the crew's panicked voices as they tried to obey both at once.

Someone grabbed his arm and pulled him to his feet.

"Run, Cas!" Prisma yelled. The two of them ran toward the hatch. Although the *Riptide* had a head start, the other ship was approaching quickly from behind.

Prisma slid down the ladder, and Cas followed. Gunshots filled the air as he ducked into the hatch.

In the medic cabin, Prisma locked the door from the inside and grabbed the sword hidden under the cot. Cas pulled his own sword out of his belt. Above him, he could hear shouting, gunshots, and cannon fire.

"Who are they? Why are they attacking us?" Prisma asked.

"Could they be a Navy ship?" he asked nervously.

Prisma shook her head. "I've never seen a Navy ship with colorful sails."

Cas tensed as heavy footsteps hurried down the ladder. They stopped just outside the cabin, and his heart began to pound as someone tried the door handle.

There was a moment of silence. Then a hole was blasted in the door. Prisma screamed and ducked beneath the desk. Cas jumped back, tripped, and fell onto the floor.

The door flew open and a tall, hulking man stepped inside, gun drawn. His dark eyes looked between the two.

"Drop your swords and get up to the deck. Now," he growled. Cas and Prisma obeyed. On the deck, they found the rest of the crew surrounded by armed pirates. Alistair and Nyx were being tied to the mast.

"Bring those two over," the captor demanded. Prisma and Cas were shoved toward the mast and bound with thick ropes, arms pinned at their sides.

"What's happening?" Prisma asked Alistair. "Who are these people?"

"I don't know," he said.

"What do you mean, you don't know?"

"I've gotten on a lot of people's bad sides. I don't recognize these particular people, but I'm sure they have their reasons."

"Stop talking," one of the men snapped. "Our captain's the one who wants to see you."

"And who's your captain?" Alistair asked.

Someone stepped from the red-sailed ship to the *Riptide* and strode toward them. The deck went eerily silent, and their attackers parted to allow him through.

He was tall and slim, wearing a wide-brimmed black hat and long crimson coat, with long, straight black hair and pale skin. He wore tinted glasses and a cruel smile on his angular face. On his shoulder sat a strange-looking black lizard with red eyes. The creature was longer than Cas's forearm.

Cas heard Alistair catch his breath and turned to see that his friend was wide-eyed and white-faced.

"Good to see you again, Alistair," the man said, voice dripping with malice.

"You . . . you can't be here," Alistair stammered.

"Why? Because I'm dead?" He stepped closer, his smile turning into a scowl. "Because you blew up my ship?" Alistair didn't answer. "Well, I survived. My first mate informed me about your little gunpowder trick, and we jumped overboard before the explosion. Unfortunately, we didn't have time to get the rest of the crew, but luckily my good friends arrived with my *new* ship shortly after. Do you like it? It's the fastest ship this side of Torokai; the *Red Death*."

The man backed away and smiled at his captives. "I don't believe we've been properly introduced. I'm Captain Lucien. And I assume you're Alistair's new crew?"

"No," Nyx spoke up. "He's part of *my* crew."

Lucien looked back and forth between the two.

"You're not even the captain, Alistair?" He laughed.

"No, he's not. And you will address me as the one in charge here, not him," Nyx said. He turned to her.

"Alright, then. You destroyed my ship and tried to kill me. Your subordinate stole something very valuable from me. I intend to get it back, and then kill every last one of you." He spun back around to Alistair. "Now, where is it?"

"I don't have it," Alistair said coldly. Lucien drew his sword and traced the tip along the scars that crisscrossed Alistair's face.

"If you tell me, I'll kill you quickly. If you make me search for it, I'll give you a matching set of these on the other side," he growled.

"I told you; I don't have it. I threw it in the ocean, like I should've done a long time ago."

"You're lying."

"I'm not."

"We're going to tear this ship apart if we have to, Alistair!" Lucien yelled, teeth bared in fury. "And it better be here, for your sake. If it's gone, things are going to be much worse for you and your friends."

"If I may ask, what are you looking for? I will gladly help you find it," Nyx asked, shooting a glare at Alistair.

"The Eye of the Sea," Lucien said.

Nyx paused. "Actually, I don't know what that is. You're on your own."

"I'm not surprised. Alistair likes to keep his most valuable possessions to himself." Lucien leaned in again, lowering his voice to a menacing whisper. "I'll ask you one more time; where is it?"

"At the bottom of The Well. Perhaps you should go look for it," Alistair replied. Lucien spun toward his ship and shouted.

"Ragna! Bring out the bargaining chip!"

Cas watched as a blonde woman emerged from below deck, dragging someone along with her. At first, he couldn't figure out who it was, as his long graying hair covered his face. But as they stepped onto the deck of the *Riptide*, Cas recognized him as the mapmaker from Yarlford.

"Kal?" Alistair cried.

Gagged with his hands tied behind his back, Kal was shoved down to the deck in front of the mast. He had clearly lost weight since Cas last saw him, and his face was bruised and clothes stained with dried blood. He didn't meet Alistair's eyes.

"Your friend has been very helpful so far. He's the one who told us where to find you," Lucien said.

"Let's see if he keeps helping us," Ragna said, pulling out a curved knife and holding it to Kal's throat.

Cas jumped as a crack of thunder echoed across the water. He looked up and realized the black clouds were getting close.

"I'm guessing Kal has never been keelhauled?" Lucien asked with a smile. "Would you like to tell him about it, Alistair?" Alistair didn't answer, eyes blazing with rage. "No? That's alright, we'll show him. Ragna, get the ropes!"

"Wait!" Alistair said, voice breaking. He paused, staring down at his feet. "I hid it down in the cargo hold. In one of the boxes."

Lucien's smile widened. He snapped his fingers and gestured to his crew.

"Get down there and start looking." His men disappeared one by one down the hatch. "You're making a good choice, Alistair."

Cas felt something cold touch his hand. He glanced down, and realized it was Alistair's metal hook. He had looped the sharp surface under the ropes, and was beginning to cut through them.

"We had such a good thing going, Alistair," Lucien was saying as he paced back and forth along the deck. "You as captain and me as first mate, stealing and killing and torturing . . . it was so much fun! Remember when you taught me how to strangle someone with their own intestines? That was the Alistair of legend. That was the Demon of the North Sea. Then . . . you got old. And you got weak." Alistair stopped cutting for a moment, his lip curling in anger.

"Weak?" he snarled.

"Yes, weak. You stopped using the Eye, and you got soft. You started letting our victims leave alive. You were talking about *retirement*. It's the law of nature, Al. Once the leader loses their edge, they need to be replaced by someone stronger." He shook his head. "You should've just died the first time I tried to kill you. Now you've lost your precious ship, you've lost the Eye again, and you've ruined countless innocent lives. Your old crew, your new crew, Kal, all the messenger vessels I had to destroy . . . And what did you gain? A few extra years?"

A flash of lightning lit up the sky, followed almost immediately by an ominous rumble of thunder. The smell of rain grew thicker in the air.

"But I'm not a monster," Lucien continued. "How's this sound; since you told me where the Eye is, I'll kill your new crew quickly. Bullet to the head. And I won't have as much fun with you as I'd like to. Let's revive an old classic: tied to the mast on a sinking ship. Seems like a fitting end for you."

"We still get to have *some* fun with you, of course," Ragna said, licking her lips to reveal a tongue split down the center like a snake's.

"First we can feed his fingers to Scylla," Lucien said, ticking his lizard under its chin. "She likes those. Don't you, my sweet?" The lizard licked his hand and cocked her head, slit-pupil eyes trained on those tied to the mast.

Cas felt the ropes loosen. Alistair's hook sliced through the last bit of fiber, and the restraints fell away.

Immediately, Nyx lunged for the sail rope and pulled it with all her strength. The sail unfurled, catching the wind. The *Riptide* pitched forward.

Lucien and Ragna lost their footing and tumbled to the deck. Below, Cas heard Lucien's crew shouting. He knew they would be up the ladder in seconds.

As Lucien climbed to his feet, teeth bared in rage, Alistair ran to meet him. Cas held his breath as, for one terrible moment, Lucien's sword arched through the air.

Alistair dodged the blade by inches and kicked Lucien hard in the chest. He let out a cry and fell overboard, splashing into the water as the *Riptide* sped away.

Ragna jumped up as the rest of her companions began to emerge onto the deck. The rain pounded down as the crew of the *Riptide* took up their blades and pistols and attacked.

A man came around the mast and swung his heavy sword at Cas, who ducked away at the last second. The man slashed at him again, and this time the blade lodged itself in his wooden leg. The two paused for a moment, as the man tried to figure out why his sword hadn't hit flesh.

Cas took the opportunity and jumped back, pulling the hilt right out of the man's hands. Yanking the blade out of his leg, he turned on his attacker. The pirate drew a long knife from his belt.

Above the rain and thunder, he could hear Lucien's shouts as he commanded his crew back to their ship.

As the *Riptide* pitched and rolled with the increasingly choppy waves, Cas nearly lost his balance. His attacker lunged forward. Cas found his footing and thrust the sword toward the pirate.

The blade pierced the man's chest, sliding inside with a sickening sound like a knife passing through a rotting fruit. The pirate's expression turned from a menacing scowl to terror as he realized what was happening.

Lightning flashed and thunder boomed as Cas and the man stared at each other for what felt like minutes. Blood leaked out from around the blade as the man staggered back. Cas watched in silent horror as the light in his eyes faded. He fell backward, over the side of the ship and disappeared beneath the churning waters below.

Cas was frozen in place. He looked from the dark sea to the dark blood on his hands.

"Cas!" Nyx's voice rose above the chaos. He turned to see her at the helm, as the last few enemies retreated overboard. The *Red Death* was approaching fast through the pouring rain. "Tie yourself in!"

Cas grabbed a length of rope, but it was ripped from his hands by the howling wind. The mast creaked ominously as the sails strained.

"Captain!" Tig yelled. "The mast is gonna break, we have to stow the sails!"

"Not yet!" Nyx commanded. Cas heard a crack as the wood took the immense strain.

The *Red Death* seemed to pause. As a flash of lightning lit the scene, he saw the crew scrambling to raise the sails to keep their masts intact. The ship disappeared behind the curtain of rain as the *Riptide* sailed deeper into the storm.

"Now!" Nyx shouted. "Raise the sails, quickly!"

Cas leapt into action along with the others. As he grabbed a sail rope, it was suddenly torn from the mast and vanished into the sea. The rigging was snapping from its moorings under the force of the wind.

A wave broke over the deck, knocking Cas off his feet. As he tumbled toward the edge of the ship, he realized with a pang of regret and terror that he hadn't yet tied himself in.

He was washed off the deck, and for a brief moment he was falling down to meet the black waters. Then something tightened around his throat and he came to a sudden stop, dangling above the waves.

He choked and clawed at the cord around his neck before finding a foothold on a porthole below him. The stranglehold loosened as he slipped his fingers under it and pulled it off, and he climbed onto the deck, panting.

Looped around a jagged plank on the side of the ship was the golden snail shell necklace. He pulled it free, realizing he would have been swept away and probably drowned if it hadn't caught the plank.

"Thanks, Jesper," he whispered as he tucked it back into his shirt.

"Land!" Gyles screamed above the gale. The bottom of the ship scraped against rock with a grating shriek. Then, with a lurch that sent the whole crew stumbling and falling to the deck, the *Riptide* came to an abrupt halt.

17

Shipwrecked

Cas stumbled onto the narrow strip of beach, clothes heavy with water and exhausted from navigating the storm as well as the crashing surf. His prosthetic leg slipped and sank awkwardly into the loose sand. The *Riptide* had wrecked on a rocky spit of land that jutted out from the island, battered by waves and wind coming off the open ocean beyond. The crew was slowly making their way to the beach.

He saw someone being dragged across the sand and limped toward them. Splinter lay on his back, head in Gryph's lap while Knives held his hand. A gash in his stomach was slowly seeping blood across the white beach. Prisma knelt next to him.

Splinter coughed weakly and looked up at Gryph and Knives.

"Before I die, I need to tell you two something . . ." he gasped, his tiny frame shaking.

"You're not dying, Splinter," Prisma said. He raised his head to look at her.

"I'm not?"

"No. You just need stitches."

He breathed a sigh of relief. "Oh. In that case, I can tell you guys later." Gryph rolled his eyes and Knives shook his head.

"Alistair!" Nyx's voice boomed across the beach. Everyone paused what they were doing and turned as she staggered out of the surf, dripping wet, pistol drawn. She headed straight for him. "You're going to wish they had killed you once I'm done with you!" His eyes went wide and he backed away. Cimik jumped between the two, blocking Nyx from reaching Alistair.

"This is the second time you've almost killed us all and wrecked my ship!" she screamed. "I'm going to turn you inside out! I'm going to skin you and hang you on my wall like the world's ugliest tapestry!"

"Nyx, calm down," Alistair said.

"Calm down? *Calm down?* I'll kill you, Alistair!" She lunged toward him. Cimik grabbed her around the waist and hoisted her over her shoulder. "Put me down! I'm the captain, I can kill whoever I want!"

"We're going to go calm down, captain." Cimik said, walking off toward the other side of the beach while Nyx flailed and clawed at her.

"When we run out of supplies, I'm going to eat you first, Alistair!" Nyx shouted before they got out of earshot. He stared after her, horrified. He glanced over at Cas.

"I think the captain's mad at you."

Alistair laughed nervously. "I think perhaps so."

He sat down on a rocky outcrop, and Cas joined him. They stared out at the sea as the rain subsided and the clouds lightened.

"Did . . . did you really strangle someone with their own intestines?" Cas asked finally.

"That was a long time ago," Alistair said simply.

"That doesn't make it okay."

"No, you're right. It doesn't," he stared down at the sand before meeting Cas's eyes. "You've seen what the Empire is like. All the senseless killings and torture and slavery and intimidation. It's not right that they're allowed to get away with it. Don't you ever want someone to have to pay for what they do?"

"I . . . I suppose so," Cas said. He thought about the cages full of rotting corpses that lined every port, the merchant ships with their torture chambers, and what happened to Scout. "I still think that strangling someone with their intestines seems slightly excessive."

"Probably is. Slightly anyway." Alistair mused, his gaze straying to Kal, who stood by the rocky walls that bordered the beach and allowing the waves to wash over his boots. "Now, if you'll excuse me, I have some catching up to do." He walked away.

As dawn broke across the island, Cas was still sitting on the rocks. He hadn't been able to sleep that night. They had decided against making a fire, as Lucien might be able to see it if he were passing by. The wind coming off the ocean combined with his soaking wet clothes had resulted in a very cold night.

But that wasn't what kept Cas from sleep. Every time he closed his eyes, he saw the terrified face of the man he had killed and the blood staining his hands.

Once the sky was bright enough, Cas began to wander down the beach, sticking to the solid rocks between the stretches of shifting sand. The coast was dotted with massive boulders, which gave way to sheer sea cliffs in both directions. Beyond the cliffs, the hills were covered in thick, impassable jungle.

"No one's coming for us, you know." He turned to see Prisma standing on the beach behind him. Her forehead was creased with worry. "We're off the map, on an uncharted island. There won't be any passing ships to see us. If we can't get out of here ourselves . . ." She blinked back tears. Cas stepped forward and embraced her.

"It'll be okay, we'll figure it out," he said. She took a shaky breath.

"I hope so."

"Everyone!" Nyx yelled, making them look up. "Wake up! Gather round! We have business to attend to!"

They joined the others sitting on the rocks while Nyx stood in front of them. She seemed much calmer now than the night before.

"First thing's first," she said, pacing back and forth. "We're stranded on a desert island, and we have to repair the ship. This is going to be difficult, obviously, since she's run aground on the reef. But, perhaps at high tide we could try to free her."

"And what if we can't?" Knives asked.

"Then we try again at the next high tide," she said curtly.

"Do you know the odds of shipwrecked people surviving?" Tig asked, running a hand across his hairless head nervously. "Slim to none."

"I was shipwrecked. I survived," Splinter pointed out.

"You weren't shipwrecked on an abandoned island in uncharted waters." Tig said.

"We're not dying on this island," Nyx snapped. "We're going to fix the *Riptide* and get out of here, and I don't want to hear anything to the contrary! It's counterproductive." She paused and turned to look at Alistair. "Now, let's address the problem."

"Who, me?" Alistair asked.

"Yes, *you*. I've thought about it, and I've decided I'm not going to kill you, this time anyway. However, if you want any hope of getting back on my ship, there will be no more secrets between us. If you want off this island you are going to tell me everything, and I mean literally everything. I want every detail of your life and every possible person that might pop back up wanting you dead. Otherwise, you can live out the rest of your days stuck on this beach—"

"Okay, okay," he interrupted. "I get it."

"Then let's hear it." She sat down in the sand, looking at him expectantly.

"What, right now?"

"Yes. Right now. You can start with Lucien and what he wants with us."

"Fine," Alistair said. "He wants this." He pulled a blue velvet box from the inside pocket of his coat, and opened it to reveal polished sea glass. Everyone stared at it for a long beat, confused.

"What is it?" Fenix asked finally.

"This is the source of my supposedly prophetic powers. It's called the Eye of the Sea. Legend has it, it came from deep in the heart of the ocean millennia ago and offers glimpses of the future. With a price, of course. Those who use it become much like the sea: unpredictable, unknowable, and prone to fits of destructive violence." He shook his head. "Anyway. I found it when I was only 19, when I raided the ship of a wealthy merchant. It was tucked away in a secret safe in his cabin. Once I realized what it was, I used it constantly. I kept it on me at all times. That's why I gained the reputation I have."

"So, you're telling me you look into that piece of sea glass and it shows you the future while making you evil," Gyles said skeptically.

"I don't expect you to believe it, but Lucien does. He stole it when he tried to kill me, and this is what I risked all of your lives to get back at The Well."

"And who is Lucien? If he's coming for us, we need to know what we're up against," Nyx said.

"Lucien was my first mate. I hired him about ten years ago, during the height of my career, back when I was doing a lot of . . . questionable things. He thrived in that kind of environment. I should've realized then that he was just a sick and evil man, but I ignored the warning signs because he was good at his job.

"I have the benefit of blaming my behavior on an ancient magical object. Lucien never looked into the Eye, and he is worse than I ever was. He was . . . *fascinated* by torture. He wanted to know how much a human could endure before they died or went insane. He delighted in it."

Cimik rubbed the bridge of her nose. "Of course," she muttered to herself. "Of course we have this guy after us. That's exactly on brand for us."

"I always thought he was creepy," Kal added.

"Anyway," Alistair continued. "As I got older, I realized what the Eye was doing to me. I realized I had become a monster. So, I locked it in my desk drawer and tried not to use it. That wasn't easy. Once you get used to having the power to see the future, it's hard to stop. But I did my best.

"As I began to avoid using it, my desire for violence faded. We became somewhat of a normal pirate ship. We still hunted and raided ships, but I wasn't going to go out of my way to hurt anyone. This didn't go over well with Lucien.

"About two years ago, I suppose he decided he'd had enough and it was time to take matters into his own hands. He organized a mutiny with some of the like-minded crew members. They pulled me out of my bed one night and tied me up, and Lucien declared himself the new captain. They forced the rest of the crew at gunpoint to go along with it.

"Then, to drive the point home, they keelhauled me and left me behind in a lifeboat to die from my injuries. That's why . . ." He looked down at his hook hand. "Why I look like this.

"But like I told you already, a passing ship found me. I stayed with them for a year or so while I recovered. Once I was well, I stole what I needed and left while they were in port one night.

"It was a few months before I met you all that I heard what became of my old crew. I was staying at a tavern when a man arrived who claimed to have met Lucien in Thawpeak. He told me Lucien was worried about dissent among the crew who had been loyal to me, so he killed them all. That left just him and about fifteen of his followers, and he was heading to The Well to meet with some other pirates. That's when I went to the Maelstrom and just waited around until I found someone willing to take me."

"Is that all?" Nyx asked.

"Yes."

"And it's the truth?"

"Yes."

"So why are you using the Eye again, if it makes you evil?" Splinter asked.

"I don't use it very often. I took it back because I knew it would be incredibly dangerous in Lucien's hands. Keeping it with me is the best way to keep everyone safe," Alistair said.

"Which is well and good, except now Lucien has the map I made. The original one," Kal said. "It's not as precise as the one I gave you, but he knows where we're going. He could just wait for us at the Quarter."

"We can worry about that once we have a ship that can get us to the Quarter," Nyx said, standing. "Everyone up, let's get to work."

The rest of the morning was spent repairing the damage caused by the storm and their attackers. Barrels and crates down in the hold were taken apart, and the wood repurposed to patch holes, while the sails were taken down to sew up the tears, and the ropes reinforced.

"What is 'keelhauling' exactly?" Cas asked quietly as he was helping to patch things up below deck.

"It's when you're tied to a rope and thrown overboard, and the crew drags you under the ship," Knives said. "All the barnacles and mussels and things that grow on the hull are kind of . . . sharp, so you get cut to pieces."

"If you don't drown or bleed out, you usually die from infections," Fenix continued. "Or, if you survive, you end up disfigured for life."

"It's done as a punishment in the Navy, for the worst crimes," Tig said. "It's rare, but it's quite a . . . spectacle. I saw one once. The guy was dead two minutes after they pulled him back onboard. Bled out right on the deck. Alistair's lucky." They all paused as Alistair's muffled voice came from above them, discussing something with Nyx. "And we probably shouldn't be talking about this behind his back."

As Cas worked, he was acutely aware of the tide rising around them. Soon, the rocky outcrop was nearly covered by the crashing waves. When the sea reached its highest, the sails were unfurled.

A horrible cracking sound was heard throughout the ship as it shifted—and then stopped. Despite the sails straining to move the *Riptide* forward, it didn't budge from where it was stuck on the reef.

Cas's heart sank. He could tell the rest of the crew was equally disappointed as they made their way back to the beach. Nyx tried to encourage them by saying they could just try again at the next high tide, but Cas had a horrible feeling in the pit of his stomach that they were trapped.

He finally drifted off to sleep well after sunset and found himself plunged into nightmares.

They were under attack from all sides. Military ships and red sails surrounded them with a hail of gunfire. But there was something else, below the ship, rising to the surface . . .

As he jolted awake, drenched in a cold sweat, it took a moment for him to realize that the shouting he heard wasn't just echoes from his dream. He sat up and looked around. With a start, he realized the *Riptide* wasn't in the same place anymore. The ship had drifted out into the lagoon on the other side of the rocks.

"Get up! Everyone get onboard!" Nyx was yelling.

Cas jumped up and waded out into the water. As the waves lapped around his waist, he found it harder and harder to keep his footing. Panic rose in his chest as the sandy bottom dropped away, and he was suddenly treading water. He realized his prosthetic leg was just dead weight now, dragging him down as he struggled to keep his head above the surf. A wave washed over him, and he emerged from it coughing and gasping, eyes stinging from the salt.

Keeping his gaze locked on the ship in front of him, he frantically swam against the current, trying to calm his wildly pounding heart. In the dark water, he felt his hand close around a rope. He pulled himself forward and then gratefully clambered onto the deck.

"How'd she get free?" Tig asked as he climbed aboard.

"No idea. Spring tide, I suppose!" Nyx said. With everyone back on the ship, the sails were opened and Nyx began to carefully steer them through the rocky shallows. Cas looked back at the island as it faded away into the night, never happier to see the land disappear.

18

Mirages

"Kal!" Nyx called down from the helm. "You're the professional navigator. How do we get back to deeper water?"

"How should I know? I've never been here before," he replied.

"Kal, you are worth your weight in gold," she said sarcastically.

The night had dragged on as the *Riptide* slowed to a crawl, dodging reefs and rocks that Gyles spotted from the nest. South of the desert island, the open ocean had been replaced by an archipelago of atolls and sandbars with precious few deep channels weaving between them.

Cas watched as they passed dangerously close to an exposed reef, rocks glistening silver in the moonlight. He listened to the melodic sound of waves lapping against the hull and felt his eyelids growing heavy. Wisps of mist rose from the water, while lights danced across the ocean as he began to drift off.

Lights? His eyes snapped open.

An orb of soft yellow hovered just above the sea. He squinted into the foggy darkness, trying to make out what it was. Suddenly, it came into focus.

There was a man standing on the rocks holding a lantern. He wore a tricorn hat and long coat, but what took Cas by surprise was that the man looked nearly identical to him, aside from being older.

"Cas!" the man called, waving to the ship.

"D-dad?" His voice came out as a whisper.

"Cas, help!" His father sounded afraid. "I'm trapped, help!"

Cas ran to the lifeboat and began to frantically lower it into the water.

"Nyx, stop the ship! My dad . . ."

His voice was cut off by a loud gunshot. His father stopped waving. For a second, he stood totally still, as blood began to run down his face from the smoking hole in his head. Then he collapsed to the rocky ground.

Cas screamed in horror. He spun around to see Niko behind him, pistol drawn.

"You killed him!" Cas shrieked. "You—"

Niko grabbed his shoulders and turned him back, pointing at the body that lay sprawled across the reef.

"That thing isn't your father," he said. Cas watched in shock as the lantern light faded, and as it did, so did his father.

In his place was a long, black, slimy creature. Its eel-like tail twitched as blue blood dripped from its shattered head, a twisted amalgamation of fangs and spines. The slowly dimming light came from a long, filamentous lure with a glowing bulbous end. Cas stared at it, unable to speak.

"Get your sword, Cas. We're under attack." Niko's words pulled him from his horrified stupor. He turned and realized the man's blue eyes were focused with an intensity he had never seen before. He loaded another round into his gun.

Looking around the deck, Cas realized everyone had abandoned their posts. They were standing around the edges, all staring off at lights flickering against the dark backdrop of the ocean. Black forms slithered across the rocks.

"What are they?" Cas gasped.

"Mirages. They reflect your desires to lure you into the water, then they eat you," Niko said.

"Lucien!" Alistair shouted, enraged, pulling out his sword as he stared down into the waves. A figure let out a hissing laugh and paddled away from the ship.

"Come get me, Alistair," it whispered. He leapt up onto the side of the ship, about to jump into the water after his enemy. Niko pulled the trigger and the creature's head exploded in a bloody spray.

Cas heard scrabbling claws against wood, and turned to see one of the creatures had grabbed onto the deck with its stubby legs and was hauling itself up. Cimik was kneeling next to it, leaning in as its fangs snapped inches from her face.

Cas ran toward it and plunged his blade into its slimy black skin. It let out a hissing shriek and fell into the water, writhing as it disappeared beneath the waves. Cimik spun to face him, furious.

"What do you think you're doing?" she yelled, drawing her blade.

He stumbled away, half expecting her to attack him, but she paused and locked her eyes on something else.

He realized most of the crew was now gathered at the bow. Ahead of them was a small rocky island, completely covered in the disgusting creatures.

"Come join us," they whispered. "Come into the water."

Niko opened fire, sending the Mirages slithering away. The crew erupted into confused, frantic shouts as they vanished.

"Zephyrine?" Cas heard Nyx yelling from the helm. She stood at the back of the ship, staring off into the water, then jumped onto the guardrail. "I'm coming, Zephyrine!"

Cas ran up the stairs and grabbed Nyx, wrestling her to the ground before she could jump.

"Get off me!" she shouted, pushing him back.

"Nyx, stop!" he cried. She paused as another round of gunshots went off.

"What's happening?" She shoved Cas off and jumped to her feet. Cas stood and felt his heart drop.

A swarm of Mirages were climbing aboard. Their sleek bodies squirmed and writhed around the sides of the ship, claws scraping deep gouges in the wood. Several had found handholds and were pulling themselves onto the deck. Nyx drew her pistol and began to shoot at them.

The crew now seemed fully free of their delusions, and had taken up arms against the attackers.

Cas heard a menacing hiss behind him. He spun around as a Mirage flopped onto the deck, its gelatinous-looking body landing against the planks with a surprisingly solid thud. Its tail flicked against the hull, propelling it toward Cas with incredible speed.

Fangs snapped inches from his face, strings of saliva and seawater spraying onto him. He slashed at the creature with his sword. Blue blood splattered across the deck.

Nyx dropped her gun and ran to the wheel, steering them away from the rocks. Despite her evasive action, more and more Mirages climbed up the hull, clinging to the side of the ship like barnacles.

Niko cried out in pain as one sank its fangs into his leg. As he shot it, another one leapt onto his back, knocking him off his feet. It reared its head up like a snake, preparing to deliver a killing strike to the neck.

In a split second, the Mirage's head was sliced clean off by Cimik.

A gust of strong wind filled the sails, and the *Riptide* picked up speed. The glistening creatures began to lose their grip and slide back into the water, unable to keep up. Those that remained on the deck slithered over the rail and plopped into the sea, vanishing into the blackness with a flick of their eel-like tails.

The deck was covered in blood, both blue and red, as well as bodies and viscera of the creatures. Cimik wiped her sword off, looking down at the sticky liquid with disgust.

"Definitely up there as one of the worst experiences I've had with pretty girls crawling out of the water," she muttered. She looked up at Nyx. "So, Captain, who's Zephyrine?"

"None of your business," Nyx said.

"Oh, come on. Is she pretty?"

Nyx smiled, getting a far-off look in her eye. "No. Not really."

"Oh."

Cas ran from the helm and knelt next to Niko as he slowly sat up. Blood was running down his leg from dozens of deep puncture wounds.

"Prisma!" Cas yelled, looking around frantically. She wasn't on the deck. He pulled off his jacket and wrapped it around Niko's leg. Then he paused.

"Why didn't the Mirages affect you?" he asked. Niko smiled weakly and shrugged. Before Cas could pry further, Prisma ran up from the hatch and helped the man to his feet, leading him down to the medic cabin.

The rest of the night was spent on constant alert. The crew scanned the waves with pistols and swords drawn, while Nyx fought to keep them as far from the rocks and reefs as she could. Finally, the shallows gave way to deeper water again, and the *Riptide* was able to return to its normal speed.

As the horizon turned from gray to pink, Prisma emerged from below and helped Cas scrub the deck clean.

"How's Niko?" he asked.

"It took a lot of stitches to close the wound, but he'll live," she muttered. "I hope we don't see more of those things."

"I hope so too."

She looked up at him. "What did you see? When you first looked at them?"

"I saw my dad," Cas said. "Or . . . I guess, I just saw an older version of me, since I don't really know what he looks like."

"I saw my parents too. That's why I knew it wasn't real."

He paused. "What do you mean?"

"My parents wouldn't be here. They abandoned me."

"How do you know they abandoned you? Maybe they're like my dad, and they're still out there somewhere . . ."

"They're not." She stopped cleaning and sighed. "They were pirates. They couldn't have a baby on the ship so they left me at the tavern. Jois raised me, and I always thought maybe someday they would come back for me, and we could travel together and be a happy pirate family . . . But when I got older Jois told me she knows them. I've met them. They've been to the tavern. They just . . . didn't want me."

"Prisma, I'm sorry—"

"I'm telling you this because I worry about you, Cas," she interrupted. "I worry you're getting your hopes up too high. That if you meet your dad, and he's not what you imagined . . . I don't want you to get hurt."

Cas was quiet. He didn't know what to say.

19

The Meeting

Many people considered Thys a paradise, despite its unusual appearances. For Draigh, it was hot, humid, and crowded, and that made for an unpleasant experience.

The islands of Thys were unique in many ways. From above, it appeared as though a single island had been cut perfectly in half with a massive knife, creating twin islands separated by a vast channel.

At sea level passing through that channel, the islands were equally strange. Two sheer cliffs rose up on either side, marble-white and banded with red and black horizontal stripes, so tall that the deep fissure between them only saw sunlight at certain times of the year and then only at midday.

Although the currents were strong and the waves crashed against the cliffs hard enough to wear the rocks smooth, the canyon had become a massive port over time. Piers jutted out to the deeper, calmer waters in the middle of the passage, allowing ships to dock with relative safety.

Above the piers, bridges crossed the channel in a maze of ropes and wood, allowing the inhabitants to walk between the islands. Carved into the cliffs were ledges and wooden scaffolding that held an assortment of taverns, inns, and walkways, bustling with activity. Higher up on the cliff tops were homes and apartments, which continued in clusters on each side along the gently sloping terrain down to the white beaches that bordered the sea.

The newly appointed admiral sat in the back of the mostly empty tavern, feeling out of place without the rest of his Navy men. The message had explicitly stated that he must be alone.

Delivered by a Navy sea-falcon, the letter had contained details of Captain Nyx and Alistair, as well as the promise of capturing them so long as Draigh agreed to meet *alone*. That part was heavily stressed; if he brought his men to the tavern, the deal would be off.

Draigh knew it was ill-advised to meet with an anonymous person without protection, but he couldn't help himself. Losing Nyx had been the most frustrating moment of his career thus far, and that included the years of grueling training he had endured to become commander. Not to mention he was now also known for letting Alistair escape.

With the death of Admiral Caine, Draigh had been hastily promoted. However, it was more a matter of necessity, as Draigh was the only officer in the fleet qualified to become admiral. After letting the pirates escape, he could see how his men and commanding officers looked at him, with disappointment and skepticism. They didn't respect him. They thought he was a failure.

He had scoured the seas for months looking for the *Riptide* and came up empty handed. By this time, they could be anywhere. This strange letter was his only hope of righting the wrong of allowing them to escape.

The tavern door swung open and a pair of people stepped inside. One was a slim woman with long blonde hair, the other a tall man in a bloodred coat and tinted spectacles. The man had a huge, black lizard clinging to his arm. They headed straight toward Draigh, and the man sat down at the table across from him while the woman stood behind his chair.

"Admiral?" the man asked, gently stroking the lizard on its spiky head.

"Yes," Draigh said. "And who might you be?"

"My name is Lucien."

"I assume you're the one who sent the letter?"

"You assume correctly." He leaned back in his chair, smiling. "Allow me to introduce myself. I am the captain of the *Red Death*, former captain of *The Queen's Curse*."

"*The Queen's Curse*? Alistair's ship?"

Lucien's smile turned into a scowl. "No, it hasn't been Alistair's ship for years. It was *my* ship."

"Fine, then. It was your ship. I assume you're a pirate? And that's why you insisted we meet alone?"

"Yes, that's correct."

"And what makes you think I would be even remotely interested in what a pirate has to say?" Draigh asked.

"Because you're an obsessive little man with a personal invest-ment in finding the criminals you allowed to escape."

Draigh quickly stood. "If you're going to insult me, I think I'll be leaving . . ."

"Calm down, soldier," Lucien said. "I summoned you here because I know where Nyx is going."

Draigh paused, then reluctantly sat back down.

"Where?"

"First thing's first. I'm not just going to *give* this information away."

"What do you want then? Money? I'm sure arrangements can be made . . ."

"No, no. I don't want money. I want to help you find them."

"Help me?" Draigh said with a laugh. "What do you mean?"

"I want a . . . partnership of sorts. You and I, backed up by the Navy, going after the *Riptide* together."

"Why?" Draigh queried.

"I have personal investments in this too. But we don't need to get into all that."

"Before I agree to anything, I need proof of your claims. I'm not just going to partner with you without assurance."

Lucien snapped his fingers, and the woman pulled a rolled-up scroll from her jacket pocket and handed it to him. He unfurled it to show a roughly-sketched map.

"This was drawn by a close, personal friend of Alistair's. Look, it has Alistair's signature on it." He gestured to a scribbled note in the corner. "He told me this is the approximate route they're taking on their quest."

"Quest? To where?" Draigh asked.

"If I tell you, you'll just arrest me and go there yourself. You're going to have to trust me if you ever hope to find them."

Draigh considered this. He didn't fancy the idea of following this stranger, a pirate no less, off into the blue with only a map containing Alistair's signature as proof. But Draigh had a fleet of ships under his command. If Lucien tried to double-cross him or lure him into a trap, he could kill him with ease.

"Alright," Draigh said finally. "I suppose I'll join you. Just be aware that if you try in any way to cross me, I will give no quarter." He extended a hand, and Lucien shook it.

The pirate suddenly tightened his grip. "Just one more condition, if you don't mind," Lucien said.

"What's that?"

"When we find them, I get Alistair," Lucien sneered.

"Deal."

20

Dead Man's Island

Out in the open ocean for months, far from other ships and only occasionally spotting uninhabited spits of land, the crew of the *Riptide* was growing bored and restless. Even Cas, who at first entertained himself by spotting whales and sea sprites and other sea life, was becoming drained. He felt as though he was beginning to lose his mind being trapped on the ship this long.

He wanted to go into port and see people. He wanted to encounter a merchant ship and hear the excitement of the crew as they hunted it down. He even began to wish they would encounter Mirages again—anything to break the monotony.

Not to mention, there was a nagging worry at the back of everyone's minds. They were running low on supplies. They had even adjusted the course back toward charted waters, hoping to stumble across a passing ship. As much as they wanted to avoid the law, it was becoming clear that they would soon have to restock.

Luckily, they were now outside of the territory of the Empire. They had entered the lands ruled by Torokai.

Cas didn't know much about history, but hanging around the docks of Valdoria he had heard plenty of political discussion. He knew the Empire and Torokai had a long history of war as each tried to expand and claim new islands as their own. Now, as they seemed to be evenly matched for decades, an uneasy truce had been called. The Empire would rule in the Northwest while Torokai ruled in the Southeast.

Torokai was governed by a council of kings and queens, each representing a different tribe from within their territory. Many of those native to the Empire touted that Torokai's government was needlessly complicated, while visitors from Torokai said it was inferior to be ruled by a single monarch. Cas had never been to Torokai, so he had no idea which was better.

As the hottest hours of the day approached, the crew was lounging in a futile attempt to stay cool. Knives, Splinter and Gryph played cards in the shade of the mast.

"Three of a kind! I win!" Knives said, proudly slapping his cards down. Gryph stared at him in confusion.

"Wha—I thought we were playing Go Fish!"

Sitting on a barrel nearby sharpening her sword, Cimik rolled her eyes.

Tig, Fenix, and Niko were down in the cannon room, ensuring everything was in working order. As Tig had reminded them once again, he didn't know if they worked, since he still hadn't gotten to use the cannons.

Kal had taken up the night shift with Alistair, helping to navigate and steer while the others were asleep. They had both retreated to his cabin hours earlier.

Nyx stood half-asleep at the helm, not terribly worried about drifting off course due to the recent lack of strong winds and currents.

Up in the crow's nest, shaded by a makeshift awning made from extra sailcloth and ropes, Gyles practiced his violin. Cas was trying to entertain himself by watching the fish swim through the ship's wake when the music stopped suddenly.

"Dead Man's Island, straight ahead!" Gyles shouted. Everyone jumped to attention. Cas leaned over the side of the ship, and saw there was a faint, hazy strip of land on the horizon.

"How do you know it's Dead Man's Island?" Gryph asked.

"It's my job to know," Gyles replied.

"What's Dead Man's Island?" Cas asked.

"Back in the early days of the Empire, they realized they had too many prisoners and not enough jails. So they tossed them onto ships and sent them out here, to a barren rocky island, and marooned them," Nyx said. "They don't do that anymore, obviously, but mostly just because it's Torokai territory now."

"Are we stopping here?" Cas asked, half hoping she would say no, and half hoping she would say yes.

"Of course not! It's uninhabited, and it's haunted!" Splinter said. Nyx was quiet. "Right, Captain?"

"There's a chance it'll have some food and water on it, and we need supplies," Nyx replied.

"I thought the point of the Empire abandoning people here is because there was no food or water," Gryph said. Nyx shrugged.

"Do you think the Empire looked everywhere, or just assumed?" The crew exchanged glances and shrugged. "There's no harm in checking."

"What about the whole haunted part?" Splinter asked.

"If we see any ghosts, we can ask them where the food is," Gyles said sarcastically.

"You're not gonna be laughing when you get killed by a ghost," Splinter muttered.

They arrived at the island as the sun was setting. The dying light cast an eerie red glow across the jagged rocks, giving them the appearance of knife blades soaked in blood. Waves pounded against the shore relentlessly, preventing entry from all sides except one small strip of rocky beach on the southern tip.

The *Riptide* anchored offshore, and a party consisting of Cas, Cimik, Tig, Nyx and Alistair rowed a lifeboat toward the island.

"I remember some of the older commanders talking about this place," Tig said as he rowed. "None of them ever actually brought prisoners here, a'course. The Empire stopped that over a hundred years ago. But about thirty or so years ago, a few Navy vessels came down here to see if they could salvage any ship parts. The officers who came back claimed they were attacked by ghostly apparitions that killed the majority of those who went on the island."

"Yes, but those were probably the spirits of people the Empire abandoned here. Of course they would be angry at them," Cimik said. "We've never bothered them before."

"Maybe they're just angry at the world in general. Kinda like you."

Cimik glared at him.

As they reached land, Cas stepped off the boat and scanned the beach. It sloped up to rugged hills covered in scrubby grass and short twisted trees.

"Doesn't look very inviting," Alistair said.

"I'd say our odds of finding any worthwhile supplies on this island are slim to none," Cimik said.

"Well, we certainly won't find anything just standing here," Nyx said. "Let's start searching."

As Cas hiked along the windswept landscape, he couldn't help but feel happy. After months at sea, he was finally back on land. He remembered last year when he first departed Valdoria, it had been so exciting and fulfilling to be sailing across the open ocean. It was strange how quickly being on a ship could turn from freedom to confinement.

Making his way through the rocky hills that bordered the sea,

Cas found that the land gradually flattened out and the vegetation grew lusher. Tall trees filled the interior of the island, and the undergrowth, although still dry and thorny, was denser here. Perhaps they would find supplies after all.

The shadows around him grew longer as the sun dipped lower on the horizon. They needed to go back, or there wouldn't be enough time to return to the ship before dark. When he turned to address the others, he realized they weren't there.

He looked around the darkening woods, heart beginning to pound as he realized the rest of the search party was nowhere in sight. He had been so wrapped up in the excitement of getting off the ship that he'd wandered off. He began to nervously trot back the way he came.

"Nyx!" He yelled into the night. "Alistair!" There was no answer.

Suddenly, there was nothing beneath his foot when he took a step. With a scream, he fell down into a dark opening in the ground. Everything went by in a blur for a moment, then he landed hard, head smacking against a sharp rock. A wave of dizziness overcame him, and then everything went black.

*

"Where is that kid?" Tig muttered. He, Cimik, Nyx and Alistair had returned to the lifeboat when darkness fell, only to realize Cas wasn't with them anymore. They had waited, hoping he had just fallen behind and was making his way back, but now it was becoming apparent that wasn't the case.

"When was the last time you saw him?" Nyx asked.

"I know he was with us when we climbed up those hills," Cimik said, gesturing up the bank. "He must've gotten separated in the woods."

"The ghosts got him, I bet," Tig said.

Nyx turned and walked to the lifeboat. "It's too dark to go look for him now. We'll have to come back in the morning."

"You're just going to leave him?" Alistair asked.

"We can't wander around the woods in the middle of the night. Unless you want to sleep on the beach, our best option is to go to the ship and come back at sunrise."

"What if he's hurt?"

She looked back at him. "Can you see in the dark?"

"Of course not."

"Then we have no way to help him now. If we try to find him, there's a good chance we'll get lost too. We'll be back as soon as we can." She pushed the lifeboat back into the waves and jumped in. Cimik and Tig followed. Alistair scanned the hills, hoping to see Cas coming toward them. Finally, he joined them in the lifeboat and they began to row back to the ship.

*

Wherever Cas was, it was very, very dark. As he first came to, he wasn't sure if his eyes were open or closed. His head was throbbing and his body was sore and bruised. He felt around, finding a lot of sharp rocks and not much else.

Then a shaft of moonlight lit the space. He realized he was lying at the bottom of a narrow, steep tunnel. Above him, he saw the trees swaying in the wind, but they seemed far away.

He tried to climb to his feet, but something was wrong. He looked down and groaned.

The wood of his prosthetic leg was shattered. Although still held together by the metal frame, the weight-bearing section was snapped in half. He unbuckled the strap and tossed the useless piece of wood and metal aside.

He couldn't walk back to the beach, but maybe he could at least climb out of the cave. He grabbed the rocky walls and pulled himself up, leaning against the side of the tunnel for balance. Steadying himself, he began to climb.

Scaling the jagged tunnel was difficult. By the time he emerged into the woods above, he was panting, sweat dripping down his face, hands and knees scratched and bloody. He sat on the forest floor, trying to catch his breath.

At first, he didn't even hear the strange snuffling sound. As it grew louder, he looked up and saw a shadow dart behind a cluster of undergrowth. He saw another shadow moving out of the corner of his eye. He scurried back toward the entrance of the cave, heart pounding.

From behind a tree, a huge creature stepped into the moonlight. It was as tall as he was, with a dog-like face and bright white fur, striding forward in a strange loping fashion with long forelimbs and shorter back limbs. It lowered its head toward him and howled a horrifically human cackle.

Out of the woods emerged more of the hideous animals, laughing in a disturbing chorus as they crept toward him.

Cas slid back into the tunnel, trying to climb backward without falling, not wanting to take his eyes off the creatures. They darted in and out of the shadows, circling him like a swarm of sharks. With one hand still holding onto the side of the steep incline, he reached to his belt to retrieve his sword.

One of the animals lunged. Cas raised his sword and slipped further down into the cave, preparing himself to feel sharp teeth sinking into his flesh at any moment.

There was a flash of bright yellow light and the animal howled in pain.

Cas looked up. Someone stood in front of the cave, brandishing a blade in one hand and a glowing lantern in the other. The creatures had retreated into the shrubs, but Cas could hear their unsettling laughter and see their eyes glinting red in the firelight.

"Prisma?" he gasped. She turned, eyes flashing with fear and determination.

"Get up, Cas! Run!" she said.

"I can't, I . . ." he was cut off when one of the creatures jumped toward Prisma. She swung her lantern defensively and it retreated to the fringes of the light, teeth bared.

In unison, several of them charged forward, cackling loudly. Prisma threw her lantern down. The glass shattered, and a plume of flame erupted between her and the animals.

The fire caught the dry undergrowth immediately. They reared back, howling and whimpering, and loped off into the woods. Prisma turned to Cas.

"Come on, we have to get back to the ship!"

"I can't, Prisma! My leg broke. My prosthetic one. I can't walk."

She paused, looking between him and the rapidly growing wall of fire. "You couldn't have told me that before I started a fire?"

"I . . . I tried!" he stammered.

Prisma slid down into the tunnel next to him as the flames drew closer.

"How'd you find me?" he asked.

"The captain and the others came back without you. They were going to come back for you in the morning, but I knew something had to be wrong. So I . . . I came after you," she said.

"You did?"

"Well, yeah! I wasn't going to leave you here all night!" As the heat from the fire grew more intense, they crawled further into the cave.

"I don't know what those things were," she said. "They look like something I read about once. I can't remember what the locals call them, but they're native to Torokai, and their name translates to 'Demon of the Red Desert.' They're supposedly afraid of fire. But these ones are white, and the book described the Demons as being red-brown to black—" She began to cough as the air filled with smoke.

Over both of their coughing and the crackle of the flames, Cas heard a distant cackle, growing closer. The form of a creature was suddenly silhouetted against the fire.

"They must not be that afraid of it," he said as it grew closer.

An arrow hissed through the air and struck the creature in the head. It collapsed to the ground. A moment later, the fire illuminated something Cas didn't expect to see.

There were several ghostly white figures approaching them through the veil of thick black smoke, almost glowing in the intense light.

"No way," Prisma gasped.

A hand reached down and grabbed Cas, hauling him out of the cave and supporting him as they quickly hurried away. He turned and saw Prisma following, along with another white-shrouded being.

They ran from the fire and into the cool, dark forest beyond. Reaching a clearing, the specter released Cas and he fell to the ground. They pushed Prisma toward him, and she carefully sat next to him and stared at the ghosts, eyes wide with terror.

As Cas beheld them in the moonlight, he realized what he had mistaken for tattered white robes were, in fact, cloaks made from hide that looked suspiciously similar to the Demons. The ghosts pushed their hoods back, revealing that their faces were painted an ashen white.

"What do you two think you're doing, setting the woods on fire?" The one who had helped Cas demanded. He was tall and muscular, with long, curly dark hair, and Cas could see patches of dark brown skin that he had missed painting. The one who had escorted Prisma was taller and slimmer with shoulder-length blonde hair.

"I . . . I'm sorry, we were being attacked." Prisma said.

"Our parents warned us about this," the first man continued. He reached back and drew an arrow from his quiver. "They had to fight off the Empire once before, and they knew they would come back someday. Now it's our turn." He fitted the arrow into the bow and drew it back, taking aim at Cas.

"Hey!" The blond man said, stepping forward. "You don't have to kill them. They're not working for the Empire, they're like, nine."

"We're seventeen, actually," Cas said.

The man rolled his eyes. "Be quiet," he said as he turned back to his friend, gently pushing the arrow down. "They're not in the Navy."

"How do you know?" his companion asked.

"They're kids. We don't need to kill kids."

"What if they're just bait?"

"You saw their ship out there. They can't fit more than a hundred on it, we can take 'em if they have something planned."

"Fine," he said, taking the arrow out of the bow. "But I want their swords. Just to make sure."

The blond man gestured at them. "Hand them over."

Cas and Prisma relinquished the swords.

"There, you happy now? You gotta relax, Bek."

"They showed up out of nowhere and started a fire. How am I supposed to take that?" Bek asked.

"We didn't know anyone lived here," Prisma said. "I wouldn't have started the fire if I knew. I was just trying to protect my friend . . ."

"Yeah, I know," the blond man cut her off. He glanced down at Cas. "What's wrong with your leg?"

"I . . ." He paused, taken aback. "I broke my prosthetic falling into that cave."

"What are you falling into a cave for? Don't you look where you're going?" .

"I'm sorry, it was dark out," Cas said indignantly.

The blond man reached up to a low-hanging dead branch and snapped it off, and offered it to Cas.

"Here. You can use that as a crutch until we can fix your leg, okay?"

Cas took the limb. The men gestured for the two to follow as they walked off into the woods. Cas struggled to keep up as they navigated the forest with incredible expertise.

"Um, who are you, exactly?" Prisma asked as they walked. "Everyone thinks this island is abandoned."

"And haunted," Cas added.

"Good. That's what we want them to think," Bek said.

"I'm sure you two are familiar with the general history of this island, right?" the blond man asked.

"Yeah," Prisma said. "The Empire used to bring prisoners here to die."

"Essentially. They assumed this island was uninhabitable, which clearly isn't true. Lots of things live here. But regardless, most of the prisoners they brought here didn't die. They survived, they built a community, and we're their descendants."

"You've been living out here all this time? Why didn't you try to find a way off the island?" Cas asked.

"Why would we want to? This is our home."

"The Empire didn't want our ancestors, and they probably don't want us either," Bek said.

"And you're the ghosts who killed the Navy men when they came back?" Prisma asked.

"*We* aren't. Our parents and grandparents were," the blond man said.

"But if the Empire returns, we intend to defend our island just like they did," Bek growled.

"We don't like the Navy either," Cas said quickly. "We're pirates."

"Oh! Excellent!" the blond man said, turning to face them. "My great-grandfather was a pirate. I'm Kio, by the way."

As the horizon began to light up with the first rays of sunrise, they stepped into a clearing. In front of them was a huge sinkhole. Inside, down in the flat basin, Cas realized there was an entire village. Huts built from wood and mud were arranged in concentric circles, and torches lit the cave with a warm yellow glow. Despite the early hour, people were already leaving their homes and hurrying about.

Kio gestured to a series of ladders and wooden walkways leading down into the sinkhole, and looked at Cas.

"You think you can climb down?"

"Yeah, probably," he said uneasily. "Why do you live down there?"

"The Demons can't climb. Plus, that's where the fresh water is. It's all underground."

"Huh," Cas said. He looked down at the thriving town, full of people preparing strange root vegetables and slabs of meat. "Could we . . . possibly ask for a favor?"

Nyx and the others seemed quite surprised when they arrived the next morning to find Prisma and a strange man dressed in white standing on the beach together, along with a pile of rough-hewn crates and bags. But they were reassured that pirates were welcome here.

Now they were loading the supplies into the lifeboats to take back to the ship, and they were no longer afraid of the ghostly villagers.

"Thank you for this," Nyx said. "The supplies, and not killing the two idiots who set your island on fire."

"Hey!" Prisma objected.

"Don't worry, the fire burned itself out and there wasn't much damage," Kio said. "Besides, we know how kids are."

"Are you sure there's nothing you want in return? We could come back with payment."

"Nah. We don't need anything. The island supplies us with all that we need." Kio paused and glanced at Bek. "Just don't tell anyone that people are living out here."

"Of course not. Just ghosts," Nyx winked at them.

As they rowed back to the *Riptide*, the pale figures disappeared back into the woods, evaporating into the morning mist as they crossed the hills.

"You sure they weren't ghosts?" Tig asked.

"Of course they aren't," Cas said. "How would ghosts build a village? How could they carry the supplies here?"

Tig shrugged. "I ain't a ghost expert."

In the other lifeboat, Cimik fiddled with Cas's prosthetic leg that she had retrieved from the cave.

"You did a good job messing this up, kid, but I think I'll be able to fix it," she called.

"Good," Nyx said, her voice taking on an ominous tone. "He'll need it where we're going."

21

Here Be Monsters

From Dead Man's Island, they sailed north—a straight shot to the Queen's Quarter. Alistair had modified the course slightly the previous night, sending them closer to the island of Zarra. But, with no land and no ships in sight, the crew was relaxing on the deck that afternoon.

"So my father was always saying, Bartholomew, I'll pay your way through school, but once you're done you better find yourself someone nice and rich and get married," Gyles said. "And I would tell him, dad, I don't want to get married. I'm not interested in that. I want to play the violin and study navigation. So, after I got kicked out of school, he told me that if I wasn't getting married, I could go figure things out for myself, and not to come home till I did."

"Your first name's Bartholomew?" Splinter asked with a laugh.

"Oh, you're one to talk, *Stephanie*," Gyles said.

Splinter hit him across the back of the head, making him drop his bottle. "I told you that in secret," he snapped.

"Stephanie? Ain't that a girl's name?" Knives asked.

"Yeah, that's why I don't use it!" Splinter said.

"There haven't been as many ghosts and demons as I was expecting on this trip," Cas said to Alistair as he joined him at the side of the ship, staring down into the sparkling blue water. "Aside from the Mirages, of course, but that was months ago."

Alistair let out a short laugh. "There's plenty out here. Just because we haven't seen them doesn't mean they're not there."

"I don't mind if they're out there, as long as I don't have to be around them."

A familiar mischievous smile crossed Alistair's face.

"I don't think you get it, kid. The ocean itself is a monster."

Cas blinked in surprise, looking out at the calm sea around them. "How so?"

"Think about it. Do you know what lies beneath your feet right now? Miles and miles of empty black abyss separate you from the next solid surface. It may look serene up here, but below us are currents that howl and rage stronger than any storm that's ever graced the land, that will pull you under and swallow you up forever given half a chance. We like to think we've conquered the sea, in our fragile little wooden ships, but the truth is we'll always be visitors to this place. If you forget that, it'll be the last thing you ever do." Alistair turned. "The monsters you should fear 'round here don't have fangs and claws. They're armed with wind and waves."

Cas laughed uneasily as Alistair disappeared into his cabin.

Gyles paused as he crossed to the hatch. "He's right, you know," he said.

"You believe that? You don't believe anything," Cas said, surprised.

"Yeah, but think about it. There's dozens of religions and cultures across the map, and each of them has their own beliefs and gods and spirits and concept of the afterlife, but the one thing they all agree on is that the sea is something otherworldly. That if you're lost to the water, you never find your way back. That can't be a coincidence," he said, and climbed down below deck.

Cas looked back into the water. Despite the heat of the day, he felt chills run through his body as he considered how deep it might be, or what might be hiding beneath the serene blue surface.

"Empire merchant ship on the horizon!" Nyx's voice snapped him out of his trance.

The crew raced to the deck and the flag was raised. This time as they approached the ship, Cas didn't feel guilty.

The merchant's sails opened fully, and the ship leapt away from the pirates. The smaller *Riptide* followed, at a distance at first, and then quickly closing in. The crew laughed and fired their guns into the air as they approached.

A bang and a flash of light made Cas instinctively drop to the deck, and the *Riptide* pulled back. A second cannon went off, and the crew ran to take cover. Cas glanced up, realizing he hadn't heard a cannonball hit the ship or the water.

"They don't have any ammunition. They're firing blanks!" Nyx shouted. "Get back to your posts!"

"Are you sure?" Knives called. "Maybe they're just pretending they don't have ammunition so they can surprise us when we get closer!"

"That's a risk we're going to take," she barked.

As the merchants began to make their getaway, the *Riptide* angled back toward it and continued the chase. Their prey fired another round of false cannonballs, but the pirates didn't flinch this time. Drawing close, Tig and Cimik tossed hooks toward the ship and caught the rigging.

As they boarded the merchant ship, Cas couldn't help but notice that most of the crew appeared to be slaves, based on their tattered clothes, scars, and apathetic state. The captain stood separately from them in his expensive clothes and hat, angrily watching as his cargo was taken.

While Cas waited on the deck, sword drawn to discourage anyone from trying to escape, he found himself dwelling on Fenix's rescue, and on what Alistair had said on the desert island; "It's not right that they're allowed to get away with it. Don't you ever want someone to have to pay for what they do?"

"It isn't right," Cas muttered. Nyx, who had been watching the captain closely, turned to look at him.

"Huh?"

"Why *is* the Empire allowed to hurt people? Just because merchants are rich, they're allowed to run their ships with slavery and torture?" Cas whispered to her.

Nyx smiled and raised an eyebrow, regarding him with interest. "What are you going to do about it, Cas?"

Before he could answer, the merchant captain lunged forward, drawing a short knife from his coat pocket. Nyx didn't react fast enough.

He slashed her across the arm, knocking the gun from her hand. She stumbled back and fell to the deck. As the merchant ran toward her, Cas swung his sword.

He caught the man in the side, knocking him to the ground. The merchant clutched his wound as Cas stood over him.

For a moment, Cas didn't move. Was he really about to kill someone, again?

No. He wasn't a murderer.

"We should tie him up below deck," Cas said. "And free his slaves."

"I like the way you think," Nyx said with a laugh. She motioned to the others.

Knives and Gryph hauled the merchant to his feet and dragged him to the hatch, Splinter following behind gleefully with a length of rope.

Nyx stood and gestured to the cabin. "How about you go search his room and see if there's anything worth taking?"

Cas pushed open the door and entered the extravagant room. A four-poster bed sat in one corner, next to floor-to-ceiling windows framed by green satin curtains, opposite from an intricately carved wooden armoire and matching dresser. Cas pulled open the drawers, pleasantly surprised to find them filled with expensive fabrics and jewelry.

He stuffed his pockets with as much loot as he could. It occurred to him that, when he was living on the streets, any one of these items could have changed his life. He could have traded these emerald rings for food or the collection of silk handkerchiefs for an apartment.

As he turned to go, he saw movement out of the corner of his eye and jumped, drawing his sword. It took a moment for him to realize there was a mirror hanging on the wall and not another man standing in the room. He hardly recognized himself.

The skinny, pale boy who had once patrolled the docks of Valdoria wasn't there anymore. He was tan and lean from working on the ship for so many months. His hair was longer, past his shoulders, and full of curls from the saltwater-laced air. Short but dark fuzz covered his chin and the sides of his face, and the innocent light was gone from his blue eyes. His gaze strayed down to his legs: one boot and one wood-and-metal shaft.

He swallowed hard. He looked, genuinely, like a pirate.

He slowly lowered his sword and returned it to his belt. For a brief moment, he wondered if this was how it had all begun for Alistair; a young man who witnessed so much pain and suffering that he no longer felt guilt for the crimes he committed. What if tying up the merchant was only the beginning?

"Cas!" Nyx yelled from outside. He tore himself away from the mirror and hurried back to the deck. The others were back on the *Riptide* already. Cas hurried down the rope and back onto his ship.

"You're free now!" Nyx shouted to the slaves. "It's your ship, do with it what you will!"

She jumped down onto the quarterdeck, and they were off. As the *Riptide's* prow sliced through the waves, Cas glanced back at the ship to see it was sailing away in the opposite direction.

He had done something good. He had helped people. Yes, it was at the expense of someone else's freedom, but that one person was a bad man who kept slaves. A person who stole the freedom of others. He was the monster, not Cas.

He turned to look north. Things had changed for him. *He* had changed. But there was no going back to the wide-eyed pickpocket he had been before. He could only go forward, to whatever lay beyond that horizon.

*

The morning air had a chill in it as Cas climbed from the crew's quarters out onto the deck. The sun had only just started to rise, casting a reddish glow across the water. Mist twisted up from the glass-flat sea in long, spiraling tendrils, growing thicker as the sky brightened.

There was something eerie about the atmosphere. Perhaps it was the fog, or the red sky, or how the lack of waves created an unsettling silence. The crew seemed to sense it, working as quietly as possible so as not to break the all-consuming stillness.

They were approaching the Quarter. Gyles had confirmed it the night before by mapping the constellations, calculating that they would be approaching the surrounding fogbanks within the next day or two.

As the sun rose higher in the sky, the mist thinned but never fully dissipated. A constant gray haze surrounded the ship, making it difficult to see more than a few yards ahead. Cas realized, as he looked across the white-tinted seascape, that he would need to get used to constant fog.

"Straight ahead!" Cas jumped as Gyles' voice broke the silence. "There's . . . something!"

The crew paused what they were doing and ran to the sides of the ship, squinting into the haze. As the *Riptide* slowly advanced, the outline of a tall, dark shape appeared.

A small angular rocky outcrop rose out of the water in front of them, hardly big enough to be considered an island. Waves washed against the sides and splashed over the top of the islet. Perched on the widest part of the ledge was a high, narrow tower.

At first, Cas thought it had to be an old lighthouse. But who would put a lighthouse out here, far from any land, in a section of the ocean where no one dares to enter?

As they drew closer, he began to notice that something was off about the structure. The tower was much taller than any lighthouse he had seen before, and lacked the trademark circular top. Instead, the building tapered to an ominous point, sticking up into the fog like the blade of a sword. The tower was old and dilapidated, with broken windows and visible cracks in the foundation, dark stone discoloring to a pale gray under the constant wind and waves.

"What *is* that?" Fenix asked as they all stared up at it.

"That," Nyx said, "is the Temple of the Drowned Queen's Congregation."

4

Part 4

22

The Journal of Captain Nyx

I have decided to recount my experiences in the Queen's Quarter, con-fusing and hazy though my memories may be, in the hopes that they may dissuade others from venturing into that cursed place. I do not know how many of these memories are true events that actually occurred and how many are fevered dreams or visions, for the Quarter blurs the lines between reality and imagination and they begin to bleed into each other.

We were in high spirits when we approached the fogbanks. There were twenty-five of us, myself included. We had all heard the legends of the Quarter over the years, but the idea of wealth beyond our wildest dreams made us push those fears to the back of our minds. We would follow the course I had plotted from the many maps I'd collected, and surely we couldn't fail.

I became a sea captain at age 17, elected to lead by my father's crew after his death. Holding a course is something I can do in my sleep. On paper, the path to where I believed the island was couldn't have been clearer. It was only a matter of maintaining the course through the fog, I told myself. I was so naive.

We came upon the old tower at sunset. We knew this would be the last charted land for many miles, so we stopped for the night, patching up the ship and replenishing our drinking water. I did not go inside the tower, or actually set foot on the island at all. But the men I sent in came out shaken, saying they had glimpsed a cloaked figure holding a lantern from the corner of their eyes.

I dismissed this. It must have been a trick of the light, or perhaps these months at sea were getting to them. I told them to sleep it off.

The next morning, we set out onto the mist-shrouded waters, deeper and deeper into the Quarter. Initially, I believed we were making good time, and traveling North in a relatively straight trajectory.

At some point, I looked down at my compass, and to my surprise, I found that we had somehow completely reversed direction. I brought the ship around so we were facing north, and we continued. But once again, when I checked the compass several minutes later, it showed we were headed south.

I had my first mate take over at the helm, thinking perhaps that I needed to rest and that my sleep-addled mind was playing tricks on me. However, he reported the same thing as me: the compass was randomly changing direction, as if we were traveling in circles. We tried to get reorientated, but the compass didn't respond to our direction anymore. The arrow simply spun round and round. We had passed the point of no return, for we were now incapable of going back the way we came.

I hardly remember why the six of us went below deck that evening. The quartermaster, cook, cabin boy, two mates and myself were busy with some tasks in the cargo hold, when we heard a commotion on deck. The crew were yelling about something, eventually calling the others in the sleeping cabin to come up and see.

As the six of us began to climb up, the voices seemed to fade out, becoming whispers before disappearing altogether. I reached the deck first, to find myself completely alone. The only sounds were the lapping of the waves against the hull and the creaking of the ladder as the others joined me.

The crew was gone. All nineteen of them had vanished into thin air.

That night and much of the next day is very hazy to me, looking back. I don't remember how we came to terms with the fact that nineteen people had seemingly faded into the fog, but we did.

I do remember that, in those moments, I had not given up hope just yet. I believed that if we pressed on, we would eventually find our way out. Perhaps we would even find the others, for surely they couldn't really have vanished. They had to have gone somewhere.

Days and nights are hard to keep track of in the Quarter. The constant fog creates darkness even when the sun is high in the sky, and therefore sunset and sunrise are only a shift between murky twilight and filtered moonlight. But I believe we had been in the Quarter three days by this point.

It was on that third night that we lost the cabin boy. I don't know how he went overboard; all I heard was a splash, followed by a scream. We searched the water, going in circles for hours to try and locate him, but never saw the boy. We did, however, hear him. That entire night we heard his screams of terror and cries for help echoing across the waves, always coming from different directions, and often from two places at once, as if something out there was mimicking him.

The cries eventually faded away as the light shifted from silver to pale pink, signaling that dawn had come. We never heard them again.

The cook was beginning to lose his grasp on reality by that point. He spent the day locked in his cabin, crying and refusing to respond to me when I tried to get him to come out. I was also starting to feel a constant, nagging sense of dread, but I pushed the ominous sensation down. I thought that I could still save what remained of my crew.

Several days passed. We floated on, lost and alone, hoping and praying we would finally emerge from the fog. The two remaining mates reported that they couldn't sleep. They said something was scratching at the hull at night, as if trying to get into the ship. The quartermaster claimed he was having horrible, vivid nightmares, and I often heard him scream in the night while I was lying awake, too afraid to sleep.

I was also hearing things. From sunset to sunrise, it seemed the ocean itself was speaking to me. It told me strange tales of life, and death, and even what lay beyond. I frequently found myself standing on the deck all through the night, staring down into the dark waves as they whispered their stories.

When the cook finally emerged from his cabin one night, he said that he, too, was unable to sleep. He said there was something down in the lower deck, hiding among the barrels and waiting for him. I asked how he knew that, as he hadn't left his room in days. He didn't answer me and returned to his cabin.

The next morning the quartermaster found his body in the cargo hold. It was flayed open, with all the organs meticulously removed. It had clearly been there for several days, as the body was beginning to rot. The smell was horrendous. No one offered an explanation as to how we had seen him alive only a few hours before. We simply tossed the body overboard.

The remaining four of us had stopped speaking by this point. We completed our duties mechanically, maintaining the ship, keeping watch for anything out of the ordinary, attempting to sleep each night with little success. I personally was so consumed with the voices of the sea that I hardly noticed what the others were doing. Night and day, reality and dreams were blurring together into a fog-shrouded trance.

I was snapped out of this state when the storm hit. I could feel my mind coming back to me, as if I was remembering who I was for the first time. I was Captain Nyx, and I was determined to survive.

The storm raged for what seemed like days, and very well could have been. Without a crew, all we could do was stow the sails and wait for it to pass. Waves and wind battered us incessantly, the darkness lit time and time again by brilliant flashes of lightning.

It was during those flashes that I caught glimpses of something gigantic emerging from the waves. It seemed to have spikes or fins like those of a fish, but taller than the masts of our ship. There were many of the creatures as well. Every time I saw them, I thought that they were here to attack us, but each time they slipped back beneath the black waters without incident.

We lost one of the mates when a huge wave slammed into us, nearly capsizing the Riptide. It broke over the deck, knocking me off my feet and nearly sending me into the seething water. When I regained the helm, I realized we were now down to three. We couldn't turn back for her, so with heavy hearts we left her to her fate.

The storm finally passed, and we lowered the sails once again. We did not know where we were going, but forward was better than nowhere.

It was only the next night when the last crew member died. I was in my cabin, lying awake in my hammock, when I heard a commotion outside. On the deck I found his body, foam and seawater dripping from his mouth. He had drowned without ever falling overboard.

The quartermaster and I were now the only two left. I remember us staring at each other in silence for a long moment. He looked pale and sickly, his eyes glassy and ringed with red. I realized I was probably in a similar state.

"We're going to die out here, aren't we?" I asked, the words coming out soft and rasping. He didn't answer. He didn't need to.

But, as we would come to find out, there are much worse fates than death in the Quarter.

I spotted the ship first. I don't know what day it was. Time had lost all meaning by this point.

I began to call out to the massive galleon as it drew close. The quartermaster joined me. For the first time in a long while, I felt a spark of hope, that perhaps our ordeal was over and we would be rescued.

As it neared, I realized that something was very wrong. The ship had rotting holes throughout its hull, the sails were tattered and stained, and I could hear the buzzing of countless flies hovering around the vessel.

There were at least ten men up on the deck, working in silence to hoist fraying ropes and rusting chains. The men were little more than corpses. They were alive, certainly, but they shouldn't have been.

Flesh hung from them in glistening threads, exposing bloody muscles and white bones beneath. Many were missing eyes, limbs, jaws . . .

I heard the quartermaster gagging. I watched in stunned, silent horror as the ship drifted by. The captain, standing at the helm, at first looked to be a normal man, but then he turned to me. A cloud of flies leapt up around him at the sudden movement, and I realized that half of his face was gone.

I turned away and didn't look back until I was certain that the ship and its undead crew were long gone. It dawned on me that perhaps it would be better to die than survive, knowing what my fate could ultimately be.

I spent much of the night pacing on the helm, pistol drawn, trying to decide what to do. Although I heard the whispers of the sea, I ignored them. That is, until I heard a different voice mixed in, a voice I recognized from one of my crew who had disappeared in the fog.

A hand grabbed the side of the ship, followed by another. They were black and slimy, encrusted with barnacles and limpets. A body was hauled up, in equally disgusting condition. Suddenly, dozens of my deceased crew were climbing aboard the ship.

They dragged themselves along the deck, calling to me to help them, to save them. Screaming, I tried to run, but of course I had nowhere to go. I huddled in a corner, watching as they drew closer, out of my mind with terror.

One of the men stood. I recognized him as my father, but, unfortunately, in the state he was in at his death: hanged, drawn and quartered. I couldn't take it anymore. I aimed my pistol and pulled the trigger.

The hallucinations disappeared immediately as the gunshot echoed across the water. The undead men vanished. In their place, staring at me with a mix of confusion and fear, was the Quartermaster, a patch of red spreading across his chest.

He collapsed to the ground, and I ran to his side. I told him that I was sorry, that I was seeing things, I didn't know it was him. He told me he knew, and that it was alright. And then he died in my arms.

I didn't handle his death well. I sobbed inconsolably and then drank myself into a stupor. When I awoke, I realized that I was really, truly alone now, and it was my own fault. I drank more to dampen my guilt and dismay.

I came to the decision that I would stay alive. I was always stubborn like that. After all, the Riptide needed me. She was all I had left now, and I couldn't abandon her. If I were to die, it would be sinking down into the sea with my ship, as a captain should.

Awakening from one of my alcohol-induced dazes, I realized that I was ravenously hungry. I couldn't remember the last time I'd eaten, only that it must have been before the quartermaster died, since he had been the one cooking. As for how long ago that was, I could only guess.

When I descended into the cargo hold, I found that all the food was rotting and infested with maggots. I threw it overboard.

The second storm hit with little warning. One second the seas were calm, the next the wind was howling and waves were crashing over the Riptide. I stowed the sails and waterproofed her as best I could, but it became clear that I couldn't handle the ship alone.

We began to take on water. I suspected this storm would be the end of us. Despite my stubbornness to survive, I couldn't help but feel relieved. At least the Riptide and I would die together.

I clung to the mast to keep from falling overboard as waves slammed into us, tossing us about like a cork. I was soaked to the bone, shaking, entirely prepared for these to be my last moments. I shut my eyes and waited.

Suddenly everything became still and quiet. The ship stopped rocking, the rain ceased, and even the thunder grew distant. At first, I thought I must be dead, as that was the only explanation I could come up with. I opened my eyes to find that the deck was bathed in an eerie blue light.

I found the source when I peeked around the mast, and stifled a gasp. Standing, or, rather, hovering, on a stationary wave just off the bow was a ghostly figure that I recognized immediately.

It was the Drowned Queen, spirit of the oceans, bringer of storms and whirlpools, an entity feared and revered by every seafarer. I had heard stories of her ever since I was a child, and yet I always assumed that they were just stories, superstitions passed down by the earliest sailors to explain natural phenomena. But there she was. And she wasn't what I expected.

She didn't look fearsome. Strange and otherworldly, yes, but hardly the evil creature I had heard legends about.

The Queen was a young woman, wearing an old-fashioned, flowing black gown, with long dark hair that floated as if underwater. She had pale gray-blue skin and eyes that glowed a deep unnatural blue. A chain trailed down from where I assumed her legs were, hidden by the dress and disappeared beneath the dark water below her.

She seemed curious about the Riptide. As I watched, she reached out and touched the ship, sending a ripple of light across the deck. This time, I gasped audibly, and she looked up at me.

I felt paralyzed by her gaze. I was terrified, staring into the glowing eyes of an ancient ocean god, knowing that at any moment she could wave her hand and destroy me. And yet, there was something strangely beautiful about her. A big, stupid smile spread across my face.

"Hello." Although her lips didn't move, I heard her voice all around me, low and melodic like waves crashing against the shore.

"Are you lost?" she asked.

"Y-yes," I stammered.

"Come closer."

I felt my heart skip a beat as I rose to my feet and cautiously walked across the storm-battered deck.

"What is your name?" she inquired.

I couldn't remember for a moment.

"Nyx!" I said eventually. "Captain Nyx."

She smiled. "Captain Nyx," her whispery voice repeated, wrapping around my ship like the ocean wind.

"What's your name?" I asked, immediately feeling ridiculous. But then I realized that, in the many legends, I had never once heard a name.

"Zephyrine," she said, then paused. "Queen Zephyrine."

I smiled again, and happened to look down. I realized with a start that my ship was floating on a plateau of calm water, high above the crashing waves. Suddenly feeling as though I were standing at the edge of a cliff, I fell to my knees and grabbed the side of the ship. Zephyrine looked down at me.

"You seemed to be in some trouble," she said.

"Y-yes, I . . . I don't know how to get out of here." My momentary infatuation with the spirit faded, and I remembered that I was trapped in the Quarter, my crew dead, and I myself was likely dying. I felt tears sting my eyes.

A cold hand touched my face, sending chills through my whole body. She raised my chin to look me in the eye again.

"Let me help you."

Before I could respond, the Riptide fell out from beneath me as the seemingly solid plateau dissolved into seafoam. I screamed as waves began to crash in from all sides and my ship plunged below the water. The last thing I remember was looking up at the Queen, who regarded me passively with her glowing blue eyes. Then a wave washed over my head, and everything faded to blackness.

Now I am staying at the Maelstrom Tavern. I was told that I returned three years after my crew and I departed. I don't know how that much time could have passed. By my estimation, we only had enough supplies for a year at most, and I dumped at least two months' worth into the ocean after it spoiled. I couldn't have survived more than a few weeks without food, and after subtracting the six months of travel, I could have only been lost in the Quarter for four months.

I was also told that when I returned, my ship was glowing with an unearthly blue light and encrusted with sea life like a wreck hauled from the bottom of the ocean.

I don't remember any of that, nor do I remember a return journey.

Nearly two and a half years of my life are gone, and I have no idea where I was or what happened to me.

Apparently, I was in and out of consciousness for the first several days at the tavern, being cared for by a young maid named Prisma. They said I was nearly dead. I don't recall much of that either.

Now, several weeks later, I am recovering. I am learning to trust my senses again; what I see and hear is real, no longer visions or phantasms. I frequently awake from nightmares convinced that I'm back in the Quarter and often have to be calmed by my caretaker.

I have been confined mostly to the private bedchamber on the second floor of the tavern. For a long time, I was too weak to walk much further than the end of the hallway. My room is small, with a cot, a desk, and a window offering a view of the ocean and the northern-most dock. Jois, the tavern keeper, has asked if I want to move into the more permanent chambers on the third floor that she and the tavern maids occupy. I had to decline.

I intend to return to my cabin on the Riptide as soon as possible. Although I have no crew to sail her, I find myself longing for her company. She is the only thing I have left from my former life, and I can't stand to be separated from her for this long. As much as she cannot sail without a captain, I cannot be a captain, or myself, without her.

I know that I am not the same person I once was. My eye turned from brown to blue, the same unnatural color as the Queen's. I still hear the whispers of the waves, speaking to me in a voice that I now know to be Zephyrine's, urging me to return to the sea.

Some stormy nights, when the waves are crashing against the docks and the entire tavern shakes and shudders at the end of its long chain, I swear I can see her in each flash of lightning. I know she is not finished with me just yet, and I welcome whatever it is that she has planned for me.

All of my friends and family are now dead. Only I and the Riptide remain. I know I must set sail once again, although I do not know to where.

For now, I will wait. And I will listen to the waves.

23

⚜

The Temple

Cas carefully stepped onto the slippery rocks, testing each footstep before fully committing his weight, climbing the short stone stairway to the entrance of the tower. His heart hammered as he approached the black doorway. But with so many of the others going in, he didn't want to seem like a scared little kid.

"Collect as much fresh water as you can," Nyx had instructed them. "There's no telling how long we'll be in the Quarter, and we don't want to run out."

Cas adjusted the flasks on his belt and walked into the shadowy interior of the temple. As his eyes acclimated to the darkness, he realized he was standing in a vast atrium with arched ceilings. A shattered crystal chandelier lay in the center of the space, while broken wooden benches littered the floor. Splinter pushed past him.

"You think these crystals are worth anything?" he asked, kneeling down next to the chandelier.

"If they were, don't you think someone would've looted them by now?" Tig asked.

Splinter shrugged and tucked a few into his pocket anyway.

As the crew spread through the vast room, Cas found himself staring at the walls. Each wall was painted with elaborate seascapes and intertwining ocean creatures. They must have once been vibrant and colorful but were now faded over the many years of exposure to the salty air. Although most of the windows were smashed and broken, some of them still contained blue and green stained glass that cast an underwater-like ambiance around the chapel.

He paused in front of the broken pulpit, staring up at the painting behind it. It portrayed a woman in a long, old-fashioned gown against a deep blue background. Her skin was the same pale gray as the stone she was painted on, with long black hair fanned out around her head like a dark halo. Her sunken eyes were a brilliant, unnatural blue that seemed to glow in the darkness.

She stood with arms outstretched, a long chain trailing down from her legs. At the base of the painting, clustered around the end of the chain, were dozens of corpse-like figures writhing, crying, and reaching up to her. Cas shuddered.

"The Queen and her victims." Alistair's voice came from behind him. He turned to see the man staring up at the painting. "Creepy, huh?"

"Very," Cas replied.

"Come on. We don't want to get left behind."

Cas glanced around the room and realized that the rest of the crew was gone. He quickly followed Alistair to the stone spiral staircase at the opposite end of the chapel.

"Did everyone here really die?" Cas asked as they ascended.

"According to legend, yes. What really happened is anyone's guess, since no one was around to explain when the Kiral authorities came to check on them."

There was a landing at each floor of the tower, and Cas peeked into the doorways as they went. One room contained rows of old beds, some still intact and others long since collapsed and broken. Another was littered with tables and what appeared to be wood-burning stoves, over which bundles of brown herbs and rotten fruit hung.

They finally reached the top floor of the tower, where the others had gathered. The space was filled with shelves containing thick leather-bound books, with scrolls and manuscripts strewn across the floor. Most were faded and warped by saltwater to the point of being illegible.

"Check this out!" Gyles was saying. He was standing at the far end of the room next to a huge window with some kind of cloth and wood apparatus beside it. The cloth was covered in dewdrops, which slowly gathered in streams and dripped into a large stone basin.

"Is that safe to drink?" Fenix asked.

"Yes. I've read about these. It's an old mist-sifting device," Gyles explained. "It concentrates fresh water from the fog and condenses it. It's just like rain."

"Thank you, Mr. Science," Knives said, scooping up water with his flask. The crew clustered around the basin. Cas handed his bottles to Tig, who began to fill them.

Cas noticed Prisma standing in the shadows away from the window, flipping through a book. He approached her, looking over her shoulder at the paragraphs of tiny handwritten text.

"What does it say?" He asked.

"It's a history book," she said, with an air of surprise. "It documents the kingdom that was once here, as best they could determine from the records that survived its disappearance."

"Interesting," he said.

"It's incredible, actually," she said.

"How old is it?"

"The book itself probably came from the early days of the Congregation. About 200 years ago. But the records it references date back to 600 years, back before the Drowned Queen was even born."

"I thought you didn't believe in the Drowned Queen."

Prisma glanced up at him. "I don't believe she came back from the dead and started a reign of terror by manipulating the ocean and the weather. I do believe there was a real person who inspired the legend, though."

"There is?"

"Yes. Princess Zephyrine the Third, daughter of King Kazamir and Queen Celestina. They lived about 500 years ago, just before the kingdom was lost."

"Zephyrine?" Cas asked. "Didn't Nyx . . ."

"Ey, kids! We're leaving!" Gryph's voice cut through Cas's thought. They turned to see the crew was disappearing down the staircase. Prisma closed the book and followed with it cradled in her arms.

"You're taking that?" Cas asked, trotting to catch up with her.

"Yeah! Should I just leave it here to rot instead?"

"Is that the best idea? What if it's . . ." Cas couldn't bring himself to say "haunted". "Never mind."

As they descended the stairs, Cas paused at one of the ledges. He could've sworn he saw something move out of the corner of his eye.

He stepped into the old kitchen, scanning the shadowy space nervously. A beam of moonlight filtered through the blue stained glass, casting shifting watery glints across the room. With a jolt of terror, he realized a dark figure was crouching in the corner.

The figure slowly straightened up, the outline of an oversized hood and flowing robes becoming apparent. Although its face was simply a dark void, Cas could feel it intently staring at him.

He stumbled back toward the stairs, too scared to speak. Then he blinked, and it was gone.

He looked frantically around the room, trying to make sense of what he had just witnessed. He found himself completely alone.

Trying to calm his pounding heart, he took a deep breath and hurried back down the stairs.

As he ran through the chapel, he glanced up at the painting of the Queen again. Her eyes seemed to follow him.

He barreled out the door, almost crashing into someone on the stairs. He started back but breathed a sigh of relief when he recognized the stout green-eyed man.

"Hey, watch where you're going!" Gyles cried.

"S-sorry," Cas muttered. His crewmate's brow furrowed in confusion.

"You alright? You look like you saw a ghost," Gyles said.

"Yeah," Cas stated, but he didn't elaborate.

He headed down the stairs and back onto the *Riptide* as quickly as he could.

24

The Queen's Quarter

"Before we go anywhere, we need to establish some rules," Nyx said. She was pacing back and forth at the helm nervously, while the rest of the crew stood on the deck below. "First, you're going to see and hear things in the Quarter that are going to scare you. It's going to get inside your head and use what it finds in there against you. Under no circumstances are you to let it. Whatever you see, whatever you hear, you have to remember that it's not real. If you keep that in mind, some of you will probably survive."

"Some of us?" Gryph asked.

"Probably?" Splinter asked simultaneously.

"Second, you are all to partner up. Find a buddy and know where your buddy is at all times. Go with them everywhere. Don't let them out of your sight, or there's a good chance you'll never see them again."

Cas felt Prisma grab his hand. He squeezed hers back.

"Third," Nyx continued, "our compasses are going to stop working. The mist is going to prevent us from seeing the sun or the stars.

However, our navigator and mapmaker have a plan to keep us oriented." Kal and Gyles smiled proudly, and Gyles gestured to Nyx.

"Map, Captain?"

She pulled the necklace from her pocket and held up a lantern, casting the map onto the sail. Everyone turned to look at it.

"This map is unique in that it shows a path which follows a shallow strip of water," Kal said, gesturing to the rocky outcrops and small islands that traveled parallel to the marked route. "It's always been a mystery how Eris Black found his way in and out of the Quarter, but I now believe that he used the shallows to stay oriented when his compass and visibility were compromised."

"How does that help us? Isn't sailing through shallow water just a danger of getting shipwrecked?" Cimik asked.

"Not necessarily," Gyles jumped in. "The rocks offer us an advantage: sound."

"Waves crashing against rocks is a unique noise that can carry a long way," Kal continued. "If we can hear it, we can follow it from island to island until we reach the destination."

"But what if we drift off course? What if we get so far away from the shallows that we can't hear the waves anymore?" Fenix asked nervously.

"Hopefully we can sort out from the map where we went wrong and adjust the course," Gyles said. "I did it plenty of times. In school, that is."

"So never in real life?" Tig asked.

"Not exactly, no," he admitted.

"That doesn't matter," Nyx said, returning the map to her pocket. "We have a plan, and we're going to stick to it as best we can."

"And if all else fails, we have a secret weapon," Alistair said.

"Yeah, if we can't find our way back we can always have Alistair look into his magical sea glass and figure out a proper course," Gyles said.

"Don't mock me, son," Alistair growled.

"Sorry."

"Alright, everyone. Keep the plan in mind. Keep the rules in mind. If you do, we might make it through this with relatively few casualties," Nyx said.

She looked out across the misty sea as the sunrise lit the water pink and yellow. "Lower the sails. The Quarter lies ahead."

Cas hadn't fully realized what everyone meant by "fogbank." He was imagining the same mist that settled over the water in the morning, or the fog that rolled down from the hills of Valdoria during cool days.

The fogbanks of the Quarter were something else entirely. They formed a massive wall of white cloud rising up in front of the ship. He half expected the *Riptide* to crash into it, for it looked as solid as a cliff face.

Instead, the prow silently passed through the barrier. A moment later, they were consumed by the thick cloud.

Cas could hardly see to the other end of the ship. The masts seemed to rise up into nothingness, vanishing into the white that surrounded them. It was as though a blanket had been thrown over him, muffling sounds and casting the crew in a ghostly haze. Now he understood why Nyx had instructed them to keep their partners in sight at all times; he had no doubt someone could simply be swallowed up in this fog and never be seen again.

"Oh, I don't like this at all," Knives muttered.

"Everyone stay as quiet as possible. We need to listen for waves breaking against the rocks," Gyles called from somewhere in the fog.

"And stay together," Nyx said from the helm.

It wasn't long before they came across the first rocky shelf. It rose out of the water, jagged and angular, barely visible until they were nearly on top of it. The ship narrowly avoided crashing into it.

"I suppose that's a good sign," Prisma whispered as they watched it pass. "At least Kal and Gyles know what they're talking about."

"I hope they can keep us on the path," Cas muttered, staring out into the whiteness. "Otherwise, we'll never find our way back."

As the day wore on, Cas found it hard to stay focused. He kept catching glimpses of movement out in the fog, like shadows passing just out of sight, but when he tried to get a better look, they would vanish. He also began to hear whispers. Every now and then, someone would call out that they heard waves or spotted land, but Gyles would remind them that they must hear it *consistently* to announce it.

Eventually, Cas and Prisma went down to the medic cabin together. It was less unsettling to be inside.

"I'm starting to understand why everyone thinks this place is haunted," Prisma said with a nervous laugh. "The fog really starts to mess with your head."

"Yeah." Cas hoped that was all it was. "So . . . if you don't believe in ghosts or spirits or anything, what do you think causes all this fog? Why would this one patch of ocean be covered all the time?"

"I don't know," she acknowledged. "But I'm sure there's some explanation for it."

They both jumped as a loud thud came from outside. Two more rhythmic, purposeful knocks followed.

"What was that?" Cas asked.

"An animal, maybe," Prisma suggested.

"Animals can knock?"

She glared at him. "Well, what do *you* think? That there's a person out there?"

Cas shrugged. "Nyx told us to ignore it."

Another knock echoed through the cabin, followed by a chilling metallic scraping across the hull.

Prisma moved from the desk to the cot next to Cas. "Yeah. We'll just ignore it like Nyx said," she stated, sounding unconvinced.

"Let's talk. We can keep our minds off it," Cas said, then paused, trying to come up with a conversational topic. "You . . . you said Jois raised you?"

"Yeah. I lived up on the third floor of the tavern with her and some of the other permanent maids. When I was younger, she tried to keep me out of the tavern as much as possible. It's not exactly safe for a child to be in a bar with a bunch of criminals, you know. So Jois would bring me books to keep me busy.

"She had come from a family of healers. Her grandfather had written manuals about all kinds of medical potions and how to treat different conditions. That's what I spent my days reading.

"But I was curious, and I always snuck down to the tavern anyway. So, she put me to work when I was old enough, washing dishes and serving drinks and food . . ." She paused when another loud scrape came from outside.

"Did you like it?" Cas asked.

"I . . . It was something to keep myself busy with. But it wasn't what I wanted to do. I wanted to be a healer."

"So . . . why did you become a pirate?"

She paused, clearly taken aback by the question.

"Why did *you* become a pirate?" she replied.

"To find my dad."

"Really? You committed piracy, impersonated a military guard, freed prisoners who had been sentenced to death, and battled monsters on the high seas *just* for the chance of finding a man you've never even met?"

Cas was silent.

"You're right. That's not the only reason," he said finally.

"You felt called to it, didn't you?" Prisma asked with a smile. Cas nodded.

"You too?"

"Yes. There's something inside me that's always drawn me to the ocean, and that day in the tavern I finally gave in."

"What do you think it is?"

"Our parents are pirates. Maybe it's just in our blood."

Cas smiled. "Yeah. I think that must be it."

"Whatever it is, I'm glad I have it. Otherwise, I never would've met you."

His smile grew bigger, and he felt his face growing hot. "Prisma, I . . ."

Before he could finish, a shout came from above. The two ran up to the deck just as a massive ship came into view through the fog.

As the crew gathered at the bow to see, Cas realized the other ship wasn't moving. The sails were little more than tattered rags and the hull was rotten and falling apart. It was a wreck, stuck on a jagged rock that rose up from the waves.

Nearby that wreck was another, in an equally poor condition. Towering up around it were massive spires of sharp rock, which continued to emerge from the fog as they sailed on.

"Welcome to the aptly named Shipwreck Island," Nyx announced. "This is one of the many places the false maps would lead to, ensuring that those who sought Captain Black's treasure would run aground and be trapped here forever." As she spoke, they approached the tallest rocks yet, and Cas realized there were many ships in varying states of decay scattered around them.

"How many wrecks do you think are here?" Splinter asked as another came into view.

"Dozens, I'd guess," Cimik said.

Then he saw movement on the old ships. The crew froze, staring into the fog. Hardly able to believe his eyes, Cas watched as humanoid figures, seemingly made from the mist itself, walked back and forth across the decks, adjusting rigging that was no longer there, hauling up anchors that had been trapped amongst the rocks for decades.

He felt a chill of terror as, behind him, a familiar voice whispered his name.

25

Ghosts of the Past

Cas turned, knowing what he was going to see but still not prepared.

Scout stood inches from him, clothes bloody and ripped, skin discolored and beginning to rot and fall away from the starkly white bones underneath. He stared at Cas with empty eyes and reached out a rotting hand to him.

Cas stumbled back, falling against the guardrail. All around him, the crew was screaming and running from their own apparitions. The *Riptide* began to drift toward the island as everyone abandoned their posts.

Scout hovered closer to him. "Why did you leave me, Cas?" Scout whispered. "Why didn't you help me?"

"I . . . I tried! I couldn't . . ."

"Why did you get to live when I died? I never did anything worse than you, but they condemned me to death while they let you go."

Tears began to run down Cas's face as the ghostly figure echoed what Cas himself had long thought. "I'm sorry . . ."

"And now what am I? A memory? A shadow of your old life that you can't free yourself from? A nightmare?"

"No!" Cas shouted through his tears. "You're my friend! You were my best friend. You were the only one I ever had. And I love you, damn it! I wish you were still with me more than anything, but you're not! You're gone, and I have to let you go."

Scout paused. A glimmer of life returned to his glazed-over eyes for a moment, and then he retreated back into the fog and disappeared.

Cas sat stock-still, staring after his friend. He realized he had been holding his breath and drew in a shaky gasp. Scout was gone.

Everything snapped into focus around him again. Niko was at the helm, his crutch tossed aside, trying to steer them away from the rocks while shouting at the crew to focus, that the ghosts weren't real. Cas jumped to his feet.

"Cas!" Niko yelled. "Get Nyx!"

Cas spun around, looking for her amongst the chaos. Finally, he noticed her cabin door was half open. He ran inside.

He found her huddled in the corner, head buried in her knees as she rocked back and forth. He knelt down beside her.

"Captain!" he said. She jolted upright, wild-eyed, and pushed him back. He grabbed her wrists and held them tight as she tried to squirm away. "Captain, we need you . . ."

"I can't do this again!" she cried. "I have to get out of here!"

"You can't! It's too late for that!" She fell back against the wall, breathing heavily. "It's going to be okay, Nyx, but we need you to stay calm and focus now!"

"We're not going to get out of here, Cas. We're all going to die," she whispered.

"No, we're not!" he snapped. She stared at him, surprised at the aggressive tone in his voice. "I don't want to hear you talk like that! It's counterproductive!"

"Don't raise your voice to me," she said, seeming to come down from her panic.

"I won't raise my voice to the captain. But I need you to be the captain."

She pushed him back and climbed to her feet. "Who's at the helm?"

"Niko."

"*Niko*? If he wrecks my ship, I'm gonna kill him," she said as she ran out of the cabin, Cas following close behind.

She raced to the helm and grabbed the wheel from Niko, narrowly avoiding a rock spike. Niko shouted at the crew.

"Everyone look at me! Look at me!" he demanded. His words seemed to briefly bring everyone back to reality. "These ghosts are not real! You have to ignore them; you can't give in to these delusions!"

"He's right." Gyles said in a shaky voice, but it quickly grew more confident. "It's just hallucinations! There are no ghosts here."

Another shipwreck reared out of the mist ahead of them. Nyx spun the wheel and just barely skirted around the vessel. Just then, the sails went limp. The *Riptide* slowly came to a halt just a few feet from the wreck. As it stopped, the panic that gripped the crew did as well.

"Is everyone still alive?" Nyx asked. "Gather around the helm."

They obeyed. Cas felt a wave of relief as he saw Prisma emerge from behind the mast.

"All accounted for. I . . ." Niko trailed off, staring at the shipwreck. Everyone followed his gaze. It was a newer ship, in better condition than the others they had passed. But Cas couldn't see anything that would have captured his attention. Was Niko finally being affected by the supernatural too?

"What's wrong?" Nyx asked.

"I know that ship," he said.

"You . . . You what?"

"I was on that ship," Niko said as he limped down from the helm and crossed to the bow.

"Where are you going?" Fenix called after him.

Niko didn't answer. Instead, he climbed onto the guardrail and jumped across to the wreck, disappearing into a gaping hole in the side despite everyone's protests.

"Is he allowed to do that?" Tig asked, looking up at Nyx.

She let out a sigh of annoyance. "Come on. We need to go find him."

"What? I'm not going in there," Splinter said.

"Stay here, then. Don't go anywhere or let anyone out of your sight," she ordered.

Cas followed Niko onto the ship. As he stepped across, the rotting boards creaked ominously. He peered around the dark space. Tattered hammocks hung from the beams, while molding blankets and pillows lay strewn across the floor.

"Niko!" Cas jumped as Nyx yelled.

There was no answer. She turned to address the others who had joined them—Gyles, Cimik and Fenix.

"Spread out and start looking for him," Nyx said.

Cas descended the ladder to the cargo hold, pausing each time the wood let out a sharp crack, worried that the old rotting rungs would give way and trap him below. Finally, he reached the hold with a splash. He looked down and realized there was knee-deep water filling the space, with waves lapping against a large, half-submerged hole in the hull.

He scanned the shadows, and his heart skipped a beat when he saw a figure standing on the opposite side of the room.

"Niko!" he cried, laughing nervously. "What are you doing?"

Niko's back was turned to him, and he stared down at a stack of collapsed boxes.

"I . . . I died here."

"What?"

"This was my ship. I came here to look for the treasure . . . but we ran aground on the rocks. The hold filled with water, and . . . I drowned."

"Niko, what are you talking about?"

Niko turned to face Cas, his eyes luminous in the dark room. "I remember everything now. I died, Cas. I was dead. Then I woke up on that island."

"You woke up after you died?"

"I know it sounds insane, but I did," he said quietly.

"Is that why you're not affected by the Mirages and the ghosts? Because you're already dead?" Cas asked, his hand instinctively going to the sword in his belt.

"I don't know."

"Are you a ghost?"

"I don't think so."

"Wait . . . this was *your* ship? Were you a captain?" Cas involuntarily let out a laugh. The idea of sweet, confused Niko captaining a ship was downright bizarre.

"Yes." His serious tone immediately made Cas's amused smile fade. "I am Captain Niko Black, the last descendant of Eris Black."

"You're *who*?" Nyx asked from the ladder. Cas turned to see her descending into the hold, brow furrowed in confusion. Niko confidently strode forward, offering his hand. She shook it.

"Niko Black. Pirate captain, treasure hunter, and possible ghost." Nyx stared at him for a long moment, taken aback by his sudden personality change.

"Huh. I wasn't expecting that."

"I, like many others, came here to find my ancestor's treasure and was lost in the process. I still don't know how I ended up on that island, but I think there's a reason you found me," he continued.

"What reason is that?" she asked.

"I'm not affected by the forces at play here. I believe I am supposed to be your guide through the Quarter."

*

With the wind stopped and the ship going nowhere, everyone took the opportunity to sleep. Cas realized, as he lay down in the medic cot and Prisma climbed into her hammock, that he didn't even know how long they had been in the Quarter. A day? A week?

He drifted off to sleep, only to be woken by a scratching sound coming from outside. The cabin was pitch black aside from a faint, watery light coming in through the porthole. Cas heard a squelch, and the light went out. He turned to see something pressed up against the glass; a dark, shifting mass made of dozens of writhing tentacles.

The tentacles parted, and he stared in horror as a distorted human face appeared in the porthole. It was the face of the man he had killed. A crack spread across the glass, and then with a crash the whole thing shattered and water rushed in.

He jolted awake, drenched in sweat. He looked around the room, unsure if he was still dreaming or truly awake this time.

The cabin was bathed in soft candlelight, and Prisma was sleeping peacefully in her hammock, swaying with the soft rocking movement of the ship. He took deep breaths to slow his pounding heart.

Wait, why was the ship moving?

He jumped out of bed and ran to the deck. Sure enough, the sails were billowing out with wind and the shipwreck was no longer in sight. He cursed and ran into Nyx's cabin.

She awoke with a start as he entered, and glared at him. "What are you doing in my room?"

"The ship's moving!"

"That's not possible, we dropped anchor for the night!" she said as she stumbled out of her hammock, pulling on her coat and hat before running outside. "Cas, wake everyone up!" she yelled.

As the crew raced up from their cabin, exchanging confused and frantic conversation, Nyx shushed them. They all grew silent.

"What do you hear?" she asked.

"Nothing," Cimik said after a long pause.

"Exactly. We've drifted away from the rocks. We're off course."

"I'll get right to correcting the course, Captain," Gyles said nervously, gesturing for Kal to follow him. They disappeared into her cabin.

"How could we have drifted anywhere?" Tig asked. "The anchor was down."

Nyx didn't respond.

Cas stared up at the sails as the wind grew stronger. Prisma joined him, seeming surprisingly unworried about their mysterious departure.

"What's with you?" Cas asked. "You're not freaked out by this?"

She considered the question with a slight smile. "Do you think all of this is a coincidence?" she asked finally.

"What? The ship drifting?"

"All of it. That you ended up with the map, that you got it to the one person who found her way out of the Quarter, that we accidentally teamed up with the last descendant of Eris Black and also a legendary pirate who can see the future? Is it possible that all of this is just . . . by chance?"

"What do you think it is?"

"I don't know. Fate? A grand design?"

Cas grinned. "I thought you didn't believe in any of that."

"I'm starting to."

They stumbled as the waves grew increasingly choppy. The *Riptide* jolted back and forth as the swells seemed to come from every direction at once. Cas could hardly believe his eyes as the waves suddenly took on a checkerboard pattern, the white foam criss-crossing into squares across the sea's surface.

"Cross sea!" Alistair shouted.

"What's a cross sea?" Cas yelled as the *Riptide* bucked and rolled.

"That!" He pointed to the waves.

"It's a very dangerous situation where waves interact as they move in from opposite directions!" Gyles yelled above the chaos.

As he spoke, a wall of white water slammed into the side of the ship. The crew grabbed on to whatever they could and held on for dear life. Cas was knocked off his feet and slid across the deck as the *Riptide* listed. He barely had time to wipe the water from his eyes before a second wave hit them. The *Riptide* turned nearly on its side, and Cas lost his grip on the guardrail.

For a moment everything was a blur. Cold water rushed up around him as he plunged into the sea. He clawed his way to the surface, just in time to see the ship disappearing behind another white-crested wave. Over the roaring sea, he heard Prisma yell his name.

Before he could even think about calling back, the wave crashed down over him. He was thrown back under the dark water, head over heels. As he frantically tried to find the surface, another wave pushed him further down.

His nose and throat burned as water flooded in. Involuntarily, he tried to cough it back up, but only managed to swallow more.

His body was no longer under his control, fighting to breathe even while his brain told him that he would drown if he did. He had to get to the surface. He *had* to. Raw, primal panic was driving him on, his mind blank with fear and adrenaline racing through his veins. Seconds felt like hours as he struggled.

But no matter how hard he tried to swim up, he kept being pulled down. His head was spinning, heart pounding in his ears, limbs and lungs burning as he fought to stay alive. The water felt like fire running down his throat.

His body gave a final small cough. His chest continued to spasm, trying to keep the water out but with no air left to do so. He suddenly felt very, very tired.

The edges of his vision grew increasingly dark. The panic faded, replaced by numbness. He was ready to die if it meant the pain would stop.

Staring up at the fading light, sinking lower into the sea, he noticed a blue glow coming from below. It grew brighter and brighter, until he was swallowed up within it.

26

The Kingdom

He was still alive.

He still couldn't breathe, though. He rolled onto his stomach and water drained out of his throat, burning just as much as it had on the way in. He caught a tiny gasp of air, then another. He began to cough, in spasms that racked his whole body until he had expelled the water from his airway.

His head was clearing. Staring down at the wet sand he was lying on, he realized he had no idea where he was. Still breathing hard, he looked up.

He was on a narrow strip of beach, overlooking a foggy gray sea. As he pulled himself up to his knees, he noticed what was on his other side: a stone seawall.

It was at least ten feet tall at the highest points, but appeared to be very, very old and dilapidated. The stones were cracked and the wall had abundant holes where pieces had fallen out. He shakily pulled himself to his feet and used a crumbling stack of rocks to climb to the top of the wall.

His mouth fell open. Beyond the wall was a sprawling town. The true expanse was hidden by the fog, but he could see blocks of dozens of huts and buildings, interspersed with stone walkways. In the distance, barely visible through the shifting mist, was a castle.

But the longer he looked, the more he felt as though something was wrong. Then he realized that the town was entirely devoid of life. Everything was dead silent, without even the usual chatter of seagulls.

He carefully climbed down to the cobblestone streets, noting puddles of saltwater filled with seaweed and mussels. His footsteps echoed strangely as he walked between the empty buildings. Although cracked and faded and overgrown with algae, he could tell they were once brightly colored. The style reminded him of some of the very oldest buildings in Valdoria.

"Hello?" he called. "Anyone here?"

His voice reverberated around the town, answering itself over and over again. As the echoes faded, everything was plunged back into the all-consuming silence.

He continued walking. Finally, he reached the vast courtyard in front of the castle and paused, looking around the flat, seagrass-carpeted space. Tide pools full of brilliantly colored anemones and starfish dotted the square.

Surrounding the courtyard were opulent, mansion-like palaces, smaller than the main castle but no less impressive. The castle itself was built from the same stone as the seawall, the turrets and archways and towers painted a resplendent deep blue. Cas wondered why that paint seemingly hadn't faded like the rest of the dwellings.

At the front of the castle was an arched doorway, which he cautiously approached. The wooden door lay in the entranceway, splintered as if it had been knocked off its hinges forcefully. He stepped over it and continued into the shadowy interior.

He followed a long hallway, admiring the intricate carvings in the stone walls of waves and twisting branches. At the end of the hallway was a circular room with several other hallways branching off. Overhead was a stained-glass dome, half shattered to produce a strange crescent-moon shape that cast the opposite side of the room in a watery blue light. Looking closer, he realized it was the same stained glass as in the old temple.

Across the room from him was an elevated platform, with elaborate patterns carved in the wall as if meant to frame a throne. But there was no throne.

He felt the hair on the back of his neck stand up. Even though he seemed to be alone in this strange city, he suddenly had the sensation that he was being watched. He began to slowly back out of the room.

He paused when he heard a whisper, thinking for a moment that he had imagined it. Then it came again, echoing down the hallway to his right.

"Hello?" Cas called. "Is someone there?"

"You're new," a cracked voice said, louder than before.

"Um, yeah," Cas said nervously. He could hear slow, shuffling footsteps coming toward him down the corridor. "I don't know how I got here. Or where 'here' is. Have you seen a ship go by?"

"There hasn't been anyone new here for a very long time," the voice muttered. He watched as the hem of a tattered dress fluttered into the light. Despite the rips and aged fabric, it was deep burgundy with gold trim and clearly made from expensive material. As the figure stepped closer, the light illuminated them further.

The dress was an old-fashioned style, with a cinched waist and full skirt, long flowing sleeves and lace swirls. The light reached their face, and Cas stumbled back, terrified.

A skeleton stared back at him. Strips of white skin still clung to the bones in places, stretched taut to the point of being nearly see-through. Clumps of hair, curled and styled as the high nobles of old, hung down from the skull, and two blue points of light shone inside the empty eye sockets.

Cas was frozen in shock as the jaw opened and a voice came from the nonexistent throat.

"They've finally returned!" she cried.

The call echoed through the empty castle. It snapped Cas out of his stupor. He turned and ran back toward the entranceway.

He splashed out into the courtyard, realizing it was now covered by ankle-deep seawater. As he paused, he heard creaking noises emanating from all around him.

The doors of the smaller palaces that surrounded the courtyard were opening. Skeletal figures stepped out, all dressed in lavish clothes and elaborate hairstyles; that is, those that still had hair. A murmur rose from the walking corpses as they gazed intently upon Cas.

"Someone's found us!" one yelled.

"The merchants must be back!" another proclaimed.

"We're saved!" came a third voice.

They began to close in, encircling Cas as they stumbled ever closer. He spotted a gap in the undead crowd and ran for it, narrowly missing their bony hands as they grabbed for him.

He raced through the streets, back the way he had come. The water grew deeper and deeper the closer he got to the seawall. He could hear a chorus of voices and splashing steps following him.

He had to slow down as the water lapped up around his knees. He could see the wall now, and realized that the waves were already to the halfway point, seafoam pouring through the gaps. He paused, scanning the wall for where he had climbed down.

"Come back!" a voice demanded from behind him, startlingly close. He spun around to see that the ghostly creatures were rapidly approaching. He bolted toward the wall and began to pull himself up, using the cracks and openings as handholds.

He felt a skeletal hand grab his ankle, yanking him back down. He clung tightly to the wall and kicked at them.

"You can't leave!" it desperately shrieked.

"She'll be back soon, you have to wait!" cried another.

"Don't leave us, please!" pleaded yet another.

"Let go of me!" he yelled, and kicked one last time. He felt his captor release their grip as a wave crashed over the wall, washing them back onto the streets. He scrambled to the top of the wall.

The sea was quickly getting higher. As he looked across the waves that pounded against the wall, he caught a glimpse of a dark shape through the fog, growing closer.

*

"Hey, I see something," Gyles said as he stared through his spyglass. The crew, exhausted and battered from navigating the treacherous cross sea, nodded and muttered. It wasn't the first time that they had seen something in the fog, it wouldn't be the last.

"Hang on . . . it's Cas!" Gyles said, voice rising with excitement.

"It's not Cas," Niko said, not looking up from where he lay flat on the deck. "Cas is dead."

"No! Really! It is! Get up!" Gyles grabbed him and pulled him to his feet, shoving the spyglass in front of his face. Reluctantly, Niko took it.

"What the . . . it is Cas!" he exclaimed. The crew jumped up, running to the side in confused excitement.

Prisma ran from below deck when she heard the announcement. She pushed her way through the group and snatched the spyglass from Niko.

She saw the hazy outline of a rocky wall rising from the waves, and even more distant, the shapes of buildings beyond. Standing on the wall, waving frantically at them, was a familiar boy.

"Cas!" she screamed.

Nyx spun the wheel, turning the ship so abruptly that everyone fell to the deck.

Cas jumped from the wall and into the water as the ship drew closer. He grabbed the ropes and climbed up the side. Cimik reached down and pulled him onto the deck.

As he rose to his feet, the crew began to question him all at once. But he didn't hear them. Prisma ran for him and threw her arms around him, embracing him tightly. Her lips met his.

They kissed for what seemed simultaneously like a long time and only a moment. The crew laughed and whistled as they parted. He smiled.

"I thought you were dead," she said, tears running down her face.

"Yeah, I did too," he replied.

"What *is* that?" he heard Nyx ask. The crew turned as they passed close to the wall, looking with amazement at the town as it was consumed by the waves.

"It's a long story," Cas said.

*

"So, they were all . . . dead?" Alistair asked. They sat in the crew's cabin, the ship anchored in the shallows for the night. They had taken the blankets and pillows from the hammocks and arranged them in a circle around the room.

"Yeah. Or, undead, I guess," Cas replied.

"Well, Cas, it sounds like you found the Drowned Queen's kingdom." Alistair said.

"How do you know that? It could be any kingdom," Gyles said.

"Really? Does any kingdom disappear into the sea every high tide? Any kingdom that's inhabited by the nobility who sentenced their queen to death, eternally paying for their sins by being trapped in their empty city while their bodies rot and their minds are consumed by madness? Are there a lot of those around?" Alistair asked. Gyles didn't respond.

"I agree with him," Nyx said. "They said 'she'll be back soon,' right?" Cas nodded. "They were talking about the Queen. She can't go on land, so she must leave the kingdom during low tide."

"She can't?" Gryph asked.

"No. She's chained to the sea," Nyx said.

"How do you know?"

Nyx smiled. "'Cause I've met her."

"Yeah, sure you have," Gryph muttered.

"Fine, don't believe me. I know what happened."

"I believe you, Captain," Niko said.

"Thanks, that means so much," she muttered.

"Based on what I read in the book I found at the tower, it does sound very similar to the real kingdom," Prisma said.

A scratching sound came from outside, like long claws being dragged across the hull.

"Why does it always do that when we're down here?" Knives asked, his voice strained.

"To try and scare you. Don't let it," Nyx said.

"I can't just not be scared. It's not a switch I can flip off," Knives admitted.

"Just try to relax. It's not real," Splinter said.

"How do you know? Maybe this one *is* real," Gryph said, nervously playing with his flaxen braid.

"It's hard to tell out here sometimes," Nyx muttered.

Cas settled back against the pillow, leaning next to Prisma. The lantern light illuminated her face in a warm glow as she smiled at him.

"I'm glad you're not dead," she whispered.

"So am I," he whispered back. He closed his eyes, listening to the others talk.

"So after the ship sank, I held on to some floating wood and washed up on Eversyn a couple days later," Splinter was saying.

"Really? You were just floating around on the ocean for *days*?" Gryph asked. "Weren't there sharks and stuff?"

"Of course there were. I'm lucky I didn't get eaten."

"I saw someone get eaten by a shark once," Knives said. "When I worked on that ship after I ran away from the Silver Isles. One of the men fell overboard and they were on him in a second. Real bloody. Kinda cool, though, in a morbid sort of way."

"I ate a shark once," Gryph said.

"What? Why?"

"Cause my parents caught it in their nets, and it was already dead, so we weren't gonna waste it."

"What's it taste like?" Splinter asked.

"Not that great."

"This is actually the first time I've left Yarlford," Kal was telling Gyles. "Well, I went to the north coast of Empiris once, but I've never been this far from home."

"You never traveled with Alistair?" he asked, surprised.

"No. That was never my thing. I only made the maps and plotted the courses, I didn't use them. The idea of being out on the sea so far from land scared me."

"Does it still scare you?" asked Gyles.

"Not as much as I thought it would," he said with a laugh.

"Yeah, I joined the Armada when I was sixteen," Cimik told Tig. "A member of the Armada was supposed to be at least seventeen, but I lied about my age because I really felt called to a job where I could destroy things alongside many good-looking women."

"Were you allowed to date in the Armada?" Tig asked.

"Yes, it was actually encouraged. They believed it developed a better bond between soldiers."

"That wasn't allowed in the Navy."

"That's because the Navy is the worst," Cimik said.

"Yeah. I only joined because it was either that or be a professor in Tallix like my father, and I ain't exactly the professor type."

"Your dad's a professor? I didn't know that."

"You never asked."

"So I should have just randomly asked, 'Hey Tig, is your dad a professor?'" she asked.

Tig just looked at her for a moment, shook his head, and laughed. "Yes, I think that would've been a good way to bring up the subject."

"Originally, I came from Empiris," Niko told Alistair enthusiastically. "I moved to Thawpeak later; it's less strictly monitored by the Empire, as I'm sure you know. Before I left for the Quarter, that is. It's kind of a family business. My father went off in search of the treasure, my grandfather, my great-grandfather . . ."

"And did any of them come back?" Alistair asked.

"No. Which didn't bode well for me, but I didn't want to be the family disappointment, y'know?"

"I don't know if I ever properly thanked you for coming back for me," Fenix muttered to Nyx. "Not a lot of captains would do that, for someone like me."

"Yeah, well, you're one of us now," Nyx said. "You're not getting out of this crew that easily."

The chatter eventually died down. As the rest of the crew drifted off to sleep, Alistair and Kal joined Nyx where she sat against the wall.

"You're the expert," Kal whispered. "How do you think Cas ended up on that island?"

"He said he saw a blue light just before he passed out, right?" Nyx asked. "It seems pretty obvious to me what happened."

"See? I told you," Alistair said smugly.

"But, even *if* we say that there's an undead ocean queen who lives here, and I'm not saying I believe that, why would she save him?

There's gotta be hundreds of people who die in the sea every day, and she doesn't help them," Kal said.

"She does things like that sometimes. Like I told you, I met someone who says the same thing happened to him." Alistair insisted.

"I don't know how much stock you should put in his story, Al," Kal said.

Nyx looked across the room, where the flickering lantern light illuminated Cas and Prisma sleeping side by side.

"How old is Cas now? Seventeen, almost eighteen? On the run from the Navy, defying the Empire. He's developing a habit of freeing slaves and giving them their master's wealth. He has no interest in the treasure, he just wants love and to help others," Nyx mused. "Maybe the Queen saved him because he reminded her of herself."

27

Lucien and Draigh

The full moon cast an eerie yellow glow over the calm sea, small waves lapping against the hulls of ships that passed silently beneath the starry sky. Among the uniform fleet of Navy war galleons, one ship stood out. It was smaller, with twin masts adorned with bloodred sails.

Draigh sat at the helm, cleaning his sword. He ran the cloth slowly, gently over the silvery blade, admiring how it caught the moonlight. He had always made sure to take very good care of this sword.

He traced his fingers along the elegantly carved hilt, to where his initials were engraved at the base. His father had the sword made special for him just before he left on his first journey as a merchant's cabin boy. But that wasn't why the sword held so much sentimental value to him. This was, of course, the blade he had used to maim Captain Nyx.

His very first encounter with pirates had been, understandably, terrifying. The ship had been boarded under the threat of death, the crew and captain held at gunpoint on the deck while the pirates took what they pleased. Draigh, only sixteen at the time, had hidden in the galley, shaking, heart pounding, certain he would be killed if he were found.

That fear turned to anger as he watched the horde of criminals carrying away their cargo. Was no one going to put up a fight to protect their belongings? Were they simply going to sit back and allow these deplorable creatures to take what wasn't theirs?

When he had first seen Nyx, he never imagined she was the captain. She didn't look much older than him, a scrawny pale girl with dirty hair and missing teeth. Fueled by anger, he had waited until she approached and then jumped out from his hiding place, swinging his sword wildly.

She screamed and fell back, blood cascading down her face. As she writhed in pain, he stood over her, adrenaline racing and his senses on fire. He enjoyed that feeling.

Before he could decide what to do next, two burly pirates ran into the room and grabbed him, holding him back while a third attended to Nyx.

"Should we kill him, Captain Nyx?" One of the men asked, putting a knife to Draigh's throat.

"Don't bother, he's not worth it," she said, before she was taken from the room. The men tossed his sword aside and followed her out, leaving him cowering in the corner.

He decided then and there that he would dedicate his life to chasing the high he had felt as he stood over the bloodied and defeated captain. Call it what you will—righteous fury, moral wrath—it was all the same to him.

He had joined the Navy as soon as he was old enough, and his passion and dedication ensured that he achieved rank faster than any of his peers. Now he was an admiral at the age of 26, an almost unprecedented accomplishment. Surely, the success came with a price: he had never had a girlfriend longer than a few months, for his work was far more satisfying than any relationship could be, and his family grew ever more distant as he consumed himself in his training. But to him, it was worth the sacrifice.

He finished cleaning his sword and returned it to its sheath while gazing out across the sea. On the horizon, he could see the fogbanks glowing in the moonlight, ghostly and unnatural against the dark backdrop of the night sky. He hadn't been thrilled to learn that Nyx was headed for the Quarter. Though he wasn't a superstitious man, he didn't relish the idea of sailing into such a dangerous location.

"Admiral!" one of the lookouts called in a shaky voice.

He stood, turning to face the man. "Yes?"

"There's something out there, swimming around in the fog. It's big. The other ships have signaled that they see it too. It's some kind of huge creature, or monster . . ."

"You afraid of a fish?" Ragna's mocking voice cut him off as she and Lucien emerged from the captain's quarters. She looked up at Draigh, slit tongue flicking out to lick her lips like a snake. "Quite the ferocious men you have here, Admiral," she mocked.

"I don't believe in sea monsters," Draigh said quickly. "Perhaps it's a whale."

"I've never seen a whale with spikes before," the lookout said.

"Tell the other ships to stay the course. I'm not letting Nyx escape because you saw a fish in the ocean."

The lookout seemed unconvinced but obeyed the orders he was given.

Lucien walked up the stairs to the helm, leaning against the guardrail as he looked Draigh up and down. "Do you wear that uniform to bed?" he asked with a smile.

"No, of course not."

"What *do* you wear to bed, then?" Lucien asked in a more serious tone.

"Excuse me?" Draigh was taken aback, making Lucien cackle. Draigh gritted his teeth, annoyed that he had let the pirate evoke a reaction from him.

"You really need to relax, soldier. We're all friends here."

"You are *not* my friend," Draigh barked.

Lucien faked a gasp of hurt and mimed stabbing himself in the heart.

Draigh rolled his eyes. "You don't want me as a friend anyway. I'm a Navy admiral and you're a pirate. We're natural enemies."

"That's *what* we are, not *who* we are."

"What's that supposed to mean?"

"If you take away the occupation, we're not all that different. We share similar goals, we hate the same people, we're both described as being cruel and sadistic . . ."

"I'm not sadistic," Draigh snapped.

"I've heard differently. Didn't your commanding officer, Admiral Caine, repeatedly file concerns regarding your obsession with killing pirates?" Lucien inquired.

"That's because they're *pirates*."

"So? Face it, Draigh, you're no better than me. The only difference is that I serve myself, and you're busy sucking the emperor's—"

"Don't you *dare* speak ill of my emperor," Draigh hissed, drawing his sword.

"Sir!" The lookout called again. "The other ship has spotted a second creature—"

"If you mention it again, I'm going to string you up on a fishhook and see for myself if they eat people!" Draigh shouted.

The lookout went pale and quickly returned to his post at the bow.

Lucien snickered. "Is that a standard punishment for Navy men? My, aren't you a compassionate and understanding admiral."

Draigh turned back to him, lowering his sword. "Fine. Maybe I am a bit sadistic. But don't compare the two of us. I'm still better than you."

Lucien stepped forward, leaning in uncomfortably close. "Keep believing that, soldier. The only difference between us is that you wear a uniform." He gave Draigh a quick kiss on the tip of the nose, then turned and retreated down the stairs.

Disgusted, Draigh wiped his face with his sleeve. "Crazy bastard," he muttered.

"Why must you antagonize him?" Ragna asked as she followed Lucien back into the cabin.

"It amuses me."

"You're not worried that if you annoy him too much, he'll arrest you?"

"Hardly," Lucien sat down at his desk, leaning back in the chair. "If he gives me any trouble, I'll just get rid of him. It's not like his men will miss him."

Scylla jumped down from her perch in the rafters, landing on the desk with a splat. Lucien scooped her up and stroked her scaly skin, speaking to the lizard in a high voice, "Who's a good girl? You are! Yes you are! Are you going to eat Alistair when I cut him up into pieces? Yes you are!"

Scylla licked her eyes. Ragna slowly backed out of the room. "I'll give you two some privacy, then."

She shut the door behind her. Lucien glared after her, Scylla cradled in his arms.

"She doesn't really understand us, does she?" he muttered to his pet. "No one ever does. Not my mother, not those other pirate ships who cast us out, certainly not that horrible merchant slaver who kept us locked up . . . But that's no matter. Soon we'll have Alistair, and the Eye, and we'll be the terrors of the North Sea again. Well, I will be. You'll still be my sweet baby girl!"

Scylla let out a contented purr.

28

The Sea's Revenge

Cas woke up still lying next to Prisma. He sat up and glanced around the room, noticing that he was the only one awake.

Gryph, Splinter and Knives were all sleeping side by side. They had, at one point, been covered by a blanket, but Splinter had pulled it away and now had it fully wrapped around himself. Alistair lay with his head gently resting on Kal's chest, one arm around him, prosthetic hook removed and slung across the hammock nearby.

The others were more spread out. Cimik, Gyles and Tig had all retired to their own hammocks, while Niko and Fenix were near the door facing each other, clearly having fallen asleep mid-conversation. Nyx was under several blankets, looking more like a lump of bedding than a person. She was muttering to herself in her sleep, but Cas couldn't make out any of her words.

There was something comforting about having them all in the same room together. Even though they were in the most dangerous, frightening part of the ocean, they were all safe here in the cabin.

He jumped as a loud knock came from the hull. The others awoke, looking around in confusion.

"What was that?" Cimik asked groggily.

"The ocean is telling us it's time to wake up," Nyx emerged from her blankets and walked out of the cabin.

The fog seemed extra thick that morning. It was almost claustrophobic standing on the deck, feeling the whiteness press in around them.

"Captain!" Alistair called suddenly, running up to the helm. "Look at this!"

As Niko and Nyx stared down at what Alistair was holding, Cas snuck a peek over their shoulders. It was the Eye, and he was surprised to see that the blue sea glass was glowing gold.

"Watch this," Alistair said, turning the wheel. The glow faded as the ship drifted off to the side. As he returned the wheel to its original position, the glow returned.

"You're seeing that too, right, Niko?" Nyx asked.

"I am."

"Take the wheel, Alistair," Nyx ordered. "Follow it."

Cas watched, transfixed by the Eye, as the glow faded and returned again and again while Alistair steered the ship. At the very edge of his hearing, he thought he could detect whispered voices hissing and calling his name as the golden light flickered tantalizingly inside the shifting surface of the glass. Alistair noticed and shooed Cas away.

"You don't need to be looking at that," he said sharply. Cas returned to the main deck.

"Shipwreck ahead!" Gyles announced. A small, rocky islet passed by, with a twin-masted ship run aground at an awkward angle. It looked to be the most recent of any of the wrecks they had passed. Cas could faintly make out the name: *Golden Lyre*. It faded into the fog as they continued.

"Slow the ship!" Gyles cried. The sails were raised and the *Riptide* slowed just as spires of rock appeared ahead of them.

The fog cleared slightly. Cas gasped as he saw that there was an island at the edge of his vision.

"Land-ho!"

"Could that be it?" Gryph asked hopefully. Alistair glanced from the Eye back up to the island, his face illuminated by the golden light.

"I recommend we investigate," he said.

The sea was unnaturally calm as the lifeboats paddled toward the island. The *Riptide* was anchored just outside the jagged ring of rocks that surrounded the land, unable to navigate closer.

From what Cas could see, the island was little more than a mound of craggy rocks rising above the water. He wasn't even sure how they would be able to climb to the top without injuring themselves on the jagged boulders.

Reaching the edge, they tied up the lifeboats and the crew stepped out onto the uneven ground. Cas noticed a narrow path twisting through the rocks, up toward the peak of the island. Nyx went first and Niko brought up the rear as they walked single file up the trail.

As Cas stumbled over the gravelly path, he nervously glanced around the island. The fog shifted and billowed in the wind, casting ominous shadows across the rocks. The deathly silence reminded him of the kingdom. He focused on the whispers and muttered conversation of those around him as they walked, trying to keep his mind off the feeling that they weren't alone here.

When they finally crested the top of the island, everyone stopped and stared in amazement.

"Is that real?" Knives asked.

"Oh, it's real," Niko said.

Cas could hardly believe his eyes. On the shore lay a shipwreck, black hull encrusted with barnacles and full of rotting holes, but the name was still visible written in white paint: *Sea's Revenge*. A black flag fluttered limply in the wind, bearing the same symbol he had seen on the map.

"We found it," Nyx said in awe. "I can't believe we actually found it."

"Look," Fenix said. Everyone turned to see that he was pointing down at the side of the island. There was a dark cave barely visible between the rocks, and, looking closer, Cas could see stairs carved into the stone.

They cautiously walked to the cave. Taking the lantern from Tig, Nyx stepped down into the tunnel. The others followed.

Cas ran his hands along the rough sides of the stairwell as they proceeded further and further into the depths. It seemed to go on forever before the floor leveled out into a narrow passageway. Eventually, the cave opened up into a wider cavern, and two tunnels branched off into darkness. Nyx chose the larger one. As they walked, Cas stepped on something soft and jumped back, before realizing he had stepped on a leather notebook.

"What's that?" Alistair asked, shining his lantern over it. Cas picked it up and opened it to the page where a red satin bookmark sat.

"What's it say?" Cas asked.

"It's a captain's log," Alistair said. He took it and began to read.

"*As my crew had disappeared and the Golden Lyre wrecked, I took a lifeboat and happened upon this island. Clearly, it was fate that my ship-wrecked here, for I've finally found the Sea's Revenge and ultimately, the treasure. I intend to find a way off this island and return with a larger ship to collect my findings. Until I can escape, I will remain here. Should anyone else come to attempt to take the treasure, I will defend it. I only hope it's still here when I return with another ship. —Captain Caspian Thane.*"

"Caspian Thane?" Cas gasped.

"Yes?" A faint voice echoed down the smaller tunnel.

Cas stared in shock, then took a step into the passage.

"Cas," Alistair said, making him pause. He turned to see that the rest of the crew was following Nyx down the bigger tunnel.

Alistair looked at them, then back at Cas. "If you're going by yourself, take this." He handed him the lantern. "And this." He pulled his pistol out of his belt and offered it to Cas. "Just in case."

"Thanks," Cas said, taking it.

"Good luck," Alistair said as he turned and joined the others.

Cas took a deep breath and walked into the passage. He followed the tunnel as it twisted and turned, stumbling on the uneven rocks.

"Caspian?" he called. There was no answer. "Caspian Thane?"

He saw a glimmer of light up ahead and increased his pace. He emerged into a small cavern with a circular hole in the ceiling, which allowed in a shaft of silvery light. A figure sat hunched over in the center of the space. He could see the outline of a long coat and a captain's hat.

"Caspian Thane?" he asked tentatively.

The figure raised his head but did not acknowledge Cas.

"*Captain* Caspian Thane," the figure replied. Cas let out a relieved, giddy laugh and stepped forward.

"I can't believe I found you." The lantern light played across his father's face as he turned. Cas froze.

White bone and torn flesh glinted in the firelight. He stared at Cas with wild eyes and a skeletal grin.

Cas dropped the lantern, and it smashed on the rocks, the light going out.

Caspian Thane rose to his feet and pulled his cutlass from his belt. "You're here to steal the treasure," his low, menacing growl echoed.

"N-no!" Cas stammered.

"I haven't spent the last fifteen years of my life guarding the treasure, *my* treasure, to have someone come and take it from me."

Without warning, Caspian swung his sword. Cas ducked away and the blade struck the wall, sparks flying from the contact.

"No! I'm not here for the treasure!" Cas cried. He narrowly avoided the blade as it cut through the air toward him again.

"I'll slice you open and hang you from the rocks for the birds!" Caspian snarled.

"I'm your son! I'm Lyra's child!" he insisted.

Caspian didn't hear or didn't care. He plunged the blade into the rocks inches from Cas. "I'll feed pieces of you to the sharks!"

"It's me, dad! Caspian Junior!" He dodged the sword again, stumbling and falling to the ground. Caspian put his boot on Cas's chest, holding him down with his full body weight as he raised the cutlass over his head. Cas felt his hand go instinctively to his belt, closing around Alistair's pistol.

"You'll never take my treasure, you filthy little thief!" he shouted, exposed teeth flashing white in the misty moonlight.

Tears welled up in Cas's eyes. "Dad, please . . ."

The sword swung down toward him. Cas closed his eyes and pulled the trigger.

The gunshot was as deafening as an explosion in the tiny cavern. Cas opened his eyes to see his father disintegrate into dust and bone fragments. In place of the decaying captain stood a glowing blue apparition.

Cas slowly rose to his feet, staring at the ghostly figure as it stared back at him. Long hair and a long beard framed a handsome but familiar face, blue eyes shining with sadness as they looked at Cas.

"Dad?" Cas whispered.

The ghost nodded.

Cas fell into his arms, head buried in his chest, tears running down his face. Even as he hugged his father, he could feel the man growing less solid, less tangible, the blue glow fading.

Cas had so much he wanted to say, and he knew there wouldn't be time to say it. Drawing in a ragged breath, he looked up into his father's eyes as they sparkled with tears.

"Jesper says hi," he said.

His father smiled. "I'm sorry, Cas. I'm sorry about everything." His voice was faint. Cas's hands passed through his father's form, and the apparition faded into the mist.

Cas fell to his knees and began to sob.

*

Nyx emerged from the tunnel, her lantern illuminating a huge cavern with a pool of water in the center. Her mouth fell open. Covering the floor were piles of gold coins, jewelry, boxes, chests, and ornate weapons. She let out a triumphant laugh as the treasure glittered in her lantern light.

"We found it!" she shouted. The rest of the crew raced in, their confused muttering turning to cries of joy and laughter. "Grab as much as you can now. We'll bring the ship closer and load the rest up at high tide," Nyx commanded.

The crew spread throughout in the vast room, stuffing jewels and coins into their pockets and bags.

"I never thought I'd live to see it," Alistair muttered as he looked around the golden-glowing room.

Nyx turned her attention to the far side of the space, where another small cavern branched off the main one. A golden glimmer came from inside. She made her way across the cave toward it.

Gryph, pockets full of gold and draped in countless necklaces and rings, approached a stack of boxes and began to examine them more closely. He saw something glittering between two of the wooden chests and reached in. Something grabbed him.

He yanked his arm out. Attached to his wrist was a skeletal hand, with a large diamond ring on the middle finger. He screamed in horror.

The boxes were suddenly pushed by something on the other side, and he curled into a ball as they fell on him. Standing over him was a rotting corpse dressed in the style of a pirate from the early days of the Empire. As Gryph watched in terrified silence, the undead creature drew its sword from its tattered sheath.

"Death to the thieves!" its rasping voice echoed through the cavern.

As if on command, dozens of other corpses burst out from piles of treasure, from hiding places in the walls, and from the pool. Drawing rusting swords and ancient pistols, they charged at the crew.

Nyx stepped into the smaller cavern, smiling as she saw exactly what she had wanted to see: more treasure. She hurried inside, but something tripped her. She fell to the ground awkwardly as she tried not to break the lantern she carried.

A nearly see-through wire was wrapped around her ankles. Sparks caught her eye. She watched as the glowing embers fell from the wall to the floor, and caught fire on something.

Tearing off the wire, she jumped to her feet. Multiple trails of gunpowder weaved their way through the piles of gold. She followed the trails with her eye and realized it ended in a giant cluster of powder-covered barrels.

"You've got to be kidding me," she muttered.

She turned and raced out of the room, screaming at her crew to run.

As she came around the bend and back into the main cavern, a dark figure reared up in front of her.

With a shriek of terror, she dropped to the floor as the figure swung a huge sword at her head. His blade buried itself in the cave wall. As he struggled to pull it out, she drew her sword and stabbed him in the chest.

To her surprise, her blade crunched through brittle, dusty bones. She paused, and slowly looked up into the man's face. A skull stared back at her.

She pulled her sword from the chest cavity and swung it at the skeleton's head. The strike shattered its neck, and she watched as the body collapsed to the ground.

As she ran into the main chamber, she entered a scene of chaos. Rotting skeletal figures were battling her crew amongst the piles of treasure.

"And you must be the captain," a low, gravelly voice came from beside her. She spun around to see a man, dressed in a tattered satin coat stained with centuries-old blood, his face a mask of bone and blackened flesh, with the remnants of a bright ginger beard still clinging to his exposed jawbone. What she assumed was a bullet hole ran straight through his chest to reveal a glimpse of shattered ribs and putrefying muscle.

"Eris Black?" Nyx guessed.

"This is *my* treasure," said the corpse as he stepped forward, brandishing a rusting pistol.

"And what are you gonna do with it?" Nyx asked. "Let it rot here with you?"

His bony hand fired the gun, missing Nyx by inches.

She turned and ran, screaming at her crew to follow.

Alistair was locked in a fierce swordfight with two pirates in tattered coats, skirting around the outside rim of the pool. As one of them pushed his sword aside, the other stepped forward to strike. Kal leapt down from the rocks above and sliced the skeletal pirate's head clean off.

As they heard Nyx yelling, the two paused and looked up at her.

The remaining enemy took his chance and swept his sword

toward Alistair. He jumped back at the last second, but the tip of his blade caught his jacket pocket, tearing it open. Kal countered the undead man's sword, flipping it out of his hand, then stabbing him through the chest. A cloud of dust and bone exploded as the corpse collapsed in a heap.

The blue velvet box slipped from Alistair's pocket and splashed into the pool. He spun around, eyes wide with panic, and began to desperately search for it in the dark water.

Around him, the rest of the crew was following Nyx's advice and running.

"Alistair!" Nyx yelled. "We have to get out of here, the place is gonna blow!"

He ignored her. Kal grabbed his coat and pulled him to his feet, but he shook free of his grip and lunged back toward the water.

"I have to get it back!" he cried.

"You're not going to stay here and die, Alistair!" Kal snapped.

"Leave me alone!"

"Get up, you crazy old man!" Kal shouted, grabbing him by the collar and hauling him to his feet. "I'm not leaving you down here, and you're not dying for a lousy piece of sea glass!"

Alistair stared back at him in shock, clearly not used to being spoken to in such a manner.

"Okay," he said shakily after a moment. Kal dragged him away from the water and they quickly followed Nyx down the tunnel.

"After them!" the voice of Eris Black came from behind. "Don't let them escape!"

*

Cas was leaving the tunnel as the others came running out toward the stairs.

"What's going on?" he cried.

"Run!" Splinter yelled as he went past.

"Wha—what about the treasure?" Cas asked.

Prisma grabbed his hand and pulled him along. "The treasure's not worth dying for!" she shouted.

Cas glanced back at the passage as dozens of skeletal pirates staggered after them. His eyes widened in terror as he turned and ran.

He emerged from the cave and followed the crew as they stumbled down the path, as fast as the narrow, winding trail allowed. He half fell into the lifeboat just as they pushed off, rowing frantically back toward the *Riptide*. The ghostly pirates emerged from the cave and ran down the trail toward them, swords drawn and glinting in the light.

When they were a few hundred paces from the shore, a huge explosion racked the island, flames shooting out of the cave entrance and shaking the entire landmass violently. The crew ducked down in the lifeboats as rocks and embers were thrown up into the air.

For a moment, everything grew still.

Then the island collapsed in on itself. The rocks fell inward and vanished under the boiling ocean, waves rushing in to fill the void. The flat sea around them became turbulent white water as the shockwaves emanated from the destroyed island.

The crew clung to the sides of the boats as they were tossed to and fro. The sea settled just as quickly as it began, and they found themselves amidst serenely calm water. The island was gone.

"That was quite different than I had imagined it would be," Nyx said finally.

29

Leviathans

Their collective treasure hauls equaled a few boxes of gold and jewels. The crew stared down at it, somewhat underwhelmed.

"It seems like there should be more," Knives said.

"Well, there is more, but do you wanna go look for it at the bottom of the ocean?" Tig asked. Knives shook his head.

As the others returned to their positions on the ship, Alistair hung back in the corner of the cargo hold, staring down at the floor.

Kal approached him. "You want to talk about it, or are you just going to stand around feeling sorry for yourself?"

"I lost it, Kal," Alistair said. "My most valuable possession. The only thing that made me who I was . . ."

"That *thing* didn't make you anything aside from violent and angry," Kal snapped. "*You* made you a great pirate. I immensely prefer you without it."

"I'll never be able to see the future again."

"Then I suppose you'll just have to wait and see what happens, like the rest of us. It's not so bad, really."

Alistair smiled slightly. "I suppose I could get used to it. But I intend to complain about it."

"I don't doubt that," Kal said, leaning closer. He kissed Alistair softly, making his smile grow wider.

Cas sat on a barrel on the deck, staring out across the foggy sea in silence. Prisma joined him.

"So, what happened?" she asked.

"I . . . um . . ." Cas looked down at the deck, trying to figure out what to say. "I didn't find him."

Prisma took his hand, and seemed like she was about to say something, but Niko's shout interrupted her.

"Up ahead!"

All at once, they were out of the fog. Cas shut his eyes against the bright sunlight.

"What happened? Are we out of the Quarter?" Gyles asked, surprised.

"That's the least of our problems," Niko replied.

As Cas's eyes adjusted to the sudden bright light, he realized with sinking horror that they were not alone.

A fleet of Navy ships in formation lay ahead of them, with two familiar vessels at the head: the *Vindicator* and the *Red Death*.

"Captain! I recommend we retreat back into the fogbank!" Niko said.

"And do what? Wait? They'll still be here when we come back out, *if* we come back out," Nyx replied.

"Then what do you suggest? Fight off a whole Navy fleet?" Tig asked.

"We make our final stand, and if we die, we die like pirates!"

Cas didn't particularly care to die. But if his options were hiding in the Quarter until he ended up like his father or going out in a fight with the Navy, he would take the latter.

"Tig!" Nyx cried. "It's time to unleash the cannons."

"Finally!" he said as he disappeared down the hatch, motioning for Fenix and Niko to follow.

Cas watched as the enemy's sails unfurled and they began to approach. The *Riptide* raced to meet them. He could feel his heart hammering as he counted the ships: a dozen, two dozen . . . They were hopelessly outnumbered. There was no getting out of this alive.

"What is that?" Gyles screamed. Cas turned to see a row of huge sleek black spikes rising out of the water off the side of the ship. They towered up above the masts, but despite the size of the animal, they hardly created a ripple as they quickly plunged back into the water.

A second set of spikes approached off the other side, smoothly rising up and silently slipping beneath the sea just like the first.

Cas watched as the two massive black shapes swam alongside the *Riptide*, quickly passing it and heading directly toward the fleet.

"Big, big fish. Really big fish," Cas heard Fenix call from below deck.

"Those things are *not* fish. Those things are monsters!" Splinter yelled.

Suddenly, a huge, black-green, serpent-like creature reared up out of the water and gripped one of the Navy vessels in its gigantic mouth. The creature shook it back and forth like a dog with a bone. Screams and the cracking of wood filled the air as the beast bit down on the ship, fangs slicing through the masts and snapping the hull in two.

The second creature leapt straight out of the waves like a breaching whale, capsizing several ships simultaneously. As it sank back beneath the waves, it took with it hundreds of men.

"I always knew those things would eat ships!" Nyx yelled.

The fleet broke formation. The surviving ships fled from the monstrous animals, scattering like a flock of birds in the presence of a hawk.

But two ships kept their course, pushing on through the chaos toward the *Riptide*. The *Vindicator* and the *Red Death* were quickly closing the distance between them.

Nyx brought the *Riptide* about so the side was facing the oncoming attackers. As soon as they were in range, she shouted the order to fire.

A volley of cannonballs shot through the air toward their enemies. The *Vindicator* and *Red Death* rapidly swung abreast and returned fire. One cannonball narrowly missed the mast of the *Riptide*, while another smashed a hole in the hull. Cas dove to the floor as a shower of wood fragments rained down on him.

The *Vindicator* drew adjacent to them. Grappling hooks latched onto the deck and rigging. Men in uniform and pirates swung side by side onto the *Riptide*.

Cas jumped up, drawing his sword. The crew charged at their attackers.

Another round of cannon fire exploded from the *Riptide*, and the *Vindicator* was peppered with gaping holes. The point-blank cannon shots into the side of the ship caused it to list sharply to the side, and the ropes connecting the two ships stretched and snapped with whip-like cracks, sending officers plunging into the water.

"Captain! Look out!" The yell from behind Nyx made her spin around. Climbing onto the hull was Draigh, sword held between his teeth, eyes blazing with fury. He grabbed the hilt of the sword as he leapt over the rail and lunged at her, swinging the blade wildly. She dodged out of the way and countered with her own strike. He deflected it.

"We can't keep meeting this way," she said with a smile.

"Stop trying to be cute, Nyx," he growled as he swung his sword again.

She blocked the blow. "It's just the way I am."

The two locked swords again and again, one gaining the upper hand only to lose ground to the other, evenly matched in skill.

"You won't be making clever comments when you're choking on your own blood," Draigh spat.

"You really need to relax. This level of stress can't be healthy."

"I'll relax once I eradicate you thieves from the sea once and for all!" he roared.

He swung his sword with his full strength, knocking the blade from Nyx's hand. In the same swift movement, he slashed her across the stomach as she tried to jump back. She cried out in pain and fell to the ground, blood oozing between her fingers as she grabbed her wound. He stood over her, sword raised, a crazed smile on his face.

"So long, Captain Nyx," he hissed.

Before he could move, she leaned back and kicked him in the groin. He dropped his sword and staggered back. She took the opportunity, drawing a short knife from her belt and leaping to her feet.

With a scream of fury, she plunged the knife into his face, burying the blade up to the hilt in his eye socket.

He stood completely still for a moment, blood trickling down his shocked face. Then he took a stumbling step back, tripped over the guardrail, and vanished into the water below.

"Alistair!" A voice boomed across the waves. The crew and their attackers all froze and looked to see the *Red Death* halted several yards away, cannons ready and aimed at the *Riptide*. Immediately, the remaining soldiers and pirates ran to their ropes and swung back to the other ship.

Lucien stood at the helm, speaking into a megaphone.

"Yes?" Alistair called back.

"The fleet's gone, it's just us now. Let's make this easy. Get in a lifeboat, bring me the Eye, and I'll leave your crew alone. I won't kill anyone but you. If you don't, I'm going to give the order to fire."

"I don't actually have the Eye. I know I said that before, but this time I really don't."

"You have two minutes to decide. You can keep lying or you can save your friends. Your choice."

With a resigned sigh, Alistair dropped his pistol and walked toward the lifeboat.

"What are you doing?" Kal cried.

"I'm giving him what he wants," Alistair said. "I'm sure he's going to try to kill you anyway, so as soon as I get close to the ship you need to get away as fast as you can. Hopefully he'll be too distracted with me to care about you."

"You can't do that! He'll kill you!" Kal implored.

"Better me than you."

"One minute," Lucien yelled.

"It's no secret I haven't exactly been a good crewmate to you all. I've lied to you, I've put you in danger, I've manipulated you, and it's time I pay for everything I've done. I deserve this. You don't." Alistair climbed into the lifeboat, and grabbing the pulley rope, he lowered himself down.

"We can't let him do this," Kal said in a strained voice.

"We won't," Cas said, then turned and ran to the helm.

*

The *Riptide* unfurled its sails and began to pull away as Alistair's lifeboat was hauled up onto the *Red Death*. Alistair watched them for a moment, hoping they would get away quickly enough. Then multiple hands grabbed him and threw him roughly to the deck.

Lucien sauntered down from the helm, a smug smile on his face. Although Alistair always tried to appear strong, Lucien knew that he was afraid. The fear in his eyes was intoxicating.

"Where is it, Alistair?" Lucien asked as he stood in front of his old captain.

"I was telling the truth. I don't have it," Alistair said as he kneeled on the deck. "I lost it in the Quarter." Lucien's smile faded.

"You *lost* it?" he snarled. He had seen Alistair lie plenty of times during his time working on *The Queen's Curse*, and much to his indignation, this didn't seem to be one of those times.

"It's gone, Lucien. It's over," Alistair said. For a moment, Lucien stood in silence. Then he struck Alistair across the face, hard enough to knock him flat on his back. Lucien paced frantically, his crew watching nervously as he worked himself into a rage.

"You shouldn't have lost it, Alistair. Like I told you, things are going to be much worse for you if I don't get it back. First, we're going to burn you. With candles, then torches, then iron. After that I'm going to skin you alive. Once I've had my fun with that, we're going to drown you. I intend to watch your soul leave your eyes as it's condemned to the waves for all eternity!"

"Captain!" A scream of terror came from the lookout, who, until just then, had been enraptured by the scene playing out before him. They looked up just in time to see the prow of the *Riptide* slam into the *Red Death's* hull, piercing it cleanly through. The pirates were all thrown to the deck.

With a sickening crack, the *Riptide* pulled away, leaving a jagged hole behind. Seawater rushed in, and the *Red Death* lurched as it began to sink.

Alistair leapt to his feet and grabbed a sword that had fallen to the listing deck. As the remaining pirates raced about in a panic trying to save the ship and themselves, he went after Lucien.

Lucien drew his sword and charged to meet Alistair, blades crashing together as they fought between the chaotic rush of the crew. Neither were prepared to surrender; the moment they locked swords they both knew it would be to the death.

"Why isn't he escaping?" Cas cried from the helm of the *Riptide*, trying to stay close enough for Alistair to make his retreat while staying out of gunshot range. The *Red Death* slipped lower and lower in the water.

"Because he's stupid and stubborn," Kal muttered. He cupped his hands around his mouth and yelled. "Lucien!"

Lucien paused for just a moment, but it was a moment too long. Alistair shoved Lucien against the mast and plunged his blade into his former first mate's gut, pushing it through up to the hilt.

Lucien let out a gurgling gasp and stared down at the sword, watching as a thick stream of blood seeped around the blade and soaked through his shirt. He grabbed the hilt and pulled. He realized with sinking horror that the blade had been driven into the mast, pinning him in place.

He met Alistair's eyes as his enemy backed away toward his own ship. Water rushed over the deck, and the *Red Death* sank ever faster.

"This isn't over, Alistair," he said weakly.

"It *is* over, Lucien," Alistair replied. He turned and ran for the lifeboat, cutting through the ropes with his knife and leaping in.

As he rowed away, he could hear Lucien's enraged screams and threats and curses continue for several moments. Then they stopped suddenly. Alistair never looked back.

*

"Be careful!" Nyx snapped. Prisma paused, needle hovering inches away from the captain's flesh.

"I'm going to need you to stay still," she said. Nyx sighed and looked away, cringing as Prisma stuck the needle through her wound again. "I know. I'm sorry."

"Don't be. It's not your fault it hurts," Nyx said.

"There," Prisma said as she finished sewing. She began to wrap bandages around Nyx's waist. "You're going to have to take it easy for a couple weeks while it heals." Nyx laughed.

"Have you ever known me to not take it easy?"

Prisma gave her an exasperated look.

"I will this time. I promise," Nyx said.

"Come on, let's see where Alistair's taking us," Prisma said, helping Nyx to her feet.

They emerged onto the deck, blinking in the bright midday sun. Nyx stepped up to the helm where Alistair stood at the wheel.

"Where are we headed?" she asked.

"For repairs? Kiral," Alistair said. "After all, Cas's steering left our bow in quite a mess. After repairs? Anywhere we please," he smiled.

"I suppose anywhere is alright with me," Nyx said.

"That's *still* not the right way!" Splinter was yelling down from the rigging. "Have you not learned port from starboard yet?"

"Of course I have! Port is the direction that's closest to the port!" Gryph yelled back.

"It's really not," Gyles called down from the crow's nest.

"It isn't?"

"No!"

"They're right, port is the one that means 'to carry,' therefore port is the side where you carry things to. Like in the cargo hold!" Knives said confidently. Splinter's shoe flew down from the mast and hit him in the head.

"Watch where you're pointing that thing! You don't need all of those anyway," Tig said as he climbed out from the hatch, followed closely by Cimik carrying multiple swords.

"Hey, they were left here by the Navy! They're good quality. Am I just supposed to toss them overboard?"

"What do you think that cloud looks like?" Niko asked, taking his spyglass away from his eye and handing it to Fenix.

"Um . . . a worm?" He passed the glass to Kal. Kal looked at it and began to snicker, then whispered something to Fenix and Niko. They began to laugh as well.

Prisma walked across the deck to where Cas stood leaning against the guardrail. He stared across the sparkling blue water, deep in thought.

"Hey," she said, making him glance up. "I wanted to talk to you earlier, before we got attacked."

"Yeah?"

"I just wanted to say that I'm sorry about your dad. I know you wanted to find your family."

He glanced from her to the crew and back at her again with a smile.

"I did find my family."

30

Epilogue

The moonless night made permanent fog of the Quarter even darker, beyond a faint silvery glow that edged each wave to mark where the black sky ended and the black sea began. The water lapped against the dark turrets of a vast submerged castle. Here, there was light, but not from above. A blue incandescence lit the waves from below.

A half-shattered stained-glass dome lay beneath the sea, the glow shining out from inside. Swarms of fish circled the towers and darted in and out of the windows, attracted by the soft light.

Down in the circular reception chamber, framed by a wall of intricate carvings, was a high-backed throne made from an inky black material that shifted and flowed like liquid. It floated inches off the floor, to make room for the long chain that snaked its way back into the darkness of the room.

The Queen sat atop the strange ethereal chair, hair flowing to and fro with the slight movement of the water, glowing eyes trained on the two men who knelt before her. The watery blue light seemed to pass straight through the both of them.

All around them, in the shadowy corners of the room, skeletal figures adorned in expensive attire and jewelry that glimmered and flashed like fish scales stood silently, looking down at the pair.

"Why have you sought counsel with me?" The Queen's voice seemed to come from every direction at once.

"We have a favor to ask of you, your highness," one of the men said in a small, honeyed voice.

"A favor?"

"We find ourselves . . . dissatisfied," the second man said. A chorus of ghastly laughter filled the chamber from the nobility.

"What did you expect? You're dead," the Queen replied.

"Yes, but we have very important tasks that were left undone," the first continued. "We had hoped that you, with your great powers and godlike wisdom, could, perhaps, help us?"

"That is not normally something I do," the Queen said. "I can extend life beyond its natural time, but bringing the dead back . . ."

"We are prepared to offer you something, if you are willing to try," the second jumped in excitedly. The Queen turned her attention to him, and he shrank before her gaze.

"What could you possibly have to offer me?" she asked.

He reached into his long, crimson coat and pulled from it a blue velvet box. It was plucked from his hands suddenly, and floated toward the Queen, opening as it did. She gazed at the shard of palm-sized sea glass inside, watching with interest as the reflective surface shifted and rippled like a windswept lake.

The two spectral men exchanged a glance as the Queen examined their offering. The first was grim and skeptical, his single eye full of doubt. The second maintained his wolfish smile, eyes glinting unpleasantly behind his cracked spectacles. On his shoulder, the dark form of a ghostly lizard flicked out her tongue to lick her eyes. Finally, the Queen spoke, snapping their attention back to her.

"Your proposal is intriguing. I suppose, given this trade, I will attempt to grant your request."

Alex Vega is an author and biologist who was raised in Pennsylvania and now lives in Maine. They write both fiction and non-fiction, including fantasy novels and nature articles. Their favorite pastimes include tide-pooling, exploring abandoned buildings, and running a cosplay blog.

www.ingramcontent.com/pod-product-compliance
Lightning Source LLC
Chambersburg PA
CBHW051314130726
47987CB00004B/1806